The Arcalypsis Flame

The Great Relics

D J. Smith

THE ARCALYPSIS

Flame

D.J.Smith

Published by David Smith

ISBN: 978-1-7380515-4-0

For Carter, Sydney, and Theo

Contents

"The Days of Fire were a time of unfathomable calamity which few records relate with reliable accuracy. What little is known of those dark times is recorded in the Great Library of Anturac and through oral traditions passed down by the intervening generations. A terrible event befell the once thriving land of Ardhia, an event which cast that great continent into the waves. The survivors, led by Danyr, made their way to the present land of Arinönde. There, they built a great city before moving on to the island of Anturac which is nestled among the protective barriers of the southern oceans."

-an account of the First Days

"Magic, in any form, is to be viewed with the greatest suspicion. Those who are inexperienced can accidentally call forth forces which they are unable to control, let alone comprehend..."

-'On Witches and Wizards' by Otho Rema

"It is hereby decreed that all those who do not adhere to the doctrines laid out in the Great Compendium are to be severely punished, regardless of race, creed, or caste."

-Order of the Bright Concordance

PART I

A FOOL'S ERRAND

Prologue

The Flame Awakens

"The magician shall first place himself in a great circle inscribed with protective runes. This is in order to prevent the entities being summoned from gaining access to his person. Such an event could prove catastrophic depending on the power of the being which is called forth. Thus, every magician must take precautions, lest he find himself face to face with a creature which would happily bring about his destruction."

-excerpt from the Red Book of Drachmuin, Chapter VII

The cat stared evilly at King Animrens as he stood in the Princess' room. He stared back, but could only meet that penetrating gaze for a minute more before he was forced to look away.

"Damn feline…" he muttered under his breath.

The cat had appeared on the castle doorstep a few months ago and despite numerous attempts to shoo it away, it remained.

King Animrens found the animal unsettling, not simply for the strange presence which it exuded, but also for its shining, silver left eye. Initially, he had believed that the creature was simply blind in said eye, but quickly realized that this wasn't the case. That bright, singular orb shone in the shadows of the castle when the creature was prowling about and several times Animrens had gasped in uncharacteristic fear when encountering the little fiend in an abandoned hallway.

Alas, his reservations were irrelevant.

The Princess had adopted the wayward creature as her own and there was little he could say on the matter. Ever since the death of her mother, the girl had become increasingly isolated. Having a pet, however, had been good for her and she had been able to withdraw herself more and more from the solitude of her studies. Her laughter, absent for so long, had been heard several times throughout the castle and it brought her father considerable joy.

And so, the cat had remained, for now.

At this time, Animrens had issues of larger import to deal with, namely: hostilities between his own kingdom of Arinönde and armed incursions of Beastmen from the Lower Wastes. Perhaps it had been the long peace which his kingdom had enjoyed, a combination of the masterful diplomacy and considerable military genius which his own father had exercised, but the incursions had struck at Animrens' sensibilities like a thunderbolt.

It was the blatant audacity of the attacks which troubled him most. The Beastmen were secretive and rarely seen in sunlight, yet they had assaulted the city of Calchie without so much as a second thought before retreating back to their hidden strongholds.

Animrens had convened his Military Council and they had unanimously agreed that a counter-attack was necessary, lest the Beastmen become too audacious with this minor victory. And so, a legion of skilled infantrymen and cavalry (small by Arinönde standards but large enough to send a message) had been dispatched to the Lower Wastes and ordered to raze any Beastmen settlements which they encountered to the ground.

The mission had proven to be a resounding success and no further incursions were documented for the time being. Peace once again reigned.

Still, Animrens remained disturbed.

He had always possessed the ability to see the larger picture, another skill he had learned at the feet of his father, and what he saw gave him pause. Yes, the Beastmen incursions had been unexpected, but they merely heralded a greater discord which awaited below the surface. Something had changed, and Animrens had consulted his court astrologers in an attempt to learn what it was. He was told that the Blood Star was rising, that haunted specter of the heavens so deeply revered by the Vampyres which had long portended doom and disorder.

There were rumblings within his own kingdom as well.

Rumours of strange cults operating in the labyrinths below the city and tales of shadowy groups which were gaining a foothold on the local black markets. There were dark stories of trafficking in sacred Ardhian relics and even in items which were fantastically difficult to procure, such as Dragon parts.

The tales had seemed quite outlandish until Animrens had seen it for himself. He had interrogated several of the criminals personally and found that they shared a stunning ignorance when it came to the identities of their own employers. These men had been motivated by profit and little else. They were small players in a far larger game.

Animrens pushed these thoughts from his mind, for now. He needed to focus on excising this cancer before it clasped onto the kingdom's vital organs.

He knew the broad sweep of history from the long lessons his father had given him. Kingdoms rose and fell, not always suddenly, but over time. Arinönde possessed the greatest military force in the Empire and it had exerted it to maintain the long peace it had enjoyed.

But Animrens could see that the decline had already begun.

The flagging discipline of the legions was perhaps the most telling example of the spreading corruption and this presented a dangerous situation. It wouldn't be difficult for those officers to rebel and demand more concessions. Concessions that would gradually become more and more outlandish.

*Before long...*Animrens thought bitterly. *They'll demand the throne.*

Princess Rionéolas Animrens sat in her study and pored over ancient alchemical texts. Her father's library was vast and it had provided a much-needed balm to her soul since the passing of her mother. Burying herself in the solitude of books had expanded her awareness of the world around her in ways which were both awe-inspiring and frightening.

She had read feverishly about the ancient histories of the Old Kingdom, learning what she could of forbidden lore from ages past. Much of what occurred in that time was shrouded in legend, but the coming of Danyr and the Ardhians was well documented.

It was only a matter of time before the Princess delved into the occult.

Her father's library was well stocked with books of magical exegesis and she pored over each of them with growing fascination. Only two books were denied to her, for they were kept under lock and key, and they were firstly: the dreaded *Liber Novum*, known by its more common name as the Red Book of Drachmuin, and the tainted The Black Cube by Albrecht Handschuh.

Through her studies, the Princess had gained considerable understanding of magic and its use. She saw how the art had been corrupted since ancient times and was now greatly watered down. This was something she hoped to one day remedy.

She was interrupted from her intense contemplation by a shrill voice in the hallway. Such was the anxiety and fear in it that she leapt from her chair and bolted for the doorway, throwing it open and running breathlessly into the hall.

For a moment, there was silence, then the voice wailed once more and she followed it towards the southern side of the castle.

As she approached, she could make out a few words: "stop it! It's getting away!"

Her mind raced. She recognized the voice as belonging to Erich, one of the castle Chaplains. She veered sharply to the left, almost tripping over her green dress as she went.

It felt as though it took an eternity to reach Erich, who was surrounded by several other Chaplains, all with the same look of fear.

Rionéolas ran down the golden staircase towards the group, "what happened?" she asked breathlessly.

Erich faced her with frantic, searching eyes, "Highness…" he paused as though the words eluded him. "We…we lost it…"

She moved forward and put a gentle hand on his robed shoulder, "…lost *what*?"

The Chaplain sighed deeply, "…the *cat*, your majesty…the cat."

Rionéolas' eyes widened, "the cat? You mean Mór? *My* cat?"

The Chaplain nodded, "it was in the Vault, Majesty…it stole one of the orbs."

Rionéolas nodded as though she comprehended what she was being told.

"We *must* inform your father…" Erich said.

Rionéolas frowned, "why would my cat steal an orb? And how did he get into the Vault?"

Erich glanced cautiously at the other Chaplains and they shook their heads in the negative.

He turned back to the Princess, "…forgive me, Majesty…but I'm afraid this is a rather sensitive issue. We *must* confer with your father before we can reveal more."

Erich and the other Chaplains departed, leaving the Princess stunned.

What could have possibly happened here? Why would a cat, *her* cat, do something like that? She imagined that perhaps the animal had developed a latent case of rabies or perhaps it was merely playing games as some cats are wont to do.

*But how did it get into the Vault…*she wondered.

Better yet, why were the Chaplains so eager to hide the truth from her?

She was no longer sure of what the answer was, but she intended to use every ounce of subterfuge at her disposal to find out.

The Village on the Moors

"The Ardhian peoples were adept in the use of magic. It came as naturally to them as breathing. This, coupled with their advanced scientific acumen made them an unstoppable force in the First Days. Their immortality allowed them a breadth of knowledge that no man could possibly gather in a single lifetime. They were, even in their diminished state after the destruction of their home, paragons of wisdom and virtue."

-'An Account of the First Days' by Alef Sabul

Ainshyre Village was far less imposing than the siblings had remembered. Surrounded by vast moors on all sides, it had the quaint appearance of a place which could be easily missed by anyone passing through the area.

Then again, not many passed through Ainshyre these days.

In comparison to the majesty of Arinönde, this tiny village with its farming community and endless, brooding spaces seemed like a well-groomed backwater.

Still, the rustic charm was undeniable.

Charlotte and Alexander Eliphas had enjoyed a relatively privileged existence in comparison to what they now faced. At seventeen and fifteen years old, respectively, they had found themselves on their own and were forced into the unsavoury predicament of being passed around by their extended family. Two weeks in their great-aunt's house and now an interminable stay at their great-uncle's.

As the horse-drawn wagon moved along the barren path, the siblings took stock of their situation. They were less than thrilled to be here, but were excited at the prospect of exploring the country. Their entire lives had been spent in the city, and so, the fresh air and wide-open spaces were a welcome reprieve.

When the time came, they would head to another great-aunt's just on the outskirts of Arinönde.

Their great-uncle's farmhouse lay at the top of a hill which overlooked the village. As the wagon came closer, the siblings caught a glimpse of the enormous barn near the rear of the property. The barn stood tall like a gambrel roofed sentinel, forbidding and majestic as the sun slowly rose behind it. The farmhouse where their great-uncle lived was made from stone and there was a small puff of smoke coming from its chimney. Next to the farmhouse was another, smaller building with a gambrel roof.

As the wagon approached the front door, it swung open and a tall, gangly old man with a cane shuffled out. He wore a tweed cap over his white hair and a collared shirt under a woolen sweater.

The old man called out from the front doorstep, "top of the mornin' children! So good to see you!"

Heartened by the warmth in their great-uncle's voice, Charlotte and Alexander leapt from the wagon and ran to give him a hug. They hadn't seen him in years, but had always been touched by his kindness and gentle demeanour.

"Careful now!" he said. "You'll crack me ribs!"

Charlotte laughed, "uncle Adair…it's good to see you."

"You too child…you too…go on in…breakfast is on the table."

Charlotte realized that she was famished and moved past her uncle towards the smell of home cooking which beckoned her forth.

Alexander followed closely behind.

Soon, the siblings were seated at a great, ornate wooden table and were devouring a plate of eggs and slab bacon which had been prepared for them.

Adair Crawley's farm, roughly twenty-five acres, had been passed down in the family for generations. He specialized mostly in wheat and had a few livestock which he relied upon for his own personal use. On Market Days, Adair would sell his grains to the locals and get a handsome return.

Crawley wheat had a fine reputation, after all.

As the siblings finished their meal, Adair shuffled in and smiled, "I'll tell ye…it's been ages since we had any children in this house."

Alexander glanced up from his plate, "…we're not really children anymore, uncle Adair."

Adair laughed, "aye…I s'pose not…yet to me, ye *are* children…I'm eighty years old, I'll tell you!"

Alexander smiled, "and what's it like to live for almost eighty years?"

Adair lowered himself to the table, sitting between the siblings. The old man looked at Alexander with a twinkle in his eyes, "still the inquisitive one, I see…you've not lost it over the years…" he leaned back and sighed. "'Tis a terrible thing…to lose one's imagination."

"How old is this farmhouse, uncle Adair?" Charlotte asked between bites.

The old man gripped his cane and glanced up at the ceiling, "oh, I'd say goin' on about three hundred years, or so…" he met Charlotte's gaze. "Not in bad shape, eh?"

Charlotte nodded, "not at all…it's beautiful. You don't see these kinds of houses in the city."

Adair grinned, "I s'pose you don't…your great-aunt kept this place spotless before she passed. As it stands now, I sometimes struggle to live up to her excellent work."

Alexander paused his eating for a moment, "…sorry to hear about aunt Edith, uncle…"

Adair smiled, "nae bother lad…she lived a good life and she suffered only briefly before she went…ye cannae ask for more."

There was a brief silence as the siblings finished their food. With their bellies full, they leaned back in their chairs and sighed.

Adair chuckled, "hit the spot, did it?"

"Uncle Adair…" Alexander asked softly. "How do you run this farm on your own?"

"Well…I wouldn't say it's *all* on me own…I've some help from the local farmhands. That's the way it is in Ainshyre, everybody helps everybody. As for makin' a livin', well, I do fairly well on Market Days and havin' this place double as an inn helps."

Charlotte frowned, "an inn?"

Adair nodded, "aye…that building next door. 'Tis where those passin' through stay."

Alexander nodded, "so, you're a landlord in a way?"

Adair chuckled, "I wouldnae go that far…let's just say I'm providin' a service to weary travellers…travellers such as yerself, for instance."

Charlotte smiled, "well…thank you so much for having us."

The old man nodded, "'twas the least I could do…I was quite fond of yer father, as ye know."

The siblings lowered their eyes for a moment. Such memories brought unexpected pain with them.

"Aye…" Adair said. "You run on outside and get a good tour of the place…I'll take care of the dishes."

Charlotte stood slowly, "we can help you, uncle…"

The old man fixed her with his blue eyes, "…I *insist*, lass."

The morning air was crisp and clear. There was scarcely a cloud in the sky and groups of grackles soared unopposed back and forth in steady permutations.

Alexander and Charlotte filled their lungs with the fresh air. It was a welcome reprieve from the smog of their former dwelling, though a part of them did miss their old home.

Growing up in the capital had been made affordable because their father had created a nice life for them there. His blacksmithing had been some of the finest in the land and people had flocked down from every corner of Arinönde to buy crafts and weapons from him. His proficiency with silver was unmatched and he had even shown young Alexander a few tricks of the trade before he had passed.

"Amazing, isn't it…" Charlotte practically whispered. "Look at the *view*…"

Indeed, all of Ainshyre seemed to be laid out before their eyes like a magnificent painting. Gambrel roofed houses and quaint huts dotted the square where the Market took place. Beyond the village were endless moors as far as the eye could see and their stark barrenness was initially disquieting to look upon.

Alexander tugged at Charlotte's sleeve and pointed into the distance, "there…what's *that*?"

Charlotte followed his finger, "what's wh-"

But then she saw it.

Initially, she felt anxiety rising in the pit of her stomach and her mind played cruel games with her before her vision finally settled back to normality.

"Oh…" she said. "It's a tree…I think…"

It was unlike any tree she had ever seen. It lay just outside of the village proper along a stretch of dirt road. Tall and black as night with a strew of white blossoms along its crown, the tree imposed its presence on the landscape like a dark watcher.

"Gives me the creeps…." Charlotte shuddered.

Alexander seemed to be positively bouncing, "we should go and check it out…"

"Nae, child…" a voice behind them said.

They turned with a start and saw their uncle leaning on his cane behind them.

"I wouldnae bother goin' there, if I was you…" the old man said.

Alexander felt slightly on edge, "…why not, uncle?"

"Ye best come inside while I tell ye a story…"

Adair turned and shuffled back into the farmhouse.

The siblings glanced at one another furtively and followed.

When they closed the door behind them and seated themselves back at the ancient table with Adair sitting between them, the old man began to regale them with his tale.

"That tree has been there longer than anyone can remember…" he said. "There are some here that say it's cursed…"

Alexander nearly laughed, "*cursed*? Come now uncle, *really*?"

The old man's face was stone, "do not take such things lightly, lad. Yer not in the city anymore. There are ancient things that lie sleeping in these parts and they're best left undisturbed…"

A shudder went through the siblings and the old kitchen suddenly seemed very cold.

Adair, sensing the rising dread in his young charges, decided to launch into a story, "t'was long ago…my own grandfather told me this tale…he said that the tree came from the stars, planted by the Most High. It brought great prosperity to the land, but soon, people forgot the Old Ways. They began to live carelessly and recklessly. So, the Most High let a famine befall the lands and it brough the people back into balance."

"The Most High?" Charlotte asked cautiously. "Is that the Ainshyre version of the Light Father?"

Adair shook his head, "nae lad...I'll not preach any of that Bright Church rubbish to ye...the Most High is older than any myth and we here in Ainshyre have been keepers of that sacred trust, which was given to us by our forefathers."

The siblings were baffled by what they were hearing, but young Alexander's curiosity had been whetted, "uncle...does the tree have some kind of, *magic*, around it?"

Adair fixed the boy with a cold gaze, "I'll say this only once more, lad, do not bother with that tree...I've told you more than I should've."

There was an awkward silence for a moment.

Adair, seeming to regret his sudden outburst, sighed and tried to change the subject, "come...let's go see how the sheep are doin'."

Alexander glanced at Charlotte from across the table and she frowned and shook her head at him.

She knew the boy's insatiable curiosity would never take 'no' for an answer and she dreaded what it would mean for them.

Out near the barn, the siblings watched the sheep as they grazed about carelessly. The sun was now high in the sky and it cast its gentle, golden hues over the land like a soft blanket.

Charlotte was admiring the farmhouse while Alexander explored the surrounding animal enclosures. Neither of them had fully come to terms with their grief and it lay beneath the surface of their consciousness, waiting to be acknowledged.

For Charlotte, the loss of her father represented a growing void in her life and a threat to her own mental stability. She was now thrust into the role of parent and provider for young Alexander whether she liked it or not. Having the aid of their great-aunts and uncles was certainly helpful, but it only lasted a brief time before they were passed off to the next one.

The worst part of it all was that their mother had died before their father abandoned them and the thought that he was still out there, living his life without a care in the world while his children suffered, was almost too much to bear.

Alexander was particularly damaged by it all. He had been on a course for success with the Bright Collegiate and would've been trained in the magical arts (a subject which endlessly fascinated him). Now, it seemed, that future was in doubt, although the Collegiate had agreed to postpone his scholarship for another year.

For now, the siblings would have to be content with their lot in life. It seemed that there was little they could do to alter it.

As Charlotte's gaze drifted away from the farmhouse, something caught her eye. Outside of the building which her uncle used as an inn, a man was sitting smoking a small pipe. Concentric circles of smoke floated up towards the wooden awning and dissipated like wisps. The building was about forty yards away and situated on a small hill, but even from this distance, Charlotte could see the man clearly.

He had a long, snow-white beard which was trim and well kept and his hair was tied into a ponytail which ran down his back. He wore a dark brown, wide-brimmed hat and a red wool cloak over simple peasant clothing. His features were strong and angular and his ears were pointed but his most defining feature was his eye. Even at this distance, the bright silver of his left eye shone in a way that was almost hypnotic.

Alexander noticed the stranger too and he was staring awkwardly in his direction.

The old man seemed to pay them no attention as he reclined and puffed on his pipe. In front of him, a group of grackles had assembled and they seemed to be either oblivious of the man's presence or fully aware that he represented no threat to them.

Charlotte turned to Alexander, "come…let's head inside."

The boy nodded without protest.

They walked briskly towards the farmhouse, unaware that the birds had assembled before the man in the chair and were watching him silently as though some form of strange communion was taking place.

A Forbidden Art

"The Ardhian nation, it is said, was ruled by an elite caste of four Priest Kings. They were worshippers of a Serpent God to which many of their great temples were dedicated. These Priest Kings were scholars, lawgivers, mystics, and of course unparalleled magicians the likes of which the world has never seen. The final line of Priest Kings ruled during the Days of Fire and led their people across the Great Ocean. Among their number were names which have become legend such as Danyr, Andarinoch, Drachmuin, and Suryan."

-'Tales of the Serpent Priests' by Joachim Van Fleet

Erich and the other Chaplains were ushered into the King's presence by a coterie of grim-faced Royal Guardsmen. They had discussed amongst themselves how much they would reveal and had deemed it necessary to be as forthright as possible.

To a man, they were afraid. They knew what these revelations meant.

King Aldus Animrens' throne room was vast and ornately decorated. Golden statues lined the long, red carpet which led to the throne and the ceilings loomed high in their gothic magnificence.

The Chaplains walked with heads bowed until they reached the King's throne where their sovereign sat, stone-faced.

Even in repose, King Animrens was an imposing figure. His long, red beard and piercing green eyes gave him the appearance of a barbarian warrior. Standing an impressive six-foot-two, the King struck fear into enemies and subjects alike and stories of his prowess on the battlefield were the stuff of legends.

It was to this most august of figures that the Chaplains brought their ill tidings. The small group stopped before the throne and bowed low.

Animrens regarded them with a slight frown, "…well?"

Erich raised his head slowly.

From one of the balconies overlooking the throne, Princess Rionéolas huddled out of sight and trained her ears so as not to miss anything.

Erich's soft voice filtered up to her, "your Highness…no doubt you have already heard what happened."

"I have…" the King's powerful voice was like thunder. "But I wish to hear it from *you*."

There was a moment of hesitation and the sound of Erich clearing his throat, then he proceeded in slow, halting tones, "Majesty…it appears your daughter's pet cat has stolen one of the orbs from the Vault."

"So I've heard…" Animrens said. "Have you found the little beast yet?"

"No, Highness… my brothers and I suspect that the situation may be far graver than previously thought. This is not merely a case of an animal getting into mischief…this was a *deliberate* act of theft."

The King's laughter echoed through the chambers, "*theft*? That's quite imaginative, Erich. I suppose I should've released more mice into the castle to keep the creature entertained!"

There was a smattering of laughter from the Royal Guards.

Erich lowered his head as though trying to ward off shame, "Majesty…you must understand…*nothing* could penetrate the Vault…not an insect, nor even a wisp of air…yet this *cat* did just that."

Animrens leaned back in his throne, the humour was gone from his face, "what are you saying, Erich?"

The Chaplain managed to meet the King's steady gaze, "what I'm saying, Majesty…is that this is the work of a *magician*."

Animrens chuckled once more, but his laughter betrayed his discomfort, "nonsense! There isn't a magician in all of Arinönde that has the ability to shapeshift like that! The Bright Collegiate doesn't even *teach* that sort of magic, if indeed, such a thing is even *possible*!"

"Your Majesty..." Erich said slowly. "We must use our powers of reasoning in this matter...I agree, such a thing *is* seemingly impossible, and yet here we are. I *watched* that cat bolt from the Vault with one of the orbs shining unmistakably in its mouth. Unless my eyes have deceived me, then I can't help but wonder if my assertion is correct."

Animrens sighed, "it is as I have always dreaded..." he stared into the distance as though his mind were trying to come to grips with the situation. "...I never liked that damn cat."

"Highness..."

The King looked up, his tone deadly serious, "what kind of sorcerer would be capable of such a feat?"

Erich, at last feeling that he was being truly acknowledged, wasted no time. "My colleagues and I have gone through all of the possibilities...as I've said, no magician in this kingdom is capable of shapeshifting. Thus, we've concluded that this individual must have come from *outside*."

"Outside?" The King's bushy red eyebrows frowned. "There isn't a single neighboring kingdom that possesses the magical lineage to produce such a thaumaturgist..."

Erich nodded as though he were leading the King towards the point he wished to make, "exactly...the only mention of such powers, your Majesty, is in the old Ardhian Chronicles."

The King leaned back in his throne, "you're not suggesting..."

"That this magician is a full-blooded Ardhian..."

Silence reigned in the throne room. The implications were staggering.

The King rose from his throne, "then we must act at once..."

Erich stepped forward boldly, "Majesty...the orb which was stolen...the Chaplain before my time once claimed that it possessed the whereabouts of the Great Relics..."

The King's eyes widened, "the Relics...but they were mere *myth* were they not?"

Erich shrugged, "the language encoded on the orb was written in an ancient Ardhian script. Our scholars have worked at it for years and only managed to decipher a few key words, which is why they believed that the Relics' locations were encoded in them..."

The King stroked his beard thoughtfully, but remained silent.

Up on the balcony, Princess Rionéolas couldn't believe what she was hearing and was spellbound by the fantastic tale.

"So…" the King said slowly. "You believe this magician was Ardhian, hence his potent magical abilities, and you believe he is after the Relics. If he truly *were* a man of Old Ardhia, he would be able to decipher the script with ease…"

Erich nodded, "precisely, sire…"

The King turned to his right and a Royal Guardsman stepped forward, "assemble the War Council immediately…"

The Guardsman nodded briskly, bowed, then turned and marched out of the throne room.

Erich's eyes darted back and forth anxiously, "Highness…I would recommend caution in this matter…"

The King turned his blazing eyes on the Chaplain, "*caution*? A renegade wizard has stolen one of our most valuable orbs and intends to use it to his own diabolical purpose. Caution is no longer an option…we must hunt down this heretic at all costs!"

"Sire…" Erich's voice was tightly controlled. "This magician…er, heretic…will obey *no* boundaries nor laws…if our forces cross too many borders, we could find ourselves in a precarious position with the other nations…"

The King waved him away carelessly, "that matters not…they will understand our reasons when we explain it to them…"

Erich nearly laughed but wisely stifled it, "sire…no one will *believe* this story."

The King looked at Erich as though his naiveté offended him, "of *course* they won't! Which is why we will stick with the basics: a heretic has stolen from the Royal Vault and must be brought to justice…our propaganda teams will do the rest."

Erich's mouth dropped, "sire…will you even know how to find this man or woman? I doubt that telling people to search for a black cat will narrow down our leads…"

He regretted the sarcastic comment as soon as it had left his mouth, but the King only turned to him and smiled as though he appreciated the Chaplain's anger as a sign of trustworthiness.

"The cat was male…" the King said. "It was my daughter's cat after all, so I might be inclined to know that…it also had another distinguishing feature: a bright silver left eye. Could a shapeshifter change such a defining characteristic?"

The Chaplain shook his head, "from what I have read, sire, the fundamental traits of the shapeshifter would remain intact..."

The King grinned broadly, "then there you have it...we are searching for a man...a man with a bright silver left eye. Put the word out on every street corner in every region of the kingdom..." the King's eyes narrowed and his face darkened as it always did when he was preparing for a great battle. "We will follow this man to the farthest corners of the earth, if need be, and when we have him, we shall re-obtain the orb and *pry* his magical knowledge from him...such a thing could prove to be a strategic boon to Arinönde which is why it is absolutely *essential* that we keep the matter of Ardhian ancestry or magic quiet."

Erich turned to the other Chaplains briefly and saw his own anxiety reflected in their faces. Returning his gaze to the King, he sighed before speaking, "sire...this man, whoever he may be...we have no idea what he's capable of...would it not be a better idea to take the path of caution?"

The King laughed, it was a harsh sound, "your caution has already cost us a valuable orb...I have made my decision and I'll not sway from it. The time for *caution* is long past. We must cut off this wizard's escape before he eludes us..."

The Chaplains had the distinct feeling that they had been dismissed. They bowed as one and left the throne room, baffled by this sudden turn of events.

On the balcony, Princess Rionéolas slunk away furtively to the safety of her study. Her mind was ablaze. Had her cat *really* been a magician? Only her diary would reveal the truth...

In the sanctity of her study, the Princess pored over her diary. She usually kept a diligent record of things which were important to her. As she scrolled through the various entries, she at last found what she was looking for:

11th Day of the Month of Blooming Flowers,
Year of our Light Father
2100

Today brought an unexpected gift. About two days ago, an adorable little cat showed up at the castle gates and wouldn't leave. The Guards complained that he meowed incessantly and I simply had to go down and see what the fuss was about.

The little creature was surprisingly well-kept and didn't look like he was in need of any food. I left him some milk anyway and he gulped it down before bolting back towards the market. I never thought I would see him again...

But he returned the next day.

The Guards tried to shoo him away with their spears, but he was remarkably deft at avoiding them. He somehow managed to scale the castle walls (an impressive feat in itself) and sat at the edge of one of the towers, lazing around in the sun. He was still in that same spot several hours later and I was observing him discreetly, laughing at his strange demeanour.

Then, quite unexpectedly, he sat up and looked right at me.

For a moment I nearly lost my breath, then I watched as he slowly descended the tower by artful means and made his way towards where I was standing. I couldn't explain it, but this cat had a ***presence*** *which I had never felt before and even at a distance, I could see his* ***silver left eye*** *which shone like the moon.*

He at last arrived at my feet, collapsed playfully, and gave me his belly. I rubbed his fur and laughed. He seemed like such a gentle soul and he had a sense of humour to boot.

I immediately began to pester Father so that we could keep him.

Father was reluctant at first, as he always was when it came to change. But gradually, I began to wear him down until he at last relented.

I was absolutely overjoyed!

I named the cat Mór, which in my mother's tongue means 'Old One'. I thought it an appropriate name, as the cat seems possessed of a wisdom and understanding which I have never seen in an animal before...

The Princess looked up from her diary and gasped. These minor details had seemed trivial before, but now, in the light of this revelation, they bore new and sinister meaning.

She returned her eyes to the pages, skimming ahead until she found another interesting note:

The castle dogs have been barking incessantly. They haven't stopped since Mór arrived...

Father is getting angered by their endless yapping. He claims the cat is more of a burden than a blessing and he has even joked (as is his way) of throwing Mór to the dogs to shut them up.

Father can be so crude...

Nevertheless, I must relate a fascinating incident which occurred the other night. It was perhaps midnight when I awoke with a start. What awoke me was not the barking of the dogs, but their total silence. For the first time since Mór's arrival, there was not a sound to be heard.

I went to the window to see if everything was alright and was stunned by what I saw: there was Mór, sitting in the middle of the dog pen. The dogs surrounded him in a ring, but there was no hostility in them whatsoever. Indeed, even from that height, I could see the ***fear*** *in their eyes and they quivered with their noses to the ground as though each were bowing in supplication to Mór.*

It was one of the strangest things I have ever seen...

The Princess put the diary down and took a few deep breaths. Her mind was racing a mile a minute and she was unsure what to make of it all.

One thing was for certain: Mór had been no ordinary cat.

The signs had been there right from the start. The way he had moved in the shadows of the castle hallways, the way he would appear and disappear without warning. Another interesting feature was that her dreams had been fantastically vivid while he had been here.

He had only been with her for a short time, but she had bonded to him instantly. At night he had lain at the foot of her bed and his presence had comforted her immensely.

Now, part of her felt that she had been had. It was as though a wool had been pulled from her eyes to reveal yet another ugly truth.

The death of her mother from consumption had been difficult enough and part of her, much to her later guilt, had cursed her mother for what she perceived as abandonment at the time when she had needed her most. Now, she felt as though she were reliving those emotions, only because of a *cat.*

*But...he was never a cat...*she thought bitterly. *They called him a magician...*

The idea of it made her shudder.

The fact that a shapeshifter had been wandering the halls and sleeping in her bed was horrifying in a way that she couldn't fully express.

But what were you looking for? she wondered. *What were you seeking in the Vault? They said the orb possessed the location of the Great Relics...*

The Great Relics.

The legendary shards which had been crafted from the *Light Spire* itself. Items of such power that they had allowed the ancient Ardhian Kings to alter the very fabric of reality.

But the Relics are the stuff of myth...aren't they?

Until today, she would've thought so, but now she was prepared to believe anything. She moved towards her bookshelf and ran her fingers gently across the innumerable volumes at her disposal. Her personal collection was sparse in comparison to the Royal Library, but she had managed to scoop up a few invaluably rare works of great antiquity.

She paused and smiled when she found what she was looking for: *The Arrival of the Gods*, by an anonymous scribe.

She pulled the volume from the shelf gently and cradled it in her arms like a child. She brought it towards the small, intricately carved wooden desk at the centre of the study and lit a candle against the encroaching darkness. She opened the large book with the practiced delicacy of a true scholar.

They said you were Ardhian... she thought in the gloom of the growing semi-dark. *So, let's see what we can learn about you...*

Word had spread quickly through the upper echelons of Animren's kingdom. There was a hidden grapevine which ran beneath the ground of common knowledge and which kept a gentle finger on the kingdom's pulse.

Most of what occurred in Arinönde was of a rather trivial nature.

The usual clashes between local governors fighting for prominence and even the occasional violent outbursts caused in local taverns were the bread and butter of the gossip mills.

But there was a shadow world which was growing in strength alongside the Black Market.

Indeed, the elites of this world had been responsible for the Black Market's increasing prominence and they held considerable investments which spanned the length and breadth of the kingdom.

They called themselves the Order of the Black Dragon.

Among them were some of the most prominent families on the Continent including both the Von Richter Banking Clan, the Barrows, and even several High Rectors of the Bright Church. The group met once every full moon to discuss matters of importance in the kingdoms. This time, however, they were meeting early. Rumours of a renegade magician had quickly filtered through to them and they were keen to discuss the implications.

The impromptu meeting took place at the Von Richter estate on the outskirts of the village of Ostur. Ostur, a small principality, was situated close enough to Arinönde that travel to and from the city was easy, yet far enough away that there was a sense of privacy and seclusion for those who wished to meet in secret.

Travelling by nondescript carriage, the Great Families arrived in droves. They were greeted by Edda Von Richter, the matriarch of the Von Richter clan and the inheritor of her now deceased husband Friedrich's vast fortune. Garbed in her finest black dress and cloak (for all members were required to wear black) she greeted the arriving members of the Order with a smile and directed them inside.

Within the sizeable estate was a vast ballroom which could fit nearly five hundred people. It was here that the black-garbed members of the Order gathered amidst a large chandelier and widely dispersed candles. Seating themselves in concentric circles around a small dais and with the sun falling in the distance, the Order convened once more to decide the fate of the kingdoms.

Edda Von Richter stood on the platform and greeted the members, "brothers, sisters…praise be to Draganathan."

"Praise Draganathan…" the members said in unison.

"Now..." Edda clasped her hands together. "I do appreciate those of you who could make it here on such short notice...as you know, the King has convened his War Council for the first time in nearly a decade."

The hooded figures around her nodded.

"You've no doubt heard the rumours: a heretic magician has plundered the Royal Vault and escaped with an orb..." she turned around the room and smiled broadly. "I'm curious to know what you make of it."

"I heard he was a shape-shifter..." a voice near the back said. "Is such a thing possible?"

Edda turned and nodded slightly, "according to the ancient legends, yes...according to today's common sense...absolutely not."

"This puts the entire Bright Church in jeopardy..." one of the High Rectors said, the anxiety in his voice clearly evident. "*We* are the stewards of magic in the realms. Our Collegiate keeps it tightly controlled and allows only what is necessary to be taught to the general public. If word gets out..."

Edda raised her hand, "fear not...the King *himself* wishes to ensure the secrecy of the situation. All of those who are in the know have been sworn to silence under penalty of death..."

The Rector sighed and visibly relaxed.

"Now..." Edda said. "The question comes to mind of what is to be done..."

"Kill the heretic!" a voice shouted. "Remove the threat he poses."

"Here! Here!" several members called out approvingly.

Edda shook her head, "that would be too simple..." she secretly cursed the unimaginativeness of the others. "The King intends to capture the magician and use him to his own ends...if the renegade thaumaturgist *is* in fact Ardhian..."

Several voices mingled together at once as a furious back and forth took place. At last, one of the Barrows, Cornelius, spoke, "such a thing is impossible...the pure-blooded Ardhians have all made the long voyage to Anturac."

"You would think..." Edda said. "But what if a few of them stayed behind? They *are* immortal after all..."

"If what you say is true…and we do have an Ardhian among us…harming him could risk war with Anturac…" one of the robed figures said. "A war we will *never* win…"

Edda smiled, "all the more reason for secrecy… if we move quickly, we can cut the heretic off before he escapes…but my approach differs from the King. Our informants tell us that the renegade stole an orb which relates to the location of the Great Relics…"

There were gasps around the room.

"The relics are a *myth*…" Cornelius said disdainfully.

Edda smiled haughtily, "just as the ability to shapeshift was deemed a myth as well…"

A grim silence followed.

Edda turned to the other side of the room, "what I'm suggesting, is that we force this magician's hand. If he *is* Ardhian, then he alone will know how to translate the ancient knowledge hidden in the orb. As such, we will pursue him furiously, tightening the noose around him but giving him *just* enough wiggle room so that he can lead us to the Relics."

Several hoods around the room nodded approvingly.

"We cannot use members of the Royal Guard for such a task…" Cornelius cautioned. "There will be delicate boundaries that will need to be breached."

Edda nodded, "which is why we will use a mercenary force to do the job for us…they will obey *no* boundaries and will be open to the highest bidder…" she gestured around the room. "And who can bid higher than *us*?"

Sporadic chuckles broke out.

"Who would we turn to for such a task?" Cornelius asked.

Edda turned to him and her face seemed to darken, "…I know just the man."

At the Feet of the Master

"It was said, that the Ardhians were attempting to create a Great Machine which would channel the power of the Light Spire and tap into the cosmos from which true magic emanates. What their purpose was remains unknown, but what **is** *known is that the experiment ended in catastrophe..."*

-"The Ardhian Lands" by Wolter Keers

"Did I ever tell you two about the Great Faerie Panic?" Adair asked.

The siblings looked up from their dinner and smiled at one another.

Adair nodded, "well…if I have…feel free to stop me at any time…" he took a sip from his mug and continued. "Back when I was a lad, there was talk amongst the villagers that one of the local children had been stolen by the Wee Folk. They said it was in retaliation because one of their sacred trees had been cut down…either way, there was an uproar in the village. Search parties went about day and night tryin' to find the child, but they had no luck…"

Alexander was leaning so far forward on his seat that he barely noticed that the table was digging into his ribs.

"Until one day…" Adair said. "They found him…the little boy was sitting by Sidhe Creek, starin' into the water…needless to say, everybody was overjoyed when he returned and people slept easy that night for the first time in days." Adair frowned. "But the peace didn't last…" he took another sip from his mug. "People started to think there was somethin' strange about that boy…his parents said he wasn't the same child they had lost…somethin' about him was different."

Charlotte looked over at Alexander, "could you stop shaking the table with your knee?" Her voice had more than a hint of irritation in it.

The boy looked up bashfully, "…sorry."

Adair chuckled for a moment, then continued, "as it stood, nobody could quite figure out what was wrong with the lad…then a rumour began to circulate that the boy was actually one of the Fair Folk in disguise. His strange behaviour would certainly warrant such a thought… but it was more likely that he was simply traumatised by the experience. Regardless, soon other people were claiming that their children were acting similarly. Before you know it…a full-on panic had broken out. A few children even died because of it…" Adair ran his fingers along the table. "Tragic times they were…one of the darker periods in Ainshyre."

Charlotte leaned on her hands, "did they ever figure out what happened?"

Adair shook his head, "nae, child…in time it was all hushed up. Not many like to talk about those days. It brings back too many memories."

Alexander sat back and crossed his arms, "have you ever seen a Faerie, uncle Adair?"

Adair grinned almost sheepishly, "not me, no…but there was one day that your great-auntie was herding some of the sheep back into the barn when somethin' caught her eye…she swore she saw a wee man sittin' in the old oak tree starin' at her and smilin'. She said his eyes shone like gems and he had a rather fearsome lookin' face. Nevertheless, she never felt threatened by him and a moment later, he was gone. She always felt that the Little People had blessed us because we had kept that oak tree."

Charlotte leaned back in her chair, "it would explain why this place has such a magical feeling to it…"

"That's just because I keep the place tidy…" Adair said with a smile.

They all had a laugh at that.

Alexander turned to Adair, "who is the old man staying at the house up on the hill?"

Adair leaned in towards the table as though afraid someone might hear him, when he spoke it was almost a whisper, "…he's one of them *cunnin' folk*. He arrived the day before you did."

Charlotte frowned, "cunning folk?"

Adair nodded, "aye…someone with special gifts."

"Like a magician?" Alexander asked, his face beaming.

Adair frowned, "I've never been sure what that word really meant lad…I hear it thrown around a lot these days…but that man is *different*. He used to come round the village when I was a wee lad not much older than you. He used to teach the village children about the healing plants in the area. The older folks never seemed to mind and always treated him with the utmost respect."

Charlotte cocked her head quizzically, "does he live nearby?"

Adair shook his head, "no…he used to wander through the mountains, particularly Vau-He Mountain just to the north. Everybody knows that's a sacred spot. I think he might've even lived there for a wee while. He comes and goes where he pleases. Regardless, I don't know where he's from and I've never bothered to ask. If a man doesn't want to reveal his secrets, who am I to pry…especially when he has such a *power* around him."

Alexander could scarcely contain his excitement but he knew better than to show it openly. He took a long gulp from his cup and placed it clumsily on the table, "Uncle Adair…do you know his name?"

Adair turned and looked at the boy for a long time, "you could go ask him yourself…I'm sure he'll be happy to tell you."

The boy's eyes widened and suddenly he felt a wave of fear wash over him unexpectedly.

Adair chuckled, "just don't pry too much…let him tell you what he *wants* to tell. If he's reticent, then don't push it…"

"Have you seen him perform any miracles?" Alexander asked.

Adair rose slowly from his seat, then turned to face the boy, "I told you; he used to come round when I was a boy…I'm almost eighty now…and I swear to you, he was an old man even in those days."

Leaving the farmhouse as the sun began to drop below the horizon, the siblings breathed in the dew of the evening air.

Charlotte prodded Alexander playfully, "you going over there or not?"

Alexander shuffled on his feet, "I don't know…"

But his sister knew him better than he knew himself. The idea was simply too tempting to deny and she wanted her brother to get it out of his system before nightfall.

She prodded him again, "go on…"

He turned to her and frowned, as though offended, "you're not coming?"

She laughed, "of course I am…but you need to go *first*…you're the one who studied *magic*, remember?"

Alexander sighed.

Slowly, they began to walk down the hill towards where the little inn was situated. The sky was a deep indigo and shadows had begun to creep along the horizon, shrouding the landscape in an air of mystery.

Charlotte glanced to her right as they walked, trying to see if she could find the oak tree uncle Adair had told them about. She saw it standing like a sentinel near the back of the farmhouse, brooding in the growing darkness. She squinted, and for a moment, she swore that she saw the glow of eyes staring back at her. A brief chill ran up her spine at the sight of those unearthly orbs, but a moment later they were gone.

*My mind is running wild…*she thought.

As they approached the inn, she could sense her brother's anxiety growing. The chair out front was empty, but there was a shadow moving back and forth in the dimly lit room. As they stepped to the front door, Alexander hesitated. He seemed to be using every ounce of his will to refrain from running away.

Charlotte kept her hands on his back, as though doing so would propel him forward.

Suddenly, the door opened and a flood of light poured out.

The siblings lifted their arms to shield their eyes but just as quickly as it had appeared, the light vanished and the entire porch of the inn seemed momentarily shrouded in darkness.

Alexander lowered his arms slowly, his knees shaking. He was deathly afraid of what would greet him when his vision cleared.

When the siblings at last gained the courage to look, they sighed at the sight of the smiling old man that greeted them. He stood with his arms folded against the frame of the door and his wide-brimmed hat and red cloak had been discarded. His single, silver eye shone brightly in the semi-dark.

"Greetings…" the old man said in a gentle voice.

"H-hello..." Alexander stuttered.

The boy suddenly turned to leave, but Charlotte gripped his shoulders and held him in place.

"We were just stopping by..." Charlotte said, keeping her voice tightly controlled. "We make it a habit to meet our neighbours."

The old man nodded, "a good habit...and who might you be?"

Feeling her tension dissolve, Charlotte extended a hand in greeting.

The old man reached forward and took it, shaking it gently before releasing.

"I'm Charlotte Eliphas...and this is..." she pushed Alexander forward.

"...Alexander," the boy whispered.

The old man laughed; it was a musical sound, "well, it's a pleasure to meet you...my name is Amyn."

Charlotte nodded, "our uncle Adair was telling us that you pass through here every now and then."

Amyn smiled, "indeed...although it's been many years since I last came here. But the village always draws me back."

"It's a special place, that's for sure..." Charlotte said.

The old man's eye twinkled, "you've no idea, child..."

Charlotte motioned down to her brother, "Alexander was accepted into the Bright Collegiate before our father passed..." she grinned slyly. "He was going to study *magic*."

Alexander looked up at her and scowled, but Charlotte didn't pay him any mind.

"Magic, eh?" Amyn seemed genuinely interested. "I studied a bit of magic myself once upon a time...but the times have changed since those days. Magic isn't what it used to be..."

Alexander perked up and his natural inquisitiveness took hold of him, "the Rectors said I had the highest marks in the class..."

"Is that so?" Amyn raised an eyebrow. "And I suppose the Rectors decide who is mouldable enough to learn the Great Art."

Alexander didn't notice the hint of irony in that statement and he plowed ahead with boyish abandon, "yes, they do! Admission to the Collegiate is quite the honour! I loved the little bit that I learned before we left..."

Amyn seemed to be moved by the boy's enthusiasm, "and, did they cancel your scholarship?"

Alexander shook his head, “no…it’s been postponed until I’m able to go back, which won’t be until we go over to our aunt Milda’s in Arinönde next year.”

“I see…” Amyn turned and disappeared into his room for a moment. When he returned, he was wearing his red wool cloak. “Night is falling rapidly, but that’s fine, conversations such as these are better had in shadow.”

The old man moved past the siblings and took a seat in the wooden chair next to the door. He reached into one of his pockets and pulled out a small, dark pipe which he packed tightly with an herbal mixture. He reached into his other pocket and pulled out a small match.

Alexander watched, disbelieving, as the match lit itself and then hovered over the small bowl of the pipe, sending forth plumes of smoke.

Amyn shook the match and cast it away, “now…why don’t you take a seat.” He gestured towards two other chairs across from him.

Charlotte nodded and moved forward, taking the first seat while Alexander shuffled over to the second.

Amyn took a puff of his pipe and sent up a small, smoky ringlet, “now…” he turned to Alexander. “You say you’re interested in magic, is that right?”

The boy nodded fervently.

“And you have been deemed to have a natural proclivity for it by the Bright Collegiate.”

Alexander nodded again as though he understood what the word ‘proclivity’ meant.

Amyn took another puff, “well…why would you waste your time with that nonsense.”

For a moment, Alexander drew back as though struck by an invisible blow.

Amyn raised his hand, “it’s not a personal attack, my boy…I only wonder why a lad as bright as yourself would be sucked into the propaganda of the Collegiate.”

“Propaganda?” Charlotte asked, a hint of irritation in her voice.

“Yes…the Collegiate teaches what I call ‘smoke and water’ magic…which means: they don’t teach a whole lot.”

Charlotte frowned, “and I suppose you know more than they do?”

Amyn's eye twinkled, "I make no claims of self-aggrandizement…all I'm saying is that the Collegiate isn't what they claim."

Alexander felt a sudden surge of anger, "the Collegiate is the most prestigious place in all of Arinönde…*all* the greatest magicians come out of there."

Amyn chuckled softly, "lad…your definition of the term *magician* must be loose indeed if you mean to tell me in all seriousness that the Bright Collegiate is churning out true thaumaturgists." He took another puff of his pipe. "If by 'magician' you mean 'scholars' then I'd agree fully. Most of these so-called 'wizards' leave the Collegiate and spend the rest of their days writing books on the subject which end up collecting dust in the Great Library."

Charlotte leaned forward in her chair, "so what? You're telling us that Alexander going to the Collegiate is a bad idea?"

Amyn frowned, "I'm not *telling* you anything…all I'm doing is stating the facts. It's up to *you* to make your own decisions."

Alexander seemed taken aback, but he rallied himself enough to delve deeper, "so, is there even such a thing as *real* magic?"

Amyn's face disappeared momentarily behind a plume of smoke, "what do *you* think?"

"This is pointless…" Charlotte said, surprised by the wave of irritation which was overcoming her. "We're talking in circles…either you know magic or you don't."

There was silence for a moment as Amyn puffed on his pipe.

Charlotte lowered her head, "sorry…forgive my disrespect…we've been through a lot lately and-"

"Your father was a blacksmith, wasn't he…" Amyn said.

Charlotte's mouth hung open for a moment, "yes…did uncle Adair tell you that?"

The old man blew another smoke ring, "you asked me if I know magic…but I think you'd need to dramatically rework your understanding of what magic is. Most of your knowledge comes from books and lectures, but I know things that are not written in any books and I'm not fond of giving lectures."

The siblings were enraptured and didn't dare to interrupt.

"Nothing is learnt overnight…" Amyn said enigmatically. "It takes *centuries* to become capable in the Art of Kings."

Alexander stood slowly from his chair, "…would you teach me?"

Charlotte turned and frowned, "Alexander, you can't ask such a thing…" she chided.

Amyn took a long puff of his pipe and smiled, "it's been a pleasure to meet you both…"

He rose slowly from his chair and his silver eye rested on Alexander for a moment before he turned and disappeared into his room. The door closed with a soft click.

The siblings were dumbfounded.

Charlotte gently smacked Alexander's arm, "why did you do that? You shouldn't have imposed yourself on him. Remember what uncle Adair said…"

The boy's cheeks flushed red with shame, "I just…I don't know…"

"Come on…" Charlotte rose from her chair. "Let's get back…" she began to walk towards the farm house without turning.

Alexander stared at the door for a moment longer, sighed deeply, then followed. He secretly cursed himself for his rashness, but he wasn't prepared to give up yet. He had seen something in that man which he had never seen in anyone: a power lurking beneath the frail façade which ran into depths unimagined.

It both exhilarated and terrified him.

He wanted to plumb those depths again, but had to tread carefully lest he be sucked under by those unfathomable waters and cast into the abyss.

The next morning was overcast and a rolling fog had swept across the landscape.

Charlotte and Alexander had eaten a hearty breakfast and helped Adair with a few morning chores.

"Now, don't you weans spend too much time idling around here, there's plenty to see in Ainshyre and you best go for a wee tour. Do some explorin'." Adair said. "The Solstice is fast approachin' and you'll want to see everythin' you can see before then."

"What happens at the Solstice?" Charlotte asked.

Adair brushed her off, "all in good time, lass. Now, head off and see what there is to see."

Charlotte nodded but she was puzzled by her great-uncle's enigmatic demeanour. He seemed to utter things which demanded further explanation and then refused to elaborate. Nevertheless, dreary as the day was, it seemed like a good day to get out.

The siblings made their way down the hill, glancing furtively at the inn to see if Amyn was in his chair.

He was not.

A wave of disappointment rolled through Alexander and he had the urge to run over and knock on the door, but then thought better of it. There were other things in the village to explore, for now.

Leaving the Crawley farm and approaching the village proper was a surreal experience, mainly due to the great tree which loomed in the distance.

Alexander couldn't take his eyes from it, "what do you suppose is so special about that tree?"

"Leave it be…" Charlotte said. "Remember what uncle Adair said." She didn't mention that the sight of the thing gave her an unexplainable feeling of dread.

Soon, they came to the long dirt road which led directly into Ainshyre itself. Large masses of weeds rose up on either side and they seemed to be ushering the siblings onward. When they at last arrived in the village, they were only mildly disappointed.

The streets were barren. Indeed, there wasn't a soul in sight.

Cobblestone houses, some with thatched roofs, lined the long road on either side. Every building looked entirely different from the other, as though each had its own individual character.

The siblings were unnerved by the silence around them and they couldn't shake the feeling of being watched.

Charlotte instinctively pulled Alexander close in a protective gesture.

As they continued, they arrived in what must've been the village square which consisted of little more than a stone fountain in the centre. Charlotte examined the fountain and was unnerved by what appeared to be a depiction of some sort of draconic creature with nine heads. Each head spouted water in a gentle stream into the large pool below.

"Strange…" Alexander said.

Charlotte looked around to see if there was anything of interest but all she could see was a dreary landscape of decaying houses. "Why don't we go towards the moors… maybe the landscape will offer up something."

Alexander's face beamed, "like some groundhogs? Or maybe we'll see a Faerie."

Charlotte smiled but a shiver ran up her spine as she remembered those unearthly eyes in the oak tree from the night before.

She motioned towards another road which led out of the village, "that way…I have a feeling we'll find something interesting."

As they walked, they were surprised to see a man round the corner and begin walking towards them with a measured gait. He was tall and blonde and must have been in his mid-forties.

Charlotte stopped for a moment and waved, "hello…"

The man smiled but continued on his way. As he passed, he spoke to them, "fine day, isn't it?"

Charlotte nodded, "it is…hopefully we'll get some sun tomorrow."

"Aye…" the man said. He stopped and turned to them. "You're stayin' at the Crawley place are ye?"

Charlotte nodded cautiously.

The man smiled, "he's a good fellow, old Adair…but he'll do himself no favours harboring so many outsiders."

Charlotte frowned and felt a pang of anxiety in her stomach.

The man raised his hands, "oh it's nothin' against you two…it's just that Ainshyre is a quiet place and we like to keep it that way. The more people come from outside…the more this village loses itself."

"We aren't staying long…" Charlotte said. She hated the defensive tone in her voice.

"Aye…please…forgive me for sayin' those things…it's improper…" he extended a hand. "Name's Faber, Arn Faber…I'm the local miller."

Charlotte took Faber's hand and felt the strength in it along with the rough callouses which seemed to dig into her palm. When he released her from his grip, it was almost a relief.

"You two are more than welcome at the Mill. It's just on the west side of the village. We make our own bread as well and we'd be happy to offer a loaf free of charge."

Charlotte nodded, "thank you, we appreciate it."

"Enjoy your stay... you seem like decent folk, which is why I'll tell you that the Solstice will be comin' on soon and it can be a dangerous time."

Charlotte's eyes narrowed and Alexander shuffled nervously next to her, "...dangerous?"

"Just be sure to stay indoors..." Faber said enigmatically and not without a hint of threat. "Especially as outsiders, you don't want to take chances...you'll do fine just so long as you stay at old Crawley's place."

The man turned and continued on his way.

Charlotte and Alexander watched him go with relief.

"Is this what *all* country folk are like?" Alexander asked.

Charlotte smiled, "no...just the ones in Ainshyre..."

They both chuckled to themselves, but they couldn't shake a feeling of unease.

Ainshyre may have been quaint, but there was something bubbling beneath the surface of this place, something that was waiting to erupt.

"Come on..." Charlotte said. "I saw a circle of stones just on the edge of the village...we should go and check it out."

"Fantastic!" Alexander was bouncing with enthusiasm.

They continued up the road and didn't see another soul. In many ways, they were thankful for it. If Arn Faber represented what the average villager was like, then it would be better if there was no further interaction with them.

As they made their way towards the village outskirts, Alexander caught a glimpse of the great tree in the distance. He felt a strange urge to run to that tree and explore whatever secrets it held, but managed to shake himself free from such foolish notions.

*What had uncle Adair said about that tree...*the boy wondered. *He said it was planted by the Most High...*

Whatever Old Gods his uncle had referred to were an enigma to him. An enigma that he desperately wanted to understand.

Wrath From Above

"After the loss of their ancient lands, Danyr and Drachmuin led their people across the Great Ocean and landed on the shores of the Continent. Suryan and Andarinoch had been lost in the Catastrophe. The Ardhians, arriving on great emerald ships, made landfall and prepared the long task of ensuring the continued survival of their race in the face of an uncertain future."

-'The Ardhian Lands' by Wolter Keers

The King convened his War Council with the utmost celerity. Never had the Council been called to action with such haste and many of them were worried that the kingdom was in jeopardy. When they at last realized what was going on, they were dumbfounded.

"Sire…" General Dolfuss said haltingly, his silver mustache shining nearly as brightly as his golden helm. "All of this trouble to capture one man?"

The King turned his green eyes towards Dolfuss and the General shrank back under that baleful gaze, "yes…must I now explain every decision I make as King?"

The General lowered his eyes, "forgive me, sire…I only stand before you wondering what kind of man we must be up against for the military might of our kingdom to be so directed upon his person."

The King sighed, "a dangerous man…a man who has managed to penetrate the Royal Vault and steal a precious orb. Such a thing in *anyone's* hands would threaten the security of the kingdom."

One of the King's lieutenants stepped forward, it was Clara Kansing, a specialist in siege warfare, "sire…you have requested that the Royal Guard be used in this instance…" she glanced at the King cautiously.

Animrens nodded, "if you're truly worried about causing a stir with our neighbour nations, fear not, our troops will only harry this criminal to the edge of our borders."

"And once he goes beyond those borders?" Dolfuss asked.

Animrens smiled, "we leave him to Mabinogan."

There were gasps from the Council and each face seemed imbued with the same sense of shock.

"...*Mabinogan*?" the disbelief in Dolfuss' voice was palpable. "The Dragon Killer?"

Animrens nodded, "this is a desperate situation and it calls for desperate measures. Each of you is unfortunately on a need-to-know basis, but I can assure you that the fate of our kingdom is at stake if we fail to act quickly."

The High Command shook their heads, unbelieving.

From a secret passage, Princess Rionéolas watched in silence. She was disturbed by the way the meeting was progressing.

"Well..." General Dolfuss said slowly. "You know that Mabinogan will *not* take up such a mantle unless it benefits him."

A thin smile crept slowly along the King's face, "barbarians...always so predictable...you can assure him that he'll be amply compensated for his troubles. He's to be used as a good pawn and nothing more."

"As you wish, sire..." General Dolfuss bowed, turned, and hastily left the chambers.

Lieutenant Kansing stepped forward, "what if the word gets out, sire? What if the people find that Mabinogan was in our employ? It would be a public relations disaster..."

The King nodded, "my dear Clara, you put *far* too much faith in the common man." He made a sweeping gesture towards the great windows which lined the hall. "Our people live in the most prosperous nation on the Continent...they care little for the trivialities of government as long as their daily needs are being met. Prosperity is anathema to revolution...therefore, we can easily explain away any indiscretions on our part."

Rionéolas gasped. She was shocked to see this side of her father. The cynical way he spoke about his subjects was the opposite of what he had told her in private. She had always believed that he truly *loved* his people as though they were his own children.

She barely recognized the man before her.

Clara nodded, "very good, sire…we'll get to it at once."

As the War Council began to disperse, the King rose from his throne and addressed them one last time, "the Hexekar will harass the heretic right into the trap which is laid for him."

The departing Council turned as one, the look of shock on their faces was palpable.

"Sire…" one of the Generals said. "That would mean you intend to involve the Bright Church…"

The King nodded grimly, "indeed…they will be *leading* the charge."

Back in the safety of her study, Princess Rionéolas tried to come to grips with what she had just witnessed. It was as though a stranger had taken up her father's body and transformed him into a different man. She couldn't reconcile the kind, loving guardian who had watched over her since birth with the cold, calculating figure that she had witnessed since Mór had vanished.

She sat at the desk in the centre of her study and ran her hands along the old books that were splayed across it. The feeling of those ancient texts grounded her and gave her a chance to think.

She wondered what was *really* going on here…

She felt forces pushing her father forward which were beyond even *his* control. Forces which had a hidden hand in running not just the Kingdom but the Continent itself.

These were deep thoughts for a sixteen-year-old…

She banished them from her mind, as they currently served no purpose. She wanted to figure out the motives behind Mór's (for she could think of no other name to call him) theft of the orb. What kind of man could mobilize the kingdom in such a way that they would risk a decade-long peace to capture him?

To her great dismay, she found that the answer eluded her.

She thought of leaving the matter be and heading into her lab to perform a few alchemical experiments, but constantly, her thoughts were dragged back to the case of the stolen orb and the mystique which surrounded it. She couldn't deny that it was exciting, certainly, the kingdom had never seen such a sudden surge of drama in years.

But mostly, the matter simply disturbed her.

So, what do we know so far…

The man was surely an Ardhian wizard and he was using the orb to find the Great Relics. These facts were obvious enough as her father's own advisors had deduced them during their discussion. What wasn't obvious was *why*? Why would this ancient magician take such a risk?

The answer won't be found in the books in my library... she realized.

She felt a mild shudder run through her. Only the forbidden books would have the knowledge she sought. In order to reach them, she would have to somehow retrieve the key to the crypts.

She shuddered once more. The Great Books were kept in the crypts because they were considered so dangerous that they needed special wards to protect them.

In this case...the wards are the bodies of the Chaplains that watched over them...

There was only one man who had the key to the crypts and the Princess knew he would not part with it willingly.

She turned to one of the large bookshelves behind her and narrowed her eyes to find what she sought. Hidden in plain sight was a small tome wreathed in black binding. She pulled it out and examined it for a moment, her eyes scanning the spidery, golden lettering.

The Witches of Bandover...

She felt a chill. The mention of the shadowed, blighted town of Bandover was enough to make ordinary folk resort to the High Sign, drawing their hands across their chest and clasping them together in order to beseech the Light Father's protection.

She knew from her earlier studies that Bandover had been a haven for a particularly powerful witch cult. Situated between Greater Valleyhold and Aringyle, Bandover was barely large enough to be considered a town and had been one of the last strongholds, along with Black Point, against the influence of the Bright Church.

Dark tales of human sacrifice and the most appalling black magic were associated with the town and for many years the Church had even put a ban on travelling there. It wasn't until the Great Purge in the year 1100 or the Year of Burning that a great contingent of Church officials descended on the town, rounded up any and all men and women suspected of witchcraft and immolated them.

The Princess was saddened by the thought of those dark times. In her mind, she imagined hundreds of innocent people being murdered simply because their knowledge had not aligned with that of the Church. She knew enough of the Church's propaganda to understand that they respected neither boundaries nor laws and often had their own agenda which they pushed with the unyielding ferocity typical of fanatics.

She brought the little book to her desk and opened it, scanning the pages. Immediately, she stumbled upon an account of a witch being interrogated by the Rectors. This particular woman was considered so prominent in the cult hierarchy that she was referred to simply as the 'Black Point Hag' by Church officials.

The account was utterly fascinating.

According to the Hag, the witches worshipped Great Beings which had come from the stars. They were called *The Sleepers* or *The Sleeping Ones* and sometimes *The Dreamers*. The witches believed these Beings, through their cosmic sleep, were responsible for stabilising the magical field which ran through the world and were thus the source of magic itself.

"And where are these so-called Beings to be found?" one of the interrogators asked, the sarcastic annoyance in his voice practically leaping off of the pages.

"Here..." the Hag had said. *"Beneath your great cities and towns...if your citizens knew the ancient secrets that lay asleep under their feet, they would flee in terror into the hills and risk life among the wolves..."*

The account then went on to describe how the Hag was locked away in the dungeon and slated for execution. When the appointed day arrived and the guards came to drag her to the pyre, her cell was bare and she was nowhere to be found.

The Princess flipped through a few more pages until something caught her eye. She quickly scanned back through the pages until she found it: an account of an invocation used by the witches to influence the minds of those around them.

She frowned as she scanned the sigils and arcane lettering. It was unusual for such a potent magical formula to be printed in a book that was available to the common folk. Then she remembered that the ability to read such symbols and use them effectively had long ago been lost through the purges. This sort of magic was not taught in the Bright Collegiate and it was doubtful that even the esteemed and illustrious instructors of that decaying organisation would have been able to understand it.

But the Princess had followed a different kind of instruction. It had led her into esoteric and occult studies which she had kept secret from her father (he would have forbidden it) and given her an understanding beyond even the so-called court magicians.

Thus, did she read the formula before her and understand it instantly.

She must be cautious. She might be the daughter of the King, but to delve into such secrets had its risk.

In many ways, she derived a kind of inspiration from Mór and the daring he had displayed in carrying out his designs. She would have to be equally daring to retrieve the forbidden books.

This magic is old... she thought as she examined the incantation before her. *Let's hope that it works...*

The Princess made her way into the Chapel which was located along the ground floor of the castle. The large, oaken pews which lined the aisles gave the place a feeling of religious reverence and sanctity.

Erich was exactly where she had expected he would be: near the rear of the Chapel sequestered in his study.

The Chaplain's eyes rose as the Princess approached him and he smiled warmly, "ahh…your Majesty. To what do I owe the pleasure?"

The Princess smiled sweetly, "I wish to examine the forbidden books…"

The Chaplain's face went white for a moment before he managed to compose himself, "uhh…Majesty…I'm afraid such a thing is impossible."

The Princess frowned, "…why? Why are they kept under lock and key?"

Erich leaned forward and whispered as though he was afraid some unseen force would overhear him, "because, Majesty…they're *dangerous*. They contain knowledge that was never meant for the sight of man."

"Have *you* read them?"

Erich cocked his head slightly, "…no…but I have seen them with my own eyes, and my predecessor *had* glanced through them…there is a dark energy which emanates from those texts and they have the potential to unhinge the mind if they aren't treated with respect."

The Princess lowered her head, "…I see."

"Forgive me your Majesty…it's just that I couldn't bear the thought of you reading those texts and succumbing to their power. The King would have my head!" He crossed his arms and his face became blank as stone. "It is for this reason that I must stand by my decision that the texts will remain untouched."

The Princess looked up and met the Chaplain's eyes for a moment, "forgive me then, my dear Erich…"

The Chaplain frowned, "…forgive?"

The Princess raised her hands and drew an imaginary circle in the air between them, then made a cross down the middle with the tips of her fingers. She closed her eyes and when she spoke, it seemed as though her voice came from somewhere far away. The language which flowed forth was not the classical High Speech of Arinönde but one which was much older, with vowels and syllables which didn't exist in the common tongue.

Erich's eyes widened with shock, then they closed and his head sagged forward.

The Princess caught him as he fell and gently eased him back onto his chair with surprising strength and skill. When she had laid his head forward with his arms underneath, the little Chaplain looked as though he had fallen asleep.

Indeed, he had.

The spell would last for exactly one hour if the text was correct, but the Princess didn't want to take any chances and desired to make this as quick as possible.

She moved towards Erich, who to her amusement was snoring loudly, and reached gently down into one of the pockets of his robe. Withdrawing the small key that was hidden there, she turned and headed down the spiral stairs towards the crypts.

As she descended, the darkness became greater and greater, until there was only the occasional torchlight to illuminate her path against the hard stone walls. She felt no anxiety, despite having never traversed these hidden depths before.

At last, she came to it: a great door wrought wholly from steel. Cold and forbidding.

Now, her heart *did* begin to race and she had to breathe deeply to steady herself as she approached the door with its arcane symbols. Some of the strange hieroglyphs were familiar to her as protective wards designed to prevent dark forces from getting in.

Or getting out… she thought with giddy exaltation.

She reached forward and grasped the cold doorhandle which sent a small chill through her. With infinite care, she inserted the key and turned. As she pushed the door open, a gentle gust greeted her and for a moment she felt the urge to abandon this foolish path and run.

Mustering her courage at last, she entered the small chamber and came into the presence of the Hidden Archive.

The Solstice

"Danyr, who would become Mage Emperor, was known as a fierce and able commander of men, but organising the Great Exodus and paving the way for Ardhian supremacy could not have occurred without Drachmuin. In the earliest days, as the Ardhians passed through what would become the first kingdoms, Drachmuin was known as the Lawgiver. Many of his edicts have survived down to the present day and are still in use by most of the provinces. Drachmuin would eventually abandon everything in search of knowledge and he began exploring the dark places of wisdom. It was he who convened the infamous Council of Magicians to pool their arcane powers into the Red Book which bears his name."

-'The Ardhian Lands' by Wolter Keers

Slowly but steadily, more and more of them began to arrive. The carriages were streaming in at a steady pace and that pace didn't seem to slacken as the day wore on.

Sitting on the porch of his great-uncle's farmhouse, Alexander stared on in awe. He could see, even from this distance, that whoever these people were, they *must* be important. The horses were well groomed and their coats shone in the evening sun. Some of the carriages had wheels of gold and their coachmen were dressed in formal attire.

Something big was happening.

The boy was distracted from his reverie by a pair of birds which were circling one another in an elegant dance. He followed their path as they dipped and glided up towards the hill where the sight of small ringlets of smoke caught his eye. Seeing Amyn reclining in his chair made the boy anxious, but he felt the urge to approach the man and apologise for his forward behaviour the other day.

Seemingly unable to control himself, he rose from the porch and began to make his way up the hill.

This is foolish... he thought.

And yet, he continued on. What felt like a few seconds later, he was standing before the old man who was smiling at him quizzically.

"Hello…" Alexander said awkwardly, the words barely forming. "I…I just wanted to-"

"Apologise?" the old man said with a smile, his silver eye twinkling.

Alexander stood, stunned.

Amyn laughed and it flowed forth like music, "my boy, there is no need. You have committed no offence…" he gestured to the seat next to him. "Come…"

Alexander moved as though summoned by an invisible force. He seated himself to the right of Amyn and looked out at the spectacular view of the village.

"What do you make of that…" Amyn asked.

Alexander frowned, "of what? Of the carriages?" he shrugged. "No idea…are they arriving for the Solstice?"

"You could say that…" Amyn took a puff from his pipe. "You must imagine that it is quite the occasion for the esteemed Lords and Earls of Arinönde to make their way to this little backwater."

Alexander gasped, "Lords and Earls? And they came all the way from Arinönde"

Amyn nodded, "yes…where else? Is Arinönde not wealthiest among the provinces? You lived there yourself, did you not?"

"Yes…" Alexander frowned as he tried to get his thoughts in order. "Which is why some of those carriages look so familiar…"

Amyn blew another ring of smoke, "why do you think they're here?"

The boy shrugged, "the Solstice? Is it some big event?"

Amyn waved him off as though he had missed the point, "yes of course, the Solstice is celebrated in all the lands as a fortuitous time…what I mean to ask is: why do you think these men and women, the very pinnacle of their respective social orders, are *here*?"

Alexander wracked his brain for the answers, but none were forthcoming.

Amyn leaned back in his seat, “what do you know of Ainshyre, lad?”

“Only what uncle Adair has told us…”

Amyn’s silver eye twinkled, “here’s a better question…what do you know about *magic*?”

The mention of *that* word drew the boy’s attention like a moth to a flame. A thin smile crept along his face, “well…I only know what I’ve read…I also know that the Bright Collegiate teaches it.”

Amyn nodded, “and you were fated to attend that prestigious institution, as you said before.”

Alexander shuffled in his seat, uneasily, “yes…you don’t seem to hold it in high regard…”

Amyn took another puff and blew out a stream of smoke, “you’re right…I don’t. And I can give you two reasons why: one is that their magic is superficial and is more the stuff of parlour tricks than the genuine article, the second is that their notions of magic are *elitist…*”

Alexander turned to the old man as though he had just spoken gibberish, “…elitist?”

Amyn chuckled, “yes…think about it…if you were destined for the Bright Collegiate, then you were surely given a rudimentary understanding of their methods, am I right?”

“I read a small description of it in one of the pamphlets which my school handed out prior to examinations.”

Amyn nodded, “good…then you know how they conduct their magical operations. There is a very good reason why they charge a significant tuition and the reason is that gold and ivory are beyond the reach of the commoners.”

Alexander frowned, visibly perplexed.

“Think on it, lad. A typical summoning spell, according to the Bright Collegiate, should be undertaken on a Monday when the moon is highest and the stars are perfectly aligned. It should require that the magician wear a white silk robe and be in possession of an ivory wand with a gold tip. He should have a golden goblet imbued with all manner of precious stones and he should have fasted for at least a week prior. He should attend the Church at least three times to ‘purify’ himself and he *must* begin his invocations with an appeal to the Light Father.”

"Yes..." the boy seemed in awe of Amyn's knowledge. "That is the standard practice for magic, isn't it?"

The old man shook his head, "...it is *not*. These are ceremonies that only a hundred years ago were conducted with a simple sprig of yew or hazel as a wand and the cathedral of nature as a backdrop."

Alexander gave him a blank look.

"There is magic..." Amyn continued. "And then there is *magic*...notice that your entire opinion on the subject has been shaped by the atmosphere in which you were raised. This is no fault of your own...you didn't choose where and when you were born...or perhaps you *did* and you've merely forgotten..." he took another puff from his pipe, then continued. "At the very least, you must eventually come to the understanding that magic, as an art, has been hijacked...and with very good reason."

"Hijacked by *who*?" Alexander was leaning so far off his chair that he was nearly tumbling forward.

Amyn nodded his head towards the distant carriages, "...who do you think?"

"The Lords?"

"Not *just* the Lords..." Amyn said, a hint of venom creeping into his voice. "But anyone with a vested interest in keeping the common man from learning too much. Magic is called the Royal Art for a reason, lad, and so these parasitic creatures before you have deemed it necessary to keep the *true* practice of it hidden from the likes of you..."

Alexander frowned and leaned back in his chair.

"Believe me, boy... there *are* individuals who are naturally gifted in the art...I can see, just by looking at you, that you're one of them. But know this...the path to magic through the Bright Collegiate will lead only to damnation."

Alexander shuddered, "...damnation?"

Amyn sighed, "yes...the gifted practitioners are filtered through the Collegiate and rapidly rise through the magical grades. They are taught more *only* if they are willing to comply with the rank and file. Those who are eventually learn an aspect of true magic, still a bastardisation of the real thing, but close enough to being practical that they can actually put it to use. Those who aren't...well...they either vanish for knowing too much or find themselves working as clerks in a backroom somewhere."

Alexander was deeply disturbed by what he was hearing. The sea of black carriages arriving suddenly seemed ominous and threatening. As his eyes wandered, they settled on the great, black tree which towered in the distance.

"What do you make of that?" the boy asked tentatively, pointing to the distant tree.

Amyn frowned, "I'm afraid there are things you aren't yet ready to be told, my boy, but know this: there is more to Ainshyre than meets the eye and *none* of it is to be taken lightly."

Alexander squinted into the distance; the sun was cresting the horizon and the onset of night seemed imminent.

"I had a dream about that tree…" the boy said enigmatically.

Amyn was watching him very closely, displaying no visible emotion.

"I was walking up towards it, through the big gate that bars the way…the dream felt so real, more real even than waking life…"

Amyn took another puff of his pipe, "…go on."

Alexander frowned as though trying to piece his thoughts together, "there's a small garden up there where the tree is…every plant and flower was alive, and I mean really *alive*…they were talking to me. I kept walking and soon, I was standing in front of the tree…everything else seemed to vanish. Then, it appeared as though the tree itself was calling to me, pulling me forward. I was powerless to stop myself and the tree opened up into a great, yawning abyss. I tried to run but I couldn't…" sweat broke out on the boy's forehead as he spoke. "I looked up and I couldn't see a tree anymore…it was more like a great, monstrous thing with long, black tendrils reaching up into the heavens…the sky was blood red and it looked as though great veins were spread across it instead of clouds."

Alexander leaned forward as though trying to catch his breath, the awful memory of the dream making his face turn white with the remembered horror.

Amyn leaned forward and rubbed the boy's back gently, "you had a vision…clearly…dreams are messages…" the old man leaned back in his chair. "Did you understand what you saw?"

Alexander managed to gather his senses and sat upright, "when I was dreaming…yes…but now that I'm awake, even as I try to remember it, everything seems hazy."

"Probably for the best…" Amyn said softly. "Some things aren't meant to be understood."

They sat in silence for a moment and watched as more carriages arrived.

"The Solstice must be very soon…" Alexander said.

"Tonight…" Amyn corrected. "The Solstice is *tonight…*"

Adair had supper laid out by the time Alexander entered.

Charlotte glanced up from her meal with a look of irritation, "where were you, silly?"

Alexander shrugged, "just watching the carriages coming in…"

Charlotte smiled slightly as though she were onto her brother, but said nothing.

"Aye…" Adair said softly. "The Solstice is upon us…it's a big deal around here."

Alexander seated himself and dove greedily into his supper.

The three of them continued eating in silence.

Adair finished first and wiped his mouth with a cloth, "you children best be gettin' up to bed…the Solstice is tomorrow after all."

Alexander looked up, "…it's tonight, though…isn't it?"

Adair looked at him quizzically, "nae lad…ye must be mistaken. By my reckonin', tomorrow is the big day."

Alexander was about to say more, but thought better of it. It was no use disputing his great-uncle over a trivial matter.

When the siblings had finished, Adair ushered them up to bed. They were confused by the sudden strangeness of his demeanour and he seemed to be rushing them along.

When they were at last settled, Adair stood in the doorway for a moment, staring in at them. "I have to head out to the barn right quick, children, the sheep always get anxious before the Solstice…you lot have a good sleep and we'll see you bright and early in the mornin'."

The old man turned, closed the door, and shuffled down the hallway.

In the semi-dark, Charlotte rolled over in her bed and faced Alexander on the other side of the room, "what do you suppose that was about?"

"Tonight…" Alexander whispered enigmatically. "The Solstice isn't tomorrow, it's tonight."

"And I suppose Amyn told you that, did he?" Charlotte said.

She heard her brother wriggle uncomfortably, "…yes."

"Alexander…I know you're fond of Amyn, but I want you to be careful…we don't know who he is or even where he came from…" she sighed as though what she was about to say brought her little joy. "You need to stay away from him…"

Alexander's ire was palpable, "you can't tell me what to do, Charlotte…"

"Listen…" she sat up in her bed. "Mum and Dad are gone…*gone*…all we have left is each other…I don't believe that Amyn is a harmful person, but he's…*different*."

"He knows magic…" Alexander said softly. "*Real* magic…"

"Yes, and lots of travelling con men can convince you that they know all kinds of things…just watch…the next time you speak to him, he'll charge you a fee to learn some of it, just like all of the other hucksters out there."

Alexander rolled over in his bed, "it's not fair…" he said bitterly. Then, unexpectedly, he began to sob quietly.

Charlotte sighed deeply. She sensed that her brother was wrestling with far more than mere anger over the limitations she had put on him. She rose from her bed and walked over to his, sitting next to him and putting a gentle hand on his back.

The boy clutched his pillow tightly, "I hate them… I *hate* Mum and Dad for leaving us…"

Charlotte rubbed his back gently, "I know…but we can't change it…not now. Better to get some sleep…"

She continued to rub his back until his breathing became steady and he drifted off to sleep. When she was at last certain that he was settled, she made her way over to her own bed.

The urge to cry suddenly swept over her and she allowed herself a few tears before forcing herself to suppress them. She couldn't abide those emotions for long; her responsibility was too great. Right now, she was the de facto parent to her little brother and if she collapsed under the strain of it all, who would look after him?

It was with these troubling thoughts that she drifted off into an uneasy sleep.

Adair Crawley went to his cupboard and removed a long, silken black cloak from it. He donned it in a swift motion and headed out the front door. He had already prepared his wagon and climbed onto it with a swiftness that belied his age.

He cast aside the cane at the front door as he went. It was as though the Solstice had imbued him with an infernal energy from some unseen source. He set the wagon in motion and the sound of the horses clopping down the hill at a steady pace seemed preternaturally loud in the still night air.

As the wagon approached the village proper, Adair was greeted by the light of hundreds of torches. When he reached the Market Square, he had to search for a spot amidst the endless carriages. People, all dressed in black, hooded cloaks, were milling about.

Indeed, the entire village was present.

If Charlotte and Alexander could have witnessed the buzzing activity in the Market, they would have scarcely been able to equate what they were seeing to the ghost town which they had explored not long after their arrival.

Adair parked his wagon next to the village well and leapt down onto the cobblestone of the Square. Moving through the sea of cloaked figures, he casually greeted several old friends as he went.

"Evenin' Adair…" old Barnabas, a fellow farmer, said with a twinkle in his eye.

Adair nodded, "Barnabas…how's your lovely wife?"

"Better now…" Barnabas smiled broadly, glancing down. "And the leg?"

Adair grinned, "…right as rain."

The two men chuckled.

"The Solstice heals all…" Barnabas said.

Adair nodded, "…praise the Most High."

"Indeed, praise the Most High."

Adair and Barnabas followed the long, torchlit procession as it made its way up the hill towards the Great Tree. Moving past stone obelisks and ancient burial grounds. A somber chorus broke out as the crowd milled along.

Adair felt a hand clasp his shoulder and when he turned, he was staring into the aged face of Lord Edelwyn Barrows, patriarch of the Barrows Family.

"Adair…my old friend…" Edelwyn said softly.

"Ahh…Edelwyn." Adair embraced the other man tightly. "It's been too long, old friend."

When they released one another, Edelwyn smiled and looked towards the Great Tree, "a glorious night it is…aye?"

Adair nodded, "aye…praise the Most High."

"Praise the Most High…" Edelwyn said.

"How's your business runnin'?" Adair asked.

Edelwyn smiled, "we recently expanded into mining, milling, and of course shipping. Thus far, it has helped immensely having access to the ports. The Order, as you know, likes to acquire ancient relics from across the world."

"The Order…" Adair said softly. "I've not been to a lodge for a meetin' in quite some time…"

Edelwyn put a hand on Adair's shoulder and smiled, "it matters not, old friend…once a member, *always* a member."

Adair nodded, "I appreciate that…"

Edelwyn turned back to the Tree, "the power is strong tonight…stronger than it's been in years…" he glanced back to Adair. "We must offer a worthy sacrifice to the Most High."

Adair grinned evilly and the light from the torches seemed to transfigure his face into that of a malignant satyr, "we may be in luck…the perfect offering quite literally landed on me doorstep not long ago..."

Charlotte woke with a start. Beads of sweat stood out on her forehead.

She sat up in her bed and breathed deeply. She looked over instinctively at Alexander to make sure he was still in his bed and was relieved to see him sound asleep.

She got up quietly and went towards the window which looked out over Ainshyre. Immediately, her eyes were drawn to a large, torchlit procession which seemed to be making its way steadily up the hill.

She ran to her brother and shook him, "Alexander…Alexander, wake up."

The boy turned over and muttered some inarticulate jargon before falling back to sleep.

This time she shook him harder, "…Alexander!"

"What!" the boy yelped with more than a hint of irritation in his voice.

Charlotte pointed towards the window, "look outside…"

Alexander got out of bed and rubbed the sleep from his eyes. He was stunned by what he saw. He turned to Charlotte, "what's going on? Is it the Solstice?"

Charlotte shrugged, "no idea…but it looks like they're coming towards the farmhouse…"

Panic flashed in Alexander's eyes, "…what do we do?"

"Depart with haste…" a voice said from the shadows behind them.

They both jumped and Charlotte had to stifle a scream.

Amyn stepped from the darkness, his white beard glimmering in the twilight, "…I'm afraid that Ainshyre is no longer safe for you."

"Are you with them?" Charlotte asked.

Amyn shook his head, "no…but we don't have much time. Grab what few possessions you can carry and nothing more…"

"We're not going anywhere…" Charlotte said, gripping Alexander's shirt tightly.

Amyn's silver eye shone brightly, "the choice is yours, my dear…"

Alexander looked up at Charlotte with a hint of desperation.

"We're waiting here for uncle Adair…" Charlotte said.

"Your great-uncle is among the mob…" Amyn said softly. "They intend to offer you as a sacrifice…"

"*What*?" Charlotte could barely comprehend what she was hearing.

Amyn stepped towards them, "there are many secrets in this village and chief among them is the fact that everyone who resides here belongs to a cult which is so old that its origins have been lost to time…"

Charlotte's eyes widened. Every fibre of her being wanted to disbelieve what she was hearing as pure fantasy, but deep down, she knew it was true. All of the warning signs had been in plain sight and she had suppressed them.

She glanced down at Alexander for a moment, then back to Amyn, "...okay...let's go."

The old man produced a small cloth bag with leather straps, "fit what you can in here, then don't dally even a *moment* longer."

The siblings hurried around the room, desperately trying to grab the few items of worth which they could take and they were quickly disheartened to realize just how little that would be.

Charlotte grabbed what clothes she could and Alexander grabbed his father's small blacksmithing hammer. There was no chance that he was leaving it behind.

With everything assembled, Amyn moved towards the window and glanced outside, "they're almost cresting the hill...move quickly through the back and be quiet as the grave...they will expect to catch you unaware and will waste a good deal of time searching the house..." he turned and headed towards the bedroom door. "That will allow us to get a head start, once outside the village limits, they'll pursue us no further."

Charlotte and Alexander followed him out of the bedroom and quickly descended the stairs.

Charlotte's mind was racing. She tried to piece together everything she had heard and still wondered if Amyn could be trusted.

Perhaps he's stealing us away...perhaps it's all a trick.

But the intuitive part of her knew better. She sensed that the old man was telling the truth.

As they exited through the rear of the farmhouse, they were immersed in the cool night air. The sky was crystal clear and the stars wheeled above in magnificent splendour.

Amyn gestured towards a clearing behind the farmhouse, "beyond the moors is the town of Argyr and from there the Great Forest..."

Charlotte's stomach tightened. She had read myths about the Forest which gave her considerable misgivings, but she didn't voice them here.

As the three of them sped off into the night, the torchlit procession halted at the front of the farmhouse.

Adair Crawley, previously incapable of descending the hill without a cane, stood tall at the head of the black-robed contingent. He breathed deeply and gestured towards the house, "in there, lads...go get 'em."

Several robed figures nodded and moved past him. At their head was Arn Faber who strode forward and pushed open the door. The group made its way upstairs, expecting little resistance, and was shocked when they entered the bedroom, finding it empty. After a few minutes of thoroughly searching the house, they emerged.

"There's no sign of 'em..." Faber said gruffly. "They must've stolen out into the night."

Adair's eyes widened, "aye...they may have been forewarned."

Edelwyn, standing at Adair's side, looked up at the farmhouse and sighed, "you failed to mention that *he* was here..."

Adair turned to him, "forgive me, old friend...I didn't think he'd interfere..." he glanced back to the farmhouse as several other robed figures moved in to search it. "This may complicate things..."

Edelwyn smiled, "perhaps...or perhaps it's just what we need..." he glanced at Adair. "As you know, there was a recent theft at the castle..."

"I'd not heard tell of it..." Adair said.

Edelwyn paused as though choosing his words carefully, "let's just say that the Order is turning its sights towards our old friend, Amyn...he may have more secrets than we ever imagined..."

Adair frowned, "but he's a folk healer, ain't he? I mean...the very best of them can even reverse the aging process..."

Edelwyn chuckled at his friend's naiveté, "he was old even when *we* were children...no folk healer could achieve that... suffice to say, there are higher powers that have taken an interest in him."

Adair nodded, but had clearly understood little.

Edelwyn didn't bother to tell him more. He had already revealed too much. The Order itself had grades and sensitive information was rarely shared with those in the lower echelons who hadn't been initiated into the higher mysteries. He doubted that old Adair would even be able to comprehend the scale of what was about to happen.

"Let them flee..." Edelwyn said softly. "They'll not get far...we will send word to the outlying towns to keep an eye out for them, for now...let us find another suitable sacrifice for the Most High..."

Adair crossed his arms and frowned, "such as?"

"Well…you know dear old Margaret who runs the bread shop? Her young niece is down for the summer."
Adair's face brightened, "aye…I suppose we best go and drag her out then."
Edelwyn lifted his hand, "no need, old friend…we have merely to ask Margaret and she'll drag her out *herself*."

The Old Magic

"When the Ardhians first arrived, they found a land which was untamed and vast. The first wars which were fought after they made landfall were called the Wars of the Beachheads. Through these battles, the Ardhians secured their settlements against the onslaught of ravenous Beastmen which assailed them only briefly. From here, they moved east and established the first kingdom from which they projected their growing power outwards. That kingdom would later be known as Arinönde."

-'The Ardhian Lands' by Wolter Keers

Princess Rionéolas entered the forbidden study and glanced up at the arcane volumes that were stacked before her. She was surprised to find only a single bookshelf in the cold, stone-lined room. There were perhaps two dozen volumes there to peruse, all of them banned by the kingdom.

A single, oaken table sat in the centre of the small room and on either wall were two oil lamps which she illuminated with one of the candles she had taken as she descended the stairs.

As the room filled with the warm glow of the lamps, the Princess moved towards the small bookshelf. She refrained from running her hands along the volumes as she normally would when searching for a book to read. These books were not to be trifled with and she didn't know what kind of elder magic might still be emanating from them.

The titles of these volumes were infamous among magical practitioners and were clearly divided. Along the bottom row: *The Eye of the Worm* by Gurr Corlich, *Abyssal Sigils* by an anonymous scribe, *The Pit of Magic* written on papyrus by renowned black magician Aurian. Each of these were potent in their own right, but they paled in comparison to the three which followed.

Here was: *The Black Cube* by Albrecht Handschuh, *The Seal of the Dragon* by Monen, and of course the supreme masterpiece which stood above them all: *The Liber Novum*…the terrible *Red Book of Drachmuin.*

It was this eldritch text which the Princess reached for.

She pulled it from the bookshelf slowly, treating it with the reverence which it deserved. This text, as the most infamous and famous magical book ever written, had haunted the Princesses' imagination since she was a child.

And yet, as she held it in her hands, it appeared rather unremarkable.

The smooth, red binding was almost certainly older than the Kingdom of Arinönde itself and despite the plainness of the exterior, there was a hoary, primeval power around it which the Princess had never felt before in any book. Her hands trembled slightly as she turned and laid it on the old wooden table.

In the semi-darkness, she sat staring at the tome as though unsure of how to approach it. At last, mustering her courage, she opened it to the first page and read:

The Liber Novum,
written in the Year of Falling Stars,
by the Priest-King Drachmuin.

She looked up and gasped. A wave of excitement ran through her. She would've loved to study this book from cover to cover for the rest of her life but knew that the Chaplains checked the study regularly and would know if it was missing.

She continued her perusal. The first few pages were an account of the Days of Fire, one which she had never read before:

The opening of the Silver Gate released the Star-Spawn into the world and brought about its ruin…but far worse than that…it drew the attention of something else…something from the Great Beyond…

The Princess shuddered. As absorbed as she was in this tale, she was pressed for time and had to flip through the book to find what she sought. As the ancient pages fluttered by, she caught brief glimpses of their contents: there were magical spells and ancient runes, circles of power and geometric sigils.

At last, a single word caught her eye: *Light Spire...*

She stopped on this particular page and continued reading:

The Light Spire is the key to it all...from this Spire are the Great Relics forged and only by reaching it can one find the power of the Arcalypsis Flame...

"The Arcalypsis Flame..." she said aloud.

She had never heard the term before. What ever could it be?

She had to force herself to continue reading. She knew of the Light Spire for it stood at the very heart of all the iconography of Arinönde and the Church. They called it the Spear of Antaryan and it was said to have brought life to the world when it fell from the heavens. According to these pages, Drachmuin had taken a special interest in it.

She suddenly realized that time had gotten away from her and Erich could awaken at any moment if he hadn't already. She summoned every ounce of her concentration, trying to retain as much information as possible.

The Light Spire...she thought. *How can it be found?* She wouldn't have the time to find out...she *had* to go.

But not without the book...

She closed the tome and gripped it to herself tightly. A kind of mad glee ran through her as she extinguished the light and bolted for the door.

Why am I doing this?

Perhaps she understood intuitively the disaster which was gathering strength. The rampant atavism and close-mindedness which pervaded the kingdom was something she could no longer abide. The old secrets *had* to be plumbed once again...

Otherwise, we will surely drown in the coming deluge...

High-Rector Renard Cartusian stepped quietly into the King's chambers and stood with his hands behind his back.

King Animrens was pacing back and forth anxiously.

"Highness..." Cartusian bowed.

Animrens stopped and faced him as though noticing him for the first time, "Renard… the day we have long dreaded has come at last…"

Cartusian stood tall and nodded, "I have nearly a thousand men standing by…"

"You'll need all of them…" Animrens said gruffly. "An Ardhian wizard is not to be underestimated."

"Are we *certain* this man is Ardhian?"

"What *else*!" Animrens said impatiently. "Magic such as that no longer exists…"

Indeed, it was baffling to imagine that such magic had *ever* existed. The King had heard stories of miracle workers and healers since he had been a boy. He had even seen the so called 'magicians' of the Bright Collegiate perform their magical ceremonies.

But he had never seen anything like this.

The King met Cartusian's deep, penetrating eyes, "the Hexekar were created for precisely this purpose: to hunt down *true* practitioners of magic…" his voice became grave. "To this end, I am entrusting you with executive powers…my will shall operate *through* you…do what you must, but remember, our goal is to bring this man in *alive*."

Cartusian nodded, "of course, sire…"

"Go then…"

"Praise the Light Father…" Cartusian said.

"His will be done…" the King replied.

Cartusian bowed once more and departed as swiftly as he had arrived.

Left alone at last, Animrens had time to think. He couldn't believe the situation that was unfolding before him. He was being pressed by all of his advisors to move with the greatest haste to contain this threat.

And Animrens, above all else, *despised* his advisors.

He was well aware that there were forces at work behind his back, shadow players who had a vested interest in forcing their politics on him through guile and deceit.

He would have none of it.

This wizard, if he truly was an Ardhian, would surely possess valuable knowledge. And knowledge was power in any arena.

Perhaps I can use him to liberate us from the yoke of Anturac…

The tithes which had to be paid to ensure the continued prosperity of the Continent were daily grating on the King's nerves. What right did Danyr have to declare Himself *Mage Emperor* and to hoard all wealth and power?

It was no secret that Anturac possessed magics and technologies far in advance of even Arinönde and it was because of this that Danyr had been able to assert His dominance for millennia uncounted.

Every child of the Empire knew the story of Danyr and His legendary arrival. He had descended upon the Continent like a ray of light and brought with Him an undying people who could craft the world to their will. Many of the ancient Ardhian monuments still stood across the provinces, a testament to that elder race's ingenuity and prowess.

The King was profoundly uncomfortable about the idea of breaching provincial borders, but he saw no other way around it. The thought of another kingdom acquiring the magus made him sick to his stomach. What kind of magical horrors would they be able to unleash upon Arinönde with so powerful a practitioner at their disposal? His Kingdom was in decline and this was the perfect means to rejuvenate it and restore it to glory.

The Von Richters and the Barrows had already pledged considerable resources to this enterprise and Animrens was surprised when a letter from Baroness Edda Von Richter had arrived offering him unlimited reserves of gold and silver to use as he saw fit.

Despite these heady developments, the King remained uneasy as the conflicts around him were beginning to grow apace.

In the south, in lands that would seem alien to the limited imagination of the common citizen, great beings waged wars for supremacy. The Eldann and the Vampyre nations were once again at odds and there were rumours of further conflict on the horizon.

Animrens would have been perfectly satisfied to allow those strange creatures to destroy themselves, but he worried that the conflict would spill over into the realm of Man. Should such a thing happen, only the intervention of Anturac would save them.

Then, of course, there were the Beastmen incursions. A minor nuisance at best, but a hindrance nonetheless.

Animrens walked over to his desk and looked at the map which was laid out on it. He ran his fingers over the top of it (akin to the way his daughter ran her own fingers along her books) circling the Kingdom of Arinönde and moving east towards the outskirts. His finger at last arrived at a small village on the moors and paused there.

Ainshyre...

There had been reports trickling in, reports of a man with a silver eye who had passed through this obscure backwater.

And where are you going from there?

Animrens let his finger drift along the map. There seemed to be two potential courses this heretic could choose to take: one was the road south which led towards Black Point, the other was through the Great Forest to the north.

The King pondered this intensely.

To head towards Black Point would seem to be the logical course. That derelict town had a port which the heretic could use to gain access to the oceans. There was a catch, however: he would have to pass through Emvale, which had a sizeable barracks.

Suppose he should head through the Great Forest? He would be difficult to track and we would have to fortify the surrounding towns. It is critical to make the right decision...

Still, the King was prepared to trust his intuition on this point. It had rarely led him astray.

The Princess bolted up the stairs and found, to her relief, that Erich was still sound asleep. She didn't want the hassle of having to explain herself to him and the book in her possession was only mildly hidden within the folds of her dress.

Moving quickly, she bounded down the halls of the castle, drawing curious gazes from several servants, at last reaching the sanctity of her study. Closing the door and panting heavily, she tried to catch her breath and steady her nerves. The excitement and dread of what she had done was still coursing through her.

She removed the book from the folds of her dress and gazed upon its hoary cover for a moment, hypnotized by the arcane power of the ancient tome. She managed to pull herself away from it and return to her senses.

She wondered how long it would take the Chaplains to realize the book was missing and dreaded the thought that Erich would be able to connect the dots. She had been the last person he had seen after all.

I'll cross that bridge when it comes...

She moved to the oaken desk at the center of her study and carefully placed the book down. Taking a seat and summoning all of her willpower, she opened to a random page and read the contents:

All of the gods are made of mind-stuff. They are consciousness itself...there is no limit to the power of the mental faculty in man...

Never had she been so spellbound by words. They flowed in a steady cadence and seemed to implant themselves in the very depths of her mind. She continued to read by candlelight late into the night, eagerly absorbing the lost secrets of the Old Magic.

The Great Forest

"Many are the legends surrounding the Great Forest. It is a place of primeval mystery and wonder. Many, too, are the spirits and guardians that are said to dwell there. Greatest amongst them is Druim, the White Stag. To see a glimpse of him portends either great fortune or imminent disaster. Any travellers venturing through these woods would do so at their own peril."

-'Forgotten Places' by Baum

They had arrived in Argyr shortly after noon the next morning. The trek had been punishing for the children, but Amyn had plucked up some wild herbs along the way which had staved off their exhaustion.

Argyr was another small town which appeared to be more bustling than Ainshyre but less aesthetically pleasing. It had a run-down, gritty appearance to it but, in contrast to the quiet village they had come from, the streets were packed. Market Days were in full swing across the empire and vendors in every town were busy selling their wares in preparation for Harvest Time.

Amyn found a local inn and paid the gruff innkeeper with several gold coins so that the children could be afforded some rest. They were both exhausted from their long trek.

"Where will you go?" Charlotte asked before plunging into her room.

Amyn gestured outside, "to get you some food…the Market is on."

"Are you not *tired*?"

But the old man had simply smiled and shook his head. Indeed, he appeared positively radiant despite the lack of sleep.

Charlotte didn't question it. She was desperate for rest, as was her brother who was practically falling asleep standing up. When they at last found their room and dove into their respective beds, oblivion took them.

Amyn made his way out onto the cobblestone street and breathed in the cool air. The sound of vendors and farmers hawking their wares created a cacophony which blended into a kind of steady background noise. He glanced left and right before making his way down the long, produce-laden rows of carriages and wagons.

He knew that he wouldn't be able to allow the children to rest for too long. Events were now moving quickly and there was little he could do to delay the oncoming deluge.

He cast these thoughts away, for now.

He roamed the streets casually and found a few things for the children. He hadn't intended to bring them with him initially, but the thought of them being sacrificed in Ainshyre like cattle had moved his conscience to take action.

These petty morals have gotten me in trouble before... he chided himself.

He couldn't afford to falter, not now. The pieces were falling into place and there was little to no wiggle room to alter their course.

A raven flew overhead and circled above him, cawing three times before flying off. Its warning had been received loud and clear: *armed forces were moving towards Argyr.*

Amyn knew that they intended to hem him in and he did a quick mental calculation to ensure that he would have enough time to elude them. If he were travelling alone, he wouldn't even think twice, but the addition of the children forced him to reconsider his options.

Then an idea came to him. He made his way towards one of the vendors.

The man gave him a snaggle-toothed smile and gestured to his wagon, "some produce, fine sir?"

Amyn nodded and reached into his pocket to withdraw several gold coins. They shone in the sunlight and the vendor's eyes widened with delight. He snatched the coins in one hurried motion and turned to grab a basket which he quickly filled with a generous heaping of vegetables.

Amyn made sure to meet the man's gaze and watched his eyes widen as he saw the glowing, silver orb which was looking back at him.

"Ehh…hope you have a wonderful day, kind sir…" the vendor stuttered.

"You as well…" Amyn said softly. He turned and headed back towards the inn.

The vendor watched him go as though he were transfixed. After a moment, he shook his head and returned to his wagon.

"Time to go, children…" Amyn said.

Charlotte groaned and Alexander rolled over, muttered something, then continued snoring.

"We don't have much time…" Amyn said. "Troops will be here in the next few hours."

"Armed forces…" Charlotte said, still in a semi-delirious state.

Amyn nodded, "I bought you some food for your journey."

Alexander, at last groping his way into the waking world, sat up and frowned through bloodshot eyes, "what…what's going on?"

Charlotte was now sitting upright, "I thought you said they wouldn't pursue us beyond the confines of the village…"

Amyn nodded, "these are not the wayward villagers of Ainshyre on our heels…these are members of the army."

Clarity appeared in Alexander's eyes at last, "…the army…but *why*? What did we do?"

Amyn sighed, "it was nothing *you* did, my boy…it's me they want."

Charlotte and Alexander looked at one another but remained silent.

Amyn nodded towards the door, "quickly now…we must make haste."

The siblings rushed from their beds, their heads awash with questions. Charlotte in particular was disturbed by the strange turn which these events had taken.

Alas, she felt helpless.

They were now caught in a whirlwind from which they couldn't possibly extricate themselves. Their once beloved great-uncle had revealed himself to be a manipulative monster and the trauma of Ainshyre was still too fresh to dwell on.

As they made ready and grabbed their packs, Charlotte cast a quick glance towards Alexander and saw her own fears reflected in his face. Could the old man be trusted? Was he a monster like their great-uncle?

These questions couldn't possibly be answered and as the three of them departed the inn and plunged into the streets, they glanced left and right before making their way up the long stretch of cobblestone road.

Vendors on either side of them called out incessantly and this droning, combined with the penetrating rays of the sun, gave Charlotte a throbbing headache. Soon, the streets began to clear as they moved further and further away from the bustling Market.

Alexander gave a sigh of relief and began to probe Amyn with questions, "so…where are we going exactly?"

The old man smiled indulgently, "we must pass through the Great Forest to reach the Tower."

"The Tower of…what was it called again?" Charlotte asked.

"Drachmuin…" Amyn replied.

Alexander frowned, "I've heard that name…but not in school."

The old man turned to him, "you wouldn't hear it from anyone at the Bright Collegiate either…it is a forbidden name…as are the names of the other Priest Kings save for Danyr whose legend has been corrupted nearly beyond recognition."

"Why exactly are they after you again?" Charlotte asked.

Amyn's gaze fell towards the ground, "because…I stole an ancient *Ardhian* relic."

That statement alone confirmed nearly every suspicion that the children had. They went silent for a moment and tried to process what they had just heard.

Ardhia was the stuff of myths and legends and to hear Amyn speak of such a primeval place made the children wonder if they were dreaming or if the old man was mad.

Amyn chuckled, "I'll understand if you don't believe me."

Alexander picked up his pace so that he could stride alongside their guide, "wait a minute… Ardhia was a *real* place?"

Amyn nodded, “as real as any of the places we have passed through.”

Charlotte held a hand to her head, “so…how exactly did you get this relic?”

Amyn pointed beyond the outskirts of Argyr, “let’s continue on our journey. Tonight, we’ll make camp on the outskirts of the Forest, and *then* I will answer your questions.”

The group continued on in silence. Despite their lack of sleep, Charlotte and Alexander felt a growing sense of both excitement and dread. They desperately wanted answers but knew that they would come in time.

They trekked for what felt like an unending eternity and would have surely succumbed to exhaustion if not for the herbs which Amyn supplied to keep them going.

The endless moors which surrounded them stood in stark contrast to the sea of trees which they were gradually approaching.

Charlotte pointed towards those primeval sentinels, “…is *that* it?” The anxiety in her voice was palpable.

Amyn nodded, “we will make camp at the base of this hill…”

The sun was already falling in the sky and preparing to dip below the horizon while the first stars were beginning to peak through.

Alexander marvelled at the sight before him, “I’ve never seen anything like it…it’s magnificent.”

“And who knows what beasts may be lurking in there…” Charlotte said.

Amyn chuckled but remained silent.

As they reached the bottom of the hill, Amyn stopped and glanced around, “this is a good spot…let us collect some brush to start a fire.”

Alexander dropped his pack on the ground and sighed, “and where are we going to get that?”

The old man pointed towards the Forest, “…where else?”

Charlotte groaned as she lowered her pack and sat on the cold earth, “you have fun with that…I’m not going anywhere near that Forest while darkness approaches.”

Amyn turned to Alexander, “well…that leaves you, my boy.”

Alexander glared at Charlotte with something close to resentment. Shoulders slumped; he followed Amyn to the tree line. The enormous pines loomed oppressively above and Alexander shuddered at the sight of them. Never had he seen trees of such obvious antiquity and their presence was so imposing that he felt as though they were watching him.

The old man sensed his discomfort immediately, "do not fear the trees, boy…as long as we show respect, they are of no threat to us."

No threat? Alexander thought with horror.

The implications of such a statement baffled him. Cautiously, he knelt and began gathering brush and twigs. When his arms were full with all that he could carry, he moved quickly back to the hill and was greeted by the laughter of his sister.

"See any ghosts?" she teased.

Alexander glared at her once more, "says the one who was too afraid to go in…"

She brushed him off, "not afraid…just *smart*."

"Sure…" Alexander grunted.

Amyn dropped a pile of brush and chuckled, "sibling rivalry, it seems, can endure any trial."

The old man knelt and produced a piece of flint. With a few skillful strokes he had ignited a small flame which quickly spread. Soon, they had a fire going and they sat in a circle as the chill of the night air encroached. The light and warmth of the fire gave them all a sense of comfort against the surrounding darkness.

Alexander, no longer able to contain himself, turned to Amyn, "so…you were talking about Ardhia…"

Charlotte waved him off, "Ardhia can wait…"

Alexander turned and scowled at her.

She ignored him, "Amyn…we need to know what's going on here…one minute we're in our great-uncle's village, now we're heading on some wild goose chase to an ancient tower."

The old man produced his small pipe from the folds of his robe and began to fill it with tobacco.

Charlotte continued, the irritation in her voice rising steadily, "we're not going to enter some forest until we have a proper explanation…"

Amyn lit his pipe and took a long draw from it. A plume of smoke emerged from his mouth and momentarily obscured his face, "I shall answer both of your questions…" he crossed his legs and sighed before turning to Charlotte. "First…the reason you are coming with me is because you would have died had you stayed in Ainshyre."

Charlotte gasped.

"I'm afraid it's true, child…" there was a hint of melancholy in Amyn's voice. "I've kept an eye on Ainshyre for many years and I have always suspected that they housed a secret cult…"

"Is that why all of those people were dressed in black?" Alexander asked.

Amyn nodded, "they follow the Old Religion."

Charlotte frowned, "I wouldn't expect to encounter a renegade Bright Church sect in a village so far from the capital."

Amyn turned to her slowly, his silver eye seemed to glow in the semi-darkness, "child…I can assure you that they are not followers of anything even remotely associated with the Bright Church."

Charlotte at last broke down, tears flowing forth unbidden, "I can't believe uncle Adair was going to *kill* us…I just can't…"

Alexander moved quickly to where she was sitting and put an arm around her. The boy was trying to be strong, but tears spilled from his eyes despite his best attempts to hide them.

Amyn lowered his head, "I would not have wished this upon either of you…and while I understand the pain you feel, we cannot afford to dwell on it too deeply. Know this: your uncle was part of a cult which predates the Bright Church and worships a god you have likely never heard of."

The children looked up with reddened eyes but remained silent.

Amyn took another draw from his pipe, "the older you get, the more you realize just how little you know…understand that there are forces beyond comprehension which move in this world and your uncle was merely a pawn in a much grander game…and yes…Ardhia *was* a real place despite what you've been told." He emptied the ash from his pipe and placed it back in his pocket. "Now…take rest…we must move again in a few hours."

Charlotte nodded and glanced down at Alexander only to see the boy fast asleep on her arm. She wiped her face and put her arms around him, drawing him close. A few moments later, she too was asleep.

Amyn watched them from across the fire. He knew that it was in his best interests to cut them loose as they would only slow his progress. But something in him held back.

Perhaps I've grown soft over the many ages...he thought.

Regardless, before daylight they would have to venture into the Great Forest, a perilous journey for most travellers.

But Amyn was certainly *not* most travellers.

He had already received the blessing of Druim, the Stag God, and could count on the way through being made clear. Those who wandered in without the proper ritual were liable to find themselves in an endless maze of trees and foliage from which they would never emerge.

Amyn leaned back and closed his eyes to get some rest. He hoped that the Royal Guard were tardier than they had been a generation ago, lest they close the gap and cut off any hope of escape. Given the current decadence of Animren's court, however, Amyn and the children probably still had a good head start.

The Mercenary King

"Arinönde has long been accused of using mercenary forces to do their dirty work. Chief among these is a small but brutal tribe which traces its ancestry to the Unterwilt. They were called the Móg Flagen. They were unlike other tribes in the area in that they were never sedentary. Warring and pillaging as they went, their services were often open to the highest bidder. It was from this tribe that the ruthless warrior-chief, Mabinogan, hailed."

-'Barbarian Tribes' by Philip of Norden

The camp fires were low and barely holding up against the fierce winds. Tents swayed back and forth and the grunts of goats and pigs mingled with the crackling of wood.

One of the tents opened slowly and a large, burly beast of a man emerged from it. Stretching his arms and breathing deeply of the cold night air, he made his way towards the nearest fire where a small group of men were gathered.

As he arrived, he was saluted in the customary greeting of his people.

"Ha Danen..." one of the men said.

"Ha Danen..." he replied.

At nearly six foot five, Mabinogan was a giant, even among his own people. His aquiline features were accentuated by a dark auburn beard and long hair which he had braided into a tight pony tail. He wore a crown made of Dragon teeth and his piercing eyes shone with the light of the fire as though he were some sort of predatory animal. His skin, like the skin of all the Móg Flagen, was a dusky, ashen grey.

When the officials from Animren's court had arrived requesting a secret meeting, they had been met with scepticism. In Mabinogan's tent, as the cold winds rustled outside, the officials had lain out an irresistible offer: apprehend a heretic wizard and the Móg Flagen would receive all of the land west of the River Sirin.

Mabinogan's mouth had dropped open. Those lands were part of a sacred ancestral site called the Unterwilt which had been lost to the armies of the empire centuries before. There were prophecies which had been handed down in the Móg Flagen oral traditions that a great Chief would one day unite the tribes and take back those sacred lands.

A Chief who was prophesied to rule the world one day.

Mabinogan could scarcely fathom his good luck, but he was always distrustful of outsiders, and rightly so.

"What guarantee do I have that you'll live up to your end of the bargain?" he had asked one of the officials.

The man, dressed in nondescript clothes but carrying an indisputable air of authority had given a terse reply, "the King has agreed to cede fifty percent of the land to you this instant…your people may begin settling it at their convenience. The other fifty percent, you'll get when the task is complete."

Mabinogan glanced at his astonished colleagues, smiled, and crossed his powerful arms, "the King must be desperate indeed to bring this man in…if he's prepared to offer us the *Unterwilt*…" he leaned forward and the officials unconsciously leaned back. "What exactly has he done?"

One of the officials appeared to be about to speak, but his colleague cut him off, "that is the King's concern…*your* concern is whether or not to accept his most gracious offer."

Mabinogan's eyes shone ever brighter, "well then…you'd better tell him I humbly accept."

The officials nodded. They had heard what they wanted.

Mabinogan laughed, "that simple, is it?" he spat on the ground. "If this man is indeed a wizard, as you say, then why not have the Bright Church deal with him? Isn't magic *their* specialty?"

The officials glanced at one another uncomfortably. The fact that Mabinogan knew that the heretic was a wizard surprised them.

"The Church cannot be seen to be involved..." one official said.

"Ahh..." Mabinogan slapped his leg. "So, it's a game of subterfuge, is it? Well...I'll have you know that the methods I intend to use could hardly be called *subtle*."

One of the officials nodded, his face a blank stare, "...you have free reign to do as you will...just so long as no essential Crown Land is desecrated."

Mabinogan grinned, "and what about those on the outskirts?"

"They are fair game..." the official said.

"Very well..." Mabinogan leapt to his feet, startling everyone in the tent. "We begin the hunt at sunrise..."

The other tribesmen smiled broadly and clasped their large hands together.

The officials seemed eager to depart and eyed the flap of the tent with growing anxiety. They moved swiftly towards it, hoping to make their way out with haste.

"One last thing..."

Mabinogan's guttural voice stopped them in their tracks. They turned slowly and faced him, their countenances white with apprehension.

The Lord of the Móg Flagen gazed down on them like a great beast of myth, "when I have this man in my possession...you expect me to bring him in alive...is that right?"

The officials nodded.

Mabinogan shrugged his broad shoulders, "that may require a few more concessions from the King..."

"Outrageous..." one of the officials blurted out, but he immediately regretted his loose tongue.

"Careful..." Mabinogan said softly. "The last envoy that disrespected me found their heads parted from their shoulders."

Now the officials could scarcely hide their fear. They stood quaking in the presence of the Barbarian.

"Inform the King that I will make my demands known at a later date...and be thankful that you return to him alive. I will bring this man in, but I will do so on *my* terms." Mabinogan said.

The officials nodded and departed quickly.

Mabinogan turned to the others in the tent. These men were his High Council and closest confidants, "be ready my brothers…first…we take the Unterwilt…and then…" his face grew dark. "We take Arinönde."

Princess Rionéolas awoke with a start. She had collapsed on the desk of her study and for a moment she couldn't orient herself to waking life.

How long have I been asleep? she wondered.

She glanced down and saw the open tome which lay before her and an involuntary shudder went through her being as she gazed at the geometric diagrams and mystical incantations. She closed the book in one swift movement and leaned forward with her hands on her head.

She wondered if Erich had figured out what she had done and a terrible wave of guilt ran through her. Surely the Chaplains were now seeking the stolen book and she would be brought before her father's throne to receive his baleful stare of disapproval.

Glancing out the window revealed the sun to be high in the sky which meant it was not yet lunch time. She found it strange that none of the servants had come in to rouse her but they must have seen the door to the study firmly closed and thought better of interrupting.

She looked down at the book and tried to remember what she had read of its contents. Her mind, though exhausted, was desperately trying to piece together the scattered bits and pieces which she had absorbed the night before. Finding these recollections to be less than satisfactory, she opened the book once more.

Through nothing short of chance, she realized that she had opened to the exact point that she had left off. The spidery text ran before her eyes:

The Light Spire is not what the myths make it out to be…it does, in fact, exist and its true meaning has been hidden from the general populace for millennia. Even we, mighty as we imagined ourselves, could not fully comprehend its mysteries. But the answers must surely lie in the Great Relics…

She paused for a moment as footsteps echoed down the hall.

She closed the book quickly and was prepared to chuck it under the table, but the footsteps continued on their way, passing by her room until they were only an echo.

She sighed deeply and re-opened to the last page:

We, through our arrogance, may have doomed our world. We have accidentally set foot in a cosmic arena which could very well bring woe to us all...

The Princess gasped. That was enough for now.

She closed the book and collapsed in her chair. She knew of her Father's preparations and the lengths that he was preparing to go to capture the elusive wizard.

She paused and put her slender fingers against her chin. She needed rest, but that would have to be put off for now. Perhaps, if the stars aligned, she would be able to make preparations of her own.

In the village of Argyr, a small regiment of heavily armed men arrived. They swept from house to house silently, interrogating villagers one by one. Their black uniforms and strange insignia made the villagers nervous and many who saw them said a silent prayer that they wouldn't set foot in their homes.

These were the Hexekar.

They were part of the Bright Church's most clandestine branch of occult police. They had virtually unlimited authority within their national boundaries. Interrogation, torture, and murder were their stock and trade.

And they were very, very good at them.

For now, their mission was to identify the trajectory of the renegade magician and to this end, they quietly questioned several people of interest within Argyr.

One such individual was a produce vendor named Calil. He had offered himself up with a snaggle-toothed grin to the Hexekar the moment they had set foot in the main square and he seemed to know instinctively what they were after.

Taking him aside into an alleyway, the officers had probed him with questions and he had spoken freely. Yes, he *had* seen a man in a red cloak with a rather curious silver eye. Even more intriguing, the man seemed to be accompanied by two children.

The officer's widening eyes and surprised expressions told Calil that this was indeed valuable information.

"You're with the Church…yes?" Calil asked with more than a fair bit of hesitation.

The Hexekar officer nodded slowly.

Calil gathered his hands together in prayerful reverence, "will my family be offered salvation?"

The officer looked at him for a moment, then smiled, "if your information leads to the capture of this fugitive, then you and your relations shall reside in the *Empyrean…*"

Calil's eyes misted with tears, "thank you…thank you."

The officer turned to one of his fellows and whispered something, then they departed.

Calil was sorry to see them go, but he had done his part and he was proud of it. One less heretic was never a bad thing.

The Hexekar congregated in the square, their black horses standing at the ready. One of the officers had a falcon on his arm and he extended his hand to receive a small piece of parchment which was inscribed with all of the necessary information which had been recovered. He slipped the parchment into a small, steel canister and strapped it to the falcon's leg. A moment later, the bird took to the sky with a screech.

The Hexekar commander turned and indicated silently that they should continue forward. The others nodded and mounted their horses. As swiftly as they had arrived, they were gone. While their visit had been short, they had created quite a stir among the villagers of Argyr who would now have gossip for months.

The Hexekar headed north towards the Great Forest. Their sources indicated that the magician and the children following him would most likely have headed that way, rather than venturing south. It was a bold move, but it would give the Hexekar the opportunity to outflank them. Should that prove impossible, then they were to drive him in the direction of Mabinogan and his lackeys.

The magician *must* be brought in alive, but the children travelling with him presented a problem. It was likely that they already knew more than they should about the situation and would therefore have to be dealt with appropriately.

The Hexekar knew how to keep people quiet, even it meant making them disappear.

Divergence

"Many are the paths to magical supremacy, and many are the pitfalls. The magician must always be sure that they are conducting their rituals with the utmost secrecy. To be boastful is anathema to true magic and will instantly reveal those charlatans who make bold claims but provide little in the way of substance."

-excerpt from the Red Book of Drachmuin

They had made their way into the woods just as the sun was cresting the horizon. The forest itself had a primeval presence to it which made the children shudder involuntarily.

Amyn led the way, guided by what appeared to be little more than instinct.

Charlotte glanced up at the forbidding, powerful trees that towered over them, "…magnificent." She could scarcely hide the awe in her voice. A moment later, she saw a raven perched on one of the trees, staring at her. The sun shone from the bird's eyes in golden flecks. Indeed, one of the bird's eyes seemed to shine with solid gold and she was utterly transfixed by the sight of it. Suddenly, it cawed and took the skies.

Amyn nodded, "this forest is the oldest of its kind. It predates the coming even of the Ardhians."

Alexander, showing no signs of exhaustion, found his curiosity piqued once more, "you seem to know a lot about Ardhia…where did you learn all of this knowledge?"

Amyn remained silent for a moment, "there is a clearing up ahead…when we arrive there, we will take rest."

Alexander frowned. His question hadn't been answered, but he hoped that the old man would be more forthcoming once they reached the clearing.

Dense foliage would have made travelling by horse impossible and Alexander had deduced that this was precisely what Amyn intended. He couldn't shake the encroaching claustrophobia and the feeling of being watched from all sides.

Amyn sensed the boy's discomfort, "do not fear…so long as we keep to the appointed path, no harm shall come to us."

Alexander didn't bother to ask what would happen if they strayed off into the blind wilderness. He imagined it would involve an unpleasant encounter with wild animals or perhaps the trees themselves would swallow them whole. His imagination began to run wild, conjuring fantastic delusions.

Charlotte seemed far more at ease. She had always had a kinship with the natural world.

Amyn pointed ahead, "there…"

Alexander and Charlotte saw what appeared to be an opening in the forest. Rays of light poured down between the trees and primordial stone obelisks littered the grounds. There was an air of sanctity to the place and the children walked cautiously as though afraid they may step on some ancient relic.

Amyn stopped and turned to them. He removed a small satchel and produced some bread and produce. He gestured to a tiny stream which was flowing to their right, "drink from there if you wish…"

Charlotte eyed the stream cautiously, "…is it safe?"

Amyn chuckled, "of course! As I said, no harm shall come to us so long as we keep the appointed path."

The children glanced at one another, then moved quickly towards the stream, cupping their hands and greedily drinking their fill. Satisfied, they returned to the center of the clearing and helped themselves to some bread.

Amyn sat on a broken stone pillar and lit his pipe. Soon, ringlets of smoke were blowing up towards the trees.

Charlotte couldn't help but look on in awe, "what…is this place?"

"An ancient site of worship…" Amyn said softly. "To the Stag God."

"Who is the Stag God?" Alexander asked between mouthfuls of bread.

Amyn's silver eye turned towards him, "the Guardian of the Forest…it is he who guides our path."

Charlotte nodded as though she understood. She felt quite content sitting in this place and enjoying the ambient peace that surrounded them. There was a feeling of safety here, as though they were being sheltered from the dangers of the outside world.

Finishing his piece of bread, Alexander turned to Amyn, "you were talking about Ardhia…"

The old man smiled, "you have an inexhaustible well of curiosity, don't you boy?"

"More like inexhaustible persistence…" Charlotte said, smiling and gently poking Alexander's shoulder.

The boy lowered his head, "it's just that…well…nothing."

Amyn blew another ringlet of smoke, "don't ever lose that, my boy…curiosity is a marvelous trait and one that more people should cultivate."

Alexander looked up, his face brightening visibly.

Amyn sighed, "you have both been through a great ordeal…yet you have persisted…this, in my opinion, makes you worthy of the knowledge I am about to impart."

The siblings leaned back, their eyes widening in anticipation.

"You asked me how it is that I know so much about ancient Ardhia…my answer to that question is because I *lived* it…" Amyn said.

The siblings gasped.

Alexander was looking on in a half-daze, "you are…*Ardhian*? But *how*?"

Amyn took another puff from his pipe, "perhaps we should start with a story…a story about the First Days."

The children were now absolutely enraptured and they dared not interrupt despite the innumerable questions they had.

Amyn emptied the ash from his pipe and placed it back within the folds of his robe, "let's start at the beginning…"

"I was born in the year of Falling Snow. It was, from what I'm told, one of the worst winters we had ever had. Ardhia was known for its temperate climate and winter for us was little more than a cool summer.

But this was different.

Snow fell for the first time in living memory. Our priests declared it an inauspicious omen. In a few years, we would come to the climax of our Great Work and the Arknama Machine would be complete. The Great Work was to be the pinnacle of our achievements…the diffusion of the magical field across the entire world.

I can see by the look on your faces that you've never heard of the magical field before…it is exactly what it sounds like: a cosmic field of power that surrounds the world and allows us to draw from it to create magical phenomena.

As I grew to adulthood, I was selected for service in the Priesthood. This was the lower degree of the penultimate rank of Serpent Priest. The Serpent Priests were semi-divine kings who had absolute authority over their respective districts. To become one was to be tested in every conceivable manner. Many were those who failed the tests. These were not low-level initiations, but life and death experiences which yielded no quarter to those without strength of will.

This was a time of great prosperity. It was the time before the Days of Fire…"

Amyn paused for a moment and a pained expression crossed his face, "that's enough for now…"

Charlotte glanced over at Alexander and could see that the boy was enrapt. She turned back to Amyn and clapped her hands, "well…I must say, that was *quite* the story Amyn…quite the story indeed."

The old man frowned slightly.

Charlotte leaned back on her hands, "I mean…it was nothing that couldn't have been read in any book in any library across the empire. You know, I was fine believing that you were a magician, perhaps even a highly skilled one…but now I see that you've been playing us for fools."

Alexander's eyes widened but Amyn remained silent.

Charlotte rose to her feet, "I think we'll be leaving now…"

Alexander turned to her, a look of horror on his face, "and go *where*?"

Charlotte shrugged her shoulders, "anywhere but here…we'll make our way out of the Forest and find the nearest village, from there, we can head back to the capital."

Amyn crossed his arms and an amused look ran across his face, "you remember how to get out of here?"

Charlotte gave the old man a scowl, "it can't be that difficult…if a wandering old mendicant can find his way through then I'm sure we can as well…"

Alexander gasped. He could scarcely believe the disrespect his sister was displaying.

"I understand…" Amyn said softly. "You have both been through a great deal…"

"You have *no* idea what we have been through…" Charlotte said coldly. "You saw two impressionable children and decided to whisk them away from their great-uncle's home with an elaborate story about a death cult. Then, you dragged them halfway across the province on a wild goose chase to fulfill some twisted goal which you've yet to reveal."

Alexander raised his hand in an attempt to stop the flow of invective, "…Charlotte."

She waved him off, "no…I've had *enough* of this. We've been bounced around like cattle ever since Father left. I'm tired of being taken advantage of by those who claim to be our elders…" she glared at Amyn, mustering all of the vitriol she could spare. "Take your huckster act somewhere else…we're taking back control of our lives." She turned and held out her hand to Alexander. "Let's go…"

The boy sat, momentarily stunned. He turned to Amyn with a look of sadness on his face, then took Charlotte's hand.

The old man's demeanour had remained unperturbed. He casually took his pipe from the folds of his robe and began to fill it with tobacco.

Alexander was pulled up by his sister. Her grip was strong and his arm felt as though it were in a vise. He looked at Amyn for a moment with pleading eyes.

The silver orb of the old man's eye gleamed in the light, "don't be foolish now…to stray from the path is dangerous."

Charlotte didn't bother to turn back, "no more dangerous than continuing onwards with *you*."

Alexander felt the grip on his arm release and he sighed deeply. He took one last look back at the clearing and the old man smoking his pipe, then turned and followed his sister into the depths of the Forest.

The trees began to close in on them and the path became tighter. The soft light of the clearing was replaced by a gloomy semi-darkness which began to encroach from all sides. It was as though the Forest itself was responding to the dark emotions Charlotte was exuding.

She muttered to herself as they went and Alexander could only make out small fragments of her speech which were coherent. He was less concerned with what she was saying and more worried about getting lost.

And they most certainly *were* lost.

"Charlotte…" he muttered.

She didn't hear him and seemed distracted by her own thoughts.

"Charlotte!" Alexander's voice echoed through the Forest.

At last, she stopped walking and the total silence which followed snapped her back to her senses. She turned to him, "…*what*?"

Alexander felt his anger rising, "do you have any idea where we are?"

"Of course I do…" Charlotte pointed ahead. "The exit is just up here."

"It's not…" Alexander said sternly. "We're lost."

"Are we?" Charlotte looked left, then right. "I could've sworn this was the way."

"You have no idea where we're going…we're walking in circles."

Charlotte clenched her hands tightly. Her younger brother's ignorance was staggering, "well…why don't *you* lead the way then?"

Alexander shuffled on his feet, "I…I don't know it."

"Exactly…" she said, not concealing the harshness in her voice. "You *don't* know…you don't know the responsibility I've had to take on ever since Father left: trying to look out for our best interests because *no one* else will... trying to make sure that we have a future. And now look at us…we're lost in the woods because we believed some old conman. We were supposed to be in *school* Alexander…" tears flowed from her eyes. "And look at us now…just *look* at us!"

The echo of her voice was followed by the stillness of the Forest and the sound of her heavy breathing.

Alexander moved forward and hugged her tightly. She wrapped her arms around him and they sobbed together. Their trials and tribulations flowing forth in a deluge of repressed emotion.

When it was over, Alexander pulled away from her and met her eyes with his own, "you've done a great job…Mom and Dad would be proud."

She smiled slightly, "perhaps not…now that I've gotten us lost."

Alexander pointed back the way they had come, "the clearing can't be far, perhaps we can find Amyn and he'll get us out of here…" he glanced at the ground, almost bashfully. "Then we can go our own way…"

Charlotte smiled slightly, "…perhaps."

There was a rustling sound behind them.

They turned in unison, suddenly feeling very exposed. Their breathing stopped and every sound seemed to be magnified a thousandfold.

The rustling continued. This time it was closer.

The Forest appeared to darken and the siblings looked at one another in unison.

"Run…" Charlotte said under her breath.

Instinct and panic kicked in and despite their better judgement, they ran. Alexander nearly tripped over a large exposed root but Charlotte grabbed hold of him with inhuman strength and pushed him forward. Soon, they were bolting blindly into the dense foliage.

Branches tore at their clothing as though the Forest itself had turned on them. The light which had trickled through the trees seemed to have vanished and now an all-encompassing darkness began to surround them. At the pinnacle of their terror, they stopped, unable to muster the strength to go any further.

As they huddled together and prepared to meet whatever was pursuing them, there was a sudden silence.

Charlotte, her face pressed hard against her brother's hair, dared to glance up and was astonished by what she saw: standing on a rise a few feet away from them was an enormous white stag. The creature had an air of majesty around it which seemed to illuminate the forest itself.

Charlotte rose slowly, utterly transfixed. She rubbed her eyes to ensure that she was not hallucinating and was surprised to see the stag still standing before them. The darkness which had shrouded their vision was gone and the Forest seemed to be bustling with life.

Alexander rose slowly, similarly hypnotized. All around them, green orbs floated in and out of view. He turned to Charlotte, "...Will-O-Wisps."

She nodded slowly, barely comprehending what he was saying. The green lights seemed to dance around them and it was as though she were seeing the Forest anew for the first time.

The stag, majestic and regal, turned slightly and began to walk away.

The siblings looked at one another with wide eyes and realized they were both thinking the same thing. They began to follow the creature, hesitantly at first, then quickening their pace to keep up. They didn't know where it was leading them, but anywhere was preferable to the secluded darkness they had just experienced.

The Noose Tightens

"The Ardhian monuments and relics that scatter the land remain shrouded in mystery. They are undoubtedly of the greatest antiquity, dating to the very first ages when Danyr Himself walked the land. Many believe they are possessed of some sort of magic, although the Bright Church has refuted these claims. Still, the power and mathematical precision of these ancient monuments cannot be denied, for they exert a certain influence upon the soul."

-'Wisdom Through the Ages' by Sanat Lan

The Princess had at last determined the proper course she would take. She had an adequate knowledge of astral projection and deemed it to be the safest means of finding her elusive quarry.

She had kept the golden chain which Mór had once worn when he had lived in the castle. It felt strange to think of that inscrutable creature as being a sort of shapeshifter and the idea of it sent chills down her spine. How many nights had she snuggled up next to that cat and felt a sense of comfort from its presence?

She cast these thoughts away. She didn't have much time.

She had been isolated in her study for long enough and it would only be a matter of time before the servants began wondering what she was up to. Normally, when she wasn't receiving lessons from one of her tutors, she wandered the castle grounds and conversed with the various tradesmen who lived just beyond the walls of the central keep. Technical matters had always intrigued her and some of her teachers often told her she had the mind of a Goblin. She took it as a compliment of course: Goblins were renowned as masters of technology.

She pulled the small, golden chain from her pocket and ran her fingers across it. She could perform the ritual standing up with her eyes closed. It required her to steady her mind and direct her thoughts. That she had a natural proclivity to magic had been touted by all of her teachers and scorned by her father, himself incapable of the most basic of magical operations or even feats of imagination.

She steadied her breath and repeated the mantra which would give her one-pointedness of mind. Suddenly, she was out of her body and looking down on herself. She smiled in her astral form and turned towards the window. The energy of the chain was still on her hands and she focused on it. She felt herself moving forward steadily, then, faster than thought, she found herself in the woods. It took her a moment to get her bearings and the sight of the enormous trees towering above her made her feel a strange sense of vertigo.

She turned and immediately she saw him: the old man sitting on a broken stone pillar seemingly absorbed in meditation.

As she approached, she kept rubbing the chain in her hand with her thumb. The old man didn't stir; indeed, he was as motionless as a stone. He had regal features and his snowy white beard seemed to shine in the semi-illuminated clearing.

Suddenly, he opened his eyes. Princess Rionéolas gasped and drew back.

A flash of light engulfed her and sent her spiralling through the void. When she awoke, still screaming, she imagined that she was back in her body. Indeed, the sensations of physicality had returned and she could feel the cold earth beneath her. She arose, slowly, and glanced around in shock.

Something had gone horribly wrong. She was not in the castle.

Then where am I? she wondered with growing horror.

Had she made some miscalculation? No. That surely wasn't possible. Something *else* had happened.

She could hear the sound of waves lapping on the shore which meant that she was on the coast. The sky had a grey tinge to it and there was a heavy mist in the air. Off to her right stood small, gambrel roofed houses and in the distance was a white church building. The architecture was unmistakeable as there was only one such building in all the empire and she had seen paintings of it numerous times before. Instantly, she felt a nauseating pall of anxiety come over her as she realized where she was.

Black Point...

Though she had never before set foot in that archaic place, she had heard enough stories and read enough lore to understand some of its history. It had been heralded as a magical threshold of unparalleled power. Since that time, the town had become a place of legends. An ancient cult had been rumoured to have taken hold of it and it had spawned numerous infamous figures including the Black Point Hag.

Even as a child, Princess Rionéolas had developed a keen dread in association with this place, as had many others.

Suddenly, she felt herself pulled forward by an unseen force. The scene around her changed, and she now stood in the center of the town. She could scarcely see any signs of life, save for a few oversized rats glutting themselves on a pile of refuse off to her right.

The scene shifted again. Now she was in a strange semi-darkness illuminated by a few candles. Looking at the harsh stone walls, which had the consistency of a cave tunnel, she deduced that she must now be underground.

But how? Who is guiding me?

As she moved forward, she realized she was in a large cavern. How large was impossible to tell, as the ceiling stretched on into the darkness and the walls on either side of her were barely illuminated. Torches were positioned in a long line leading to what appeared to be a central platform.

Whether the Princess moved on her own volition or by the will of some greater force she could no longer tell.

As she arrived at the central platform, she was stunned to see a figure in the darkness. As it inched closer to the light, she saw that it was a *woman*. She wore simple peasant garb and a small scarf over her head. In the distance around the platform, other figures shuffled about, but the Princess couldn't see clearly enough to make out their shapes.

As the woman drew closer, Princess Rionéolas gasped at the sight of her: her skin had a dark grey hue and her eyes glowed yellow. Even her clothing was dark grey, as though all colour had been drained from her being.

Only the eyes, glowing in the semi-dark, shone with a kind of eldritch light which made the Princess shiver uncontrollably.

"You have been chosen..." a voice beyond time said to her.

The Princess clenched her fists in fear, "…chosen?"

The old woman, if she could be called that, nodded, *"yes...by the Most High."*

"Who?"

"Your mission will become clearer to you as time passes... suffice to say, this reality is no longer fit for our Lord and He desires a higher realm filled with richer energies to consume. You will keep your eyes open for the signs..."

The Princess shook her head in confusion, "what signs?"

The old woman smiled indulgently, *"...you'll know."*

The Princess tried to fathom what she was being told, but before she could, she was cast backwards into a gaping abyss. When she awoke screaming from the blackness, she was lying on the floor of her study.

Moments later, the door swung open and one of the servants appeared, "highness…are you alright?"

The Princess took a moment to gather her senses, "yes…fine…I must have fallen asleep on the floor…"

"Let me help you up highness…" the servant moved forward and offered her a hand.

The Princess took it gratefully and as she rose to her feet, she realized in horror that she had left the Red Book lying open on the table. She glanced cautiously at the servant who appeared to be unaware.

She chanced a question, "is everything alright out there?"

The servant's eyes narrowed, "yes highness, of course, why wouldn't it be?"

"No one is searching about for anything?"

The servant crossed her arms and appeared dumbfounded, "no highness…has something been lost?"

The Princess shook her head, "no, no…forgive me…I've been having the strangest dreams."

The servant laughed, "ahh, dreams…dreams are messages."

The Princess looked at her for a moment, but before she could say more the servant winked at her and turned away, "cleaning will be through in an hour to do the study, highness…"

The Princess snapped out of her trance, "yes…of course…"

The servant smiled and departed.

Alone once more, the Princess tried to fathom what kind of experience she had just been subjected to. Perhaps her overactive imagination had gotten the better of her. Never, in all her numerous astral travels, had she ever been drawn away by another force. Of course, she had always known there were many intelligences in the Great Void, but to actually encounter one was jarring in the extreme.

Black Point...

The name jutted out in her consciousness like a jagged rock. Something was happening at Black Point. Something *big*. And she needed to know more about what it was.

She moved quickly to her library and snagged several books. She turned suddenly, remembered the Red Book on the table, then moved to scoop it up.

The old woman, if she was a woman, mentioned a mission...

What mission? She didn't know. It felt as though she were being drawn into something which was rapidly escaping her comprehension.

And who was it that had *chosen* her?

The name wormed its way up from her subconscious: *the Most High...*

Who is the Most High? she thought as she moved hastily out of her study. *Perhaps the better question though... is what.*

Mabinogan's men stood ready. He had selected the finest and most capable among them and ordered them to report to his tent. They now stood in single file, awaiting his inspection.

Here were some of the most ruthless barbarians to ever grace the cold steppes of the hinterlands. Half of them would have barely passed for human, as their ancestors had interbred with the Beastmen from the Lower Wastes. Their horns and tusks were a testament to what the Bright Church would have called 'abomination' but to the Móg Flagen, it was hailed as a sign of their superiority over the inferior masses of Man.

Mabinogan emerged, dressed in his finest furs, to inspect his troops. He had assembled ten of them for this task as he did not desire to make his presence known among the citizens of the empire.

Not yet, at least...

The 'men' stood at attention as he walked up and down their lines. Mabinogan himself was descended from similar stock but his lack of facial deformities could be beguiling for he possessed an animal's cunning.

Mabinogan stopped his pacing and faced his men, "hail Loch, god of the Wilt!"

"Hail the Wilt god!" the men shouted proudly.

"Now listen..." Mabinogan said gruffly. "We must find this renegade wizard for the Church. Our sources tell us that he will be accompanied by two children as well, so he shouldn't be difficult to track."

The beasts before him grunted with delight.

Mabinogan glared at them, "...the *wizard* is not to be harmed. The children I could care less about." He put his powerful arms behind his back. "Some of the best in the empire are pursuing this man...this means...that whatever he's done is of the highest importance to them. My sources tell me he *stole* something from Animrens."

There was silence for a moment as the others contemplated this.

Mabinogan continued, "whatever it is...it must be a thing of *tremendous* value. Our first order is to procure it for ourselves..."

The men grunted their approval.

Mabinogan's cat-like eyes shone in the eerie light of the moon, "hunt them down relentlessly. You will not be bound by borders nor by laws. In fact, for the first time in recorded history, the empire will be guiding our steps..." he looked down the line one last time. "Now...go forth...for the Unterwilt."

"For the Unterwilt!" the soldiers shouted in unison. They turned as one and departed without another word.

Mabinogan, alone at last to contemplate the next phase of his plans, returned to his tent. There was a great deal to think about.

Within the confines of his abode, he at last relaxed. A small fire in the center of the dwelling filled it with warmth and Mabinogan removed his heavy fur coat and tossed it to the side. Seating himself before the fire, he now plotted his next move.

He couldn't strike Arinönde directly, not yet at least. But the time was fast approaching.

He, like many other youths of the Barbarian tribes, had been educated in that splendid capital as part of a yearly trade between the Móg Flagen and the empire. For ten standard years he had been schooled in the ways of war, literature, maths and science and had been deemed promising enough to advance to the Bright Collegiate, although his lack of proficiency in magic had hindered him from obtaining lessons in the occult arts.

Nevertheless, he had thrived. So much so that he had become a threat.

The chief officials of the Collegiate had deemed that it would be an unmitigated disaster if a son of the Unterwilt were to outshine their own. To this end, they had rigged the system against him and ensured his eventual downfall. Casting him from the Collegiate in disgrace for a minor infraction and providing him no means to return home. Left to starve in the streets, the young boy had nearly perished but for his skill in stealing food from the local vendors. He had, through the grace of Loch, managed to escape the city and make his way into the hinterlands where he had been picked up by his own and nursed back to health.

From that day forward he had sworn vengeance.

He would use the very intelligence and knowledge his former teachers had given him and turn it against them.

*And on that inevitable day...*he thought with growing satisfaction. *All of Arinönde will beg for mercy.*

The Aulder Days

"And Danyr did smite down the Giants that opposed His passing and exiled the survivors into the outer reaches. No Giant has dared to show themselves since, nor have they been known to appear in the world of Men. Such is their righteous fate."

-First Canticle of the Coming of the Saviour, Bright Church text

They arrived back at the clearing wide-eyed and chastened. Amyn sat exactly where they had left him, smoking his pipe with an amused look on his face. It was as though no time had passed whatsoever.

Charlotte approached the old man with downcast eyes and a lowered head. She appeared to be searching for the right words.

"All is forgiven…" Amyn said with a wink.

She looked up into his eyes, meeting that inquisitive silver orb, "the…the stag…"

"Was Druim…the God of the Forest…yes…your eyes did not deceive you."

Her mouth hung open and her eyes had a faraway look.

Alexander couldn't contain his excitement, "he guided us back here and then disappeared! I tried to follow him but he was too quick…" the boy was practically bouncing. "And we saw Will-O-Wisps! Can you believe that?"

Amyn nodded his head slowly as if to assure the boy that he understood that these things were real and not the product of a child's vivid imagination, "there is much, much more in this Forest than you can imagine…but you should consider yourselves lucky…I managed to intervene with Druim on your behalf."

The children swallowed hard.

Charlotte sighed, "Amyn…I need to say it…I'm sorry…I mistook you for a fraud…it's just been-" she bit her lip but managed to stave off tears.

The old man leaned forward but his eyes were soft, "believe me, child, I understand..."

Charlotte nodded slowly but remained silent.

Amyn pointed behind them, "we must make our way out of here and continue east. If we're lucky, we may yet outrun our pursuers."

"Why bother waiting for us?" Alexander asked pointedly. "We abandoned you, and yet you remain here…"

The old man emptied the ash from his pipe and smiled, "because…your youth reminds me of a simpler time…" he seemed momentarily overcome with emotion but managed to gather himself and rise from the ruined pillar. "Come…" he motioned behind them. "Let us continue on."

The siblings nodded and followed. Any hesitation they may have had was wiped away by their encounter with the stag. Now, they were certain that their guide was the real thing.

The serenity of the forest around them was so intense that it had a palpable presence. The great oaks and pines which towered over them seemed less frightening than before. Now, they appeared to provide shelter from the dangers of the outside world.

Charlotte walked in silence, admiring the splendour.

Alexander, typically, was peppering Amyn with questions, "so, you *really* were born during Ardhian times?"

Amyn nodded.

The boy smacked his forehead, "how? How is that *possible*?"

"There is more possible than you can imagine…"

Now Charlotte spoke up, "but that would mean you were *thousands* of years old…do Ardhians not die?"

Amyn chuckled, "oh, we certainly do…our people are long-lived by default, of course, but our unique gift is that we can *choose* when we wish to depart this world…unless we're killed of course."

The implications of such a thing were staggering.

Alexander seemed to accept it instantly, "so…you're essentially immortal…and what was it like in ancient Ardhia? My teachers told me it was a megalithic culture with bronze and silver tools."

Amyn smiled, "your teachers are describing our situation after the Battle of the Beachheads."

"When Danyr and the Ardhians first arrived…" Charlotte said, recalling what she had read of ancient history. "They drove off the Beastmen and established the First Colony."

Amyn nodded, "yes…we had to fight every step of the way to ensure our survival…it was a difficult time for all of us."

Alexander gasped, "…did you know *Danyr*…I mean on a personal level."

The old man nodded, "Oh yes…he and I are good friends actually."

The boy was practically leaping with excitement, "you have to tell us everything…I want to hear it all."

Amyn looked at him quizzically, "the danger that surrounds us is now forgotten, I see…"

The boy stared down bashfully, "well…only if you *want* to tell it of course…"

Charlotte could scarcely hide her amusement. She had never seen her brother so excited.

As they proceeded along the path, Amyn leaned down and grabbed a long stick which he used to clear some of the brush that barred their way, "as I said before…every story must have a beginning…if you're prepared to hear it."

Both siblings nodded, even Charlotte had caught a wave of excitement.

"Very well…it will help us pass the hours as we travel…" the old man turned from them and continued along the path. "Let us start once more…"

"As I said before…I grew up in the last years before the decline of our civilization. Please understand, that even the lowest among our people were magical adepts. They would put many of your so-called magicians in this day and age to shame. We understood that the key to magic was *balance*…a balance which we tried to preserve.

"I understood this better than most…I'm not bragging, merely stating fact…it's why I was selected for the Serpent Priesthood. I can see by your eyes that you remember that term from my last exposition. Now, like all secret societies, the Priesthood had two specific teachings: an esoteric doctrine and an exoteric doctrine. The exoteric doctrine was distributed to the masses, but only the initiated could understand the esoteric one.

"I assume you wish to know what this doctrine was…the answer is not so simple. The exoteric doctrine spoke of the Great Forefather as Creator. This was something our people understood well, for all of life was imbued with a potent essence which could not be readily explained by logic. Now, the esoteric doctrine is different, it referred to the Arcalypsis Flame…

"You appear confused by that term…you've likely never heard it nor learned about it in your schools. As I've said before, the education system is corrupt and the Bright Church would have you indoctrinated to believe that magic is the privilege of the select few…but I tell you now, this is patently false.

"Magic exists in *all* things and anyone can draw upon it. It was the widening of this magical field which we sought to accomplish with our Great Work. To this end, we had created the Silver Gates…what were they, you ask? They were gateways into other realms. It was hoped that by activating these Gates in different energy centers around the world while using the Arknama Machine, we would be able to diffuse magical power to all…we were, in many ways, despite our advanced knowledge and millennia of wisdom, very naïve…the Skeags warned us against it.

"Ahh…I failed to mention the Skeags, didn't I? Understand that there are many races that inhabit this world and they do not always seek to make themselves known. The Bright Church would have you believe that Man alone is master of all things, but I tell you now, there are aeon-old beings whose achievements make those of Man seem like a fleeting dream.

"The Skeags and are such beings.

"The Skeags came from the Great Beyond and were master teachers of the arts and sciences, but it was the Dragons who were the first great teachers of all races. Their mathematics, science, astronomy, and magical prowess are unmatched. You've been taught that Dragons are mindless beasts but this couldn't be further from the truth.

"But I'm getting off track, aren't I? Now…in our blindness, we harnessed the geomantic power of Ardhia itself. Our continent was on top of a natural grid which produced a tremendous amount of power and it was this power which we sought to harness…we were convinced it would work, but, alas, we were wrong.

"The Gateways did not expand the magical field as we had hoped…but they *did* draw on the powers of other, more distant dimensions…and it was…disastrous."

Amyn stopped for a moment, as though deeply pained by the memory, then took a deep breath and resumed, "we opened a passage into another realm…a *hostile* realm. A realm filled with star-spawn and unfathomable creatures which did not take kindly to our intrusion. Thus began the Days of Fire…

"You've probably only heard of these times as myth and legend. I can assure you; they were very real and the world has yet to fully recover from them. Our people were caught off-guard by the incursion. The first two days saw the devastation of the capital and the slaughter of nearly a million innocents. These creatures were unlike anything we had ever encountered. They were not of this world and their ferocity was impossible to meet directly.

"Our cities burned and the eldritch fires of our abominable foes consumed all in their path. It was only by the sacrifice of our finest warriors that we were able to halt the incursion long enough to gather our strength. The Serpent Priests appointed four kings and gave them the Great Relics to wield as their own. Never had such power been granted to such a small group, but these were desperate times.

"The Skeags and the Dragons joined forces with us to drive the invaders back. Other races whose names have passed into legend gave their lives to hold the enemy at bay. In the hour of reckoning, as the skies turned red and molten ash filled the air, the Serpent Kings convened. Andarinoch and Suryan, along with Drachmuin and Danyr were among them and their wisdom in this Council saved many lives.

"The Dragons, led by Maledon the Elder, told us that they could combine their magics to close the Gate, but that Ardhia would fall. There was so little time to make a final decision, the hour was so desperate. We were losing ground every day and not even the ferocity of the Skeags could give the enemy pause for long.

"At last, a decision was made: to save the world, we would sacrifice Ardhia. I cannot describe the pain we felt in that moment, the utter despair, but there was no other way…Danyr and Drachmuin led what was left of our people onto boats while Andarinoch and Suryan stayed behind with the Dragons began their final ritual. We barely made it beyond the sight of our shores when the Gate collapsed on itself and irrevocably sundered our home. The waves took our lands and all that we had ever known and claimed them until the end of time. When we arrived in this new world, we were a broken people. But for the leadership of Danyr, we would not have survived…"

Amyn broke off his story and remained silent. The siblings were hanging on his every word. Never before had they been so enthralled by a tale.

"That is enough for now…" Amyn said. The tone of finality in his voice left no doubt that he had finished speaking and needed to be left undisturbed.

They walked in an uneasy silence, the siblings not daring to intrude upon their guide's private reflections. What they had heard baffled them to no end and threw everything they had ever known into question. They continued on their way, their minds ablaze with thoughts of a dark past and an uncertain future.

They reached the edge of the Forest just as the night was creeping in. Amyn insisted that they set up camp and prepare themselves for an early rise. Their plan was to make their way to Valleyhold and from there, to Nin-Ghasta where the Tower was located.

"What will happen when we reach the Tower?" Alexander asked.

"We go inside…" had been Amyn's matter-of-fact response.

Charlotte frowned, "what are we seeking there?"

Amyn turned the silver orb of his eye towards her, "transportation…"

The siblings were mystified by this enigmatic response, but the old man had lapsed into one of his deep silences which told them that any further questions would have to wait. They lay near the fire and were soon sound asleep.

Streams of Fate

"There are many myriad cults which fester within the empire. Among the most insidious of them is the Cult of the Black Dragon. It is believed to have originated among the Vampyres. Most of its human adherents are royalty and decadent aristocrats but its roots go back to antiquity. They worship a deity named Draganathan whose idols are represented as a black dragon with nine heads. What is troubling to those scholars who delve deeply into the subject (few as they may be) is their inability to trace the origins of this god to any discernible source. Strange as it may sound, most deities have a place and date of birth so to speak. The Light Father first appeared in the year one thousand in the central provinces of what is now the empire. Loch, the barbarian god, can be found through oral traditions to have originated several hundred years earlier in the Wilt. The Eldann worship of Aranya falls into their classical period. But alas, of Draganathan, we can trace nothing. He is an enigma that no amount of inquisitiveness can fathom and his origins are unknown. I must acknowledge the one fact that many scholars are too afraid to consider: that Draganathan's cult did not originate on our plane of existence. He is not a god of our world, he is a god from beyond, an Outsider."

- paper by of Professor Erebus of the Bright Collegiate

The Hexekar were closing the gap by the day. They had already traversed Aringyle just north of the Great Forest and were preparing to circle round to the south. They had set up camp outside of the town of Bangrave and calculated by noon tomorrow that they would be on the wizard's heels. They intended to be close enough to force the heretic's hand in such a way that it was hoped he would make a mistake.

Then Mabinogan would sweep in to retrieve him.

As the fires burned bright, sending up embers into the cool night air, the Hexekar gathered together and ate. A kitchen had been set up on the far side of the camp and after lining up to receive food, the soldiers gathered according to rank.

The upper echelons were all members of the Order and they convened apart from the rest of the men. They offered up a prayer to Draganathan and then commenced their meal. Their sporadic conversation eventually wound around to the Order itself and the secrets they had managed to glean through gossip and investigation. None of these men were privy to the most sacred knowledge, only the High Priests had access to that, but some of them had highly placed sources and they had coaxed them to reveal some of what they knew.

It was this information which they discussed now.

"The wizard is merely the tip of the iceberg..." one of the captains said between drinks. "The *real* prize isn't what he's stolen...the King has had that in his possession for years...what we want is his knowledge."

"Of magic?" another officer asked. "The Bright Church has access to every magical text in existence..."

"No...not magic..." the captain said. "That's what Animrens wants him for. What the Order wants is the *Relics*..."

There was a sudden silence, then one of the officers spoke with a trembling voice, "...the Great Relics? But I thought they were just myth."

The captain grinned, "yes...the Great Relics...forged from the Light Spire itself!"

The Hexekar were used to dealing with all kinds of magical artefacts, the black markets were filled with them, but the mention of the Light Spire was heady news to even the most jaded among them.

"It exists then..." one of the men in the back said. "The Light Spire..."

The captain nodded, "it does...but the eyes of Men can only glimpse it once every twenty years during an eclipse. Mark my words...this is the greatest undertaking of our career."

Another deep silence followed.

One of the officers finished his meal, leaned back and folded his arms, "so…we're not *really* trying to catch the wizard?"

The captain shook his head, "no…we're just keeping him moving. He's the only one who can decipher the map he stole from Animrens. We let him do the legwork."

"And why is the Order using Mabinogan?" the officer asked.

The captain smiled, "Mabinogan is just a pawn…the man has hated Arinönde for as long as he's been alive…they wronged him as a child, or something along those lines… the Order can use that."

The officers frowned, "use it for what?"

The captain's eyes flashed in the semi-dark, "war, my friend…the Order intends to use it to start a war."

"Where have you been?" Animrens asked. "Are you not feeling well?"

Princess Rionéolas lowered her eyes, "no…my head has been hurting."

"I can call in the family physician…" the King was watching her closely, a hint of concern in his eyes.

"It's alright, Father…I'll survive."

King Animrens laughed, "you know that your Mother always said you were stronger than most of the boys your age…you never complained, even as an infant."

The mention of her mother brought the Princess out of her reverie, "Father…what do you think Mother would say now, if she were here…"

The King's eyes softened, "your Mother was a woman of few words but when she spoke, she revealed her wisdom…" he turned towards one of the large, stained-glass windows which ran through the throne room. "Alas…I hear her voice less and less these days…"

"Father…" the Princess asked hesitantly. "What is happening? It seems that the castle has never been so busy."

"Nothing escapes you, does it my dear?" The King put his arms behind his back, assuming a more formal posture. "No doubt, you're aware of the many delegates that have passed through…as you know, one of the sacred orbs was stolen."

The Princess nodded.

"And I don't doubt that you also understand that the orb which was stolen was immensely valuable…"

"Of course…" she said softly. "But impossible to translate. The codex within is written in ancient Ardhian and that language has been dead since times immemorial on the Continent."

The King's eyes widened. He was visibly impressed with his daughter's depth of understanding. He didn't bother to question how she knew such things as she had always possessed the unique ability to discover anything she bent her will towards.

The King continued his pacing, "don't you see, daughter, the wizard is the key to all of this…his magical knowledge could be of immense benefit to Arinönde…" the King's voice became more animated as his excitement grew. "Magic in this time is a dying art…the Bright Church possesses *some* of the knowledge…far less than they would have you believe to be quite honest…" he stopped and faced her with his piercing eyes. "Just imagine what he knows…we could turn Arinönde into the greatest province in the empire, perhaps even surpassing Anturac."

The Princesses' eyes widened, "Father…Anturac *is* the empire. Danyr still resides on the throne…"

"So they say…" the King's tone had a conspiratorial note to it. "Perhaps the Mage Emperor died centuries ago and they've covered it up. Regardless, this is too great an opportunity to miss." He sighed deeply. "There are *other* forces that are seeking this man, and if we do not find him first, *they* will."

The Princess stepped forward, "let me help you, then…"

Animrens stopped his pacing, "I'll not have you going out there and risking your life…"

The Princess clenched her fists. She resented the idea that she needed to be cloistered away as though her fragility was unsuited to the outside world, "Father…let me into the Sanctum Sanctorum…I can use it to astral project."

The King's eyes widened, "impossible…only the High Rectors are allowed in the Sanctum…and what do you *mean* astral project? You *understand* such an art?"

The Princess did her best to conceal the hurt his condescension caused, "yes…there's *a lot* that I know…besides, it's the best way. I can glean their location instantly, but I need a device that channels enough power."

The King sighed, "and you believe the Sanctum is the only place which is suitable for such a purpose?"

She nodded.

Animrens moved towards his throne and seated himself.

When her father was deep in thought his eyes took on a glazed look as he retreated into his inner world. The Princess couldn't fathom the depths of that world and she did not wish to.

At last, Animrens' eyes regained their focus, "very well…I will inform the Rectors that you desire to use the Sanctum, but you *must* follow the appropriate protocol…" he clasped his hands together. "They will be reluctant to let a *woman* into their Holy of Holies…even one of such noble blood as yourself."

It was a cruel remark; one designed to get a rise out of her. She held herself together admirably.

"They've never had an *Animrens* woman to reckon with…give me a chance."

Her Father smiled. She had passed whatever secret test he was administering, "very well…prepare yourself to be on call…they will likely summon you when they choose to. You must show them the highest respect, regardless of how flippantly they treat you." He reached into his pocket and pulled out a golden locket. He looked at it for a moment, then held it out towards the Princess, "this was your Mother's…"

The Princess gasped. She had never seen the locket before and was entranced by the sight of it.

The King unclipped the golden chain and placed it around her neck gently. He could see that her eyes were misted with emotion and he smiled, "take it…for good luck. Do your best not to lose it."

The Princess nodded, "yes, Father…"

"Go…" the King gestured towards the doors. "Prepare yourself in any way that you see fit…"

The Princess bowed and departed. As she pushed through the great doors and headed back to her quarters the King smiled broadly and his eyes shone with pride.

So much like her Mother...he thought wistfully.

He turned towards the stained-glass windows and single tear ran down his cheek.

Mabinogan began setting his plans in order. There was much to do and very little time to accomplish it. Korazon, one of his most trusted lieutenants, would begin rallying the various nomadic tribes to their banner, keeping his activities as secret as possible. The goal was to raise a large enough force to set a defensive ring around the capital.

To do this would require both stealth and cunning.

It had been many ages since the tribes had been united, but a cause such as this seemed capable of at last bringing them together. Arinönde, though considered the greatest province in the empire, was now at the pinnacle of a steady decline which all great nations must eventually suffer. The growing decadence in the courts was spreading rapidly and softening the once indomitable discipline of the armed forces.

The Barbarian tribes, on the other hand, had never wavered in their commitment to hard living. Circumstances had forced them to adapt to the harshest of climates and it gave them their great strength.

It was this strength which Mabinogan now sought to gather.

He looked out over the barren vastness of his camp and pondered what his future would be. Would he rule over the desolation of Arinönde and take what he believed was his rightful place as King? He certainly felt that he was entitled to it. He had risen through the ranks of the Flagen through both cunning and carefully garnered respect. Why should the capital, too, not fall before his implacable will?

There was a growing electricity among the Flagen, one which had not existed in decades. They had languished on these steppes for generations and now they would at last take decisive action to right past wrongs. If the tribes united, as was hoped, they would be unstoppable.

Young boys in the tribes could often ride a horse before they could walk. By the time they were ten winters old they were more proficient with a bow and arrow than the grown men of other provinces. In ancient days, the tribes had been migratory, never remaining in one place for long. In those times, the Wilt had been wide open and far vaster than the small pittance it consisted of today. Hoarded like cattle into enclosed places, the tribes had nearly lost their old ways and been subverted by the very empire they despised.

But times were changing rapidly. A new era was about to begin. All it would take was a well-placed hammer blow to bring the whole rotten structure of Arinönde crashing down.

As with all great things, however, patience was required. Mabinogan was not so foolish as to underestimate his enemy and he knew that every mistake would be repaid in equal measure. The forces of Arinönde needed to make a mistake which would demoralize them to their core, something which would hasten their decline all the quicker.

Mabinogan grinned broadly.

You make the first move Animrens...and then we shall watch you stumble.

The Star Goddess

"There are numerous accounts in very old sources that speak of a tribe which called themselves the Alderamin. They worshipped a star goddess named T'anis whom they claimed had vanished after the First Days and was prophesied to return. On that day, the stars would shine brighter than they had in millennia and the tribe would return to the physical world. For now, they remain hidden from mortal eyes and they can slip between realms of existence as easily as we can walk from room to room."

-'The Hidden Peoples' by Wolter Keers

The edge of the Forest was very close. So close, in fact, that the morning light was beginning to penetrate the great trees with growing frequency. Delicate rays of sunshine shot through the din like golden columns. When they at last left those elder woods behind, they were greeted by a glorious blue sky and shining green meadows as far as the eye could see.

Alexander was glad to be out of the forest. Although he had admired the primeval splendour of the looming trees and untamed growth, he had felt watched constantly and despised it. When they at last set foot into the open pastures and fresh air, leaving that crowded realm behind, he breathed an audible sigh of relief and spread his arms wide to embrace the sun.

Charlotte had been less perturbed by the experience, despite getting lost. She couldn't shake her encounter with the white stag from her mind. Had it truly been Druim? Amyn seemed to confirm as much. The old man led the way silently and she couldn't shake a growing admiration for him. He seemed so unattached, so free from the concerns of mundane life. It was a freedom she desperately longed for herself and she began to study his every move with growing enthusiasm.

Alexander, too, had taken to their guide. After remaining silent for an interminable period, the boy found his old gumption and began to ask more questions.

"Where are we going now?"

Amyn turned only slightly, "towards Valleyhold, but first, we must pass through *the gap*."

Alexander's eyes widened, "the gap? What is that?"

The old man chuckled, "your inquisitive mind never ceases, does it my boy? A very good thing…" he turned back to the large expanse before them. "Some of the local peoples call it a 'thin place' or a gap between realms. There are many of them if you know where to look."

"And where do these gaps lead?" The boy's eyes were wide with excitement.

"To other realms…"

Alexander nodded his head as though he understood, but the concept seemed far-flung and vast. He had trouble comprehending *this* world in its entirety let alone others.

Charlotte walked at a leisurely pace behind them. She had little interest in their discussion and instead was admiring the sea of white flowers which stretched out in vast profusions along the edge of the forest.

"Have you ever seen one of these gaps?" Alexander asked.

Amyn shook his head, "they cannot be seen, boy, only *felt*…for instance, we are very, very near to the Astronomia as we speak."

"The Astronomia? What is that?"

"The realm of the Alderamin."

The boy couldn't hide his confusion.

Amyn's musical laughter rang out across the meadow, "you're wondering who the Alderamin are…they call themselves the 'Star People' in their native language. They are worshippers of the demi-goddess, T'anis."

Now, Charlotte spoke up, "T'anis? The Star Mother?"

Amyn turned only slightly, but his eyes revealed his intrigue, "you know that name? Not many do…she has been scrubbed from the history books and consigned to the land of myth, but I can assure you… she is *real*."

Charlotte's eyes widened and she clasped her hands together almost bashfully, "I've done my own research at the local library…I could only gather bits and pieces…" she lowered her gaze. "Did you…know her?"

Amyn was silent for a moment as though pulled into some long-lost memory, "…yes, I knew her…she was a glorious being."

"What happened to her?" Charlotte asked.

The old man sighed, "It is a story too vast and convoluted for this time…she vanished without a trace…the Alderamin have a prophecy which states that she will return to lead their people once more."

Alexander quickened his pace to match the old man, "and the Alderamin…are they…friendly?"

"As friendly a people as you're ever likely to meet…they will greet you warmly if you show them respect…but if you cross them," the old man made an unmistakeable gesture across his throat. "They are not a violent people, however, and prefer to keep to themselves. They are astronomers and astrologers of the highest order…in fact, many of them have the constellation they were born under imprinted on their very skin at birth and can refer to the stars simply by raising their hands to the sky, no matter where they may be."

"Amazing…" Charlotte said with obvious reverence. "As we pass through the gap…will they be able to see us?"

"Yes and no…" Amyn said. "The more psychically perceptive among them will…but remember that even though they are *right here*, they exist in another dimension entirely. It would be like trying to figure out what is happening in another room based on the barest of evidence."

"Can they cross over?" Alexander asked with mild trepidation. "Into our world?"

"The ones that know how to can, yes."

The siblings glanced around the meadow as though they expected to see eyes staring back at them from beyond the veil. They were secretly relieved when nothing revealed itself. As they proceeded on, a lightness in the air around them was the only indication that they were anywhere special. A few moments later, the feeling was gone.

Alexander promptly forgot about the Alderamin and began asking more pertinent questions, "Dragons…you mentioned Dragons before…are there any left?"

"Oh yes," Amyn said softly. "There are many of them, but they have elected to hide themselves, as so many races have in this spiritually dark age. They are content for men to believe they are either extinct or the product of myths." As they rose up on a hill, he pointed into the distance. "Look there…"

The siblings squinted and could make out a long, jagged mountain chain.

"The Dragon's Teeth…that's what those mountains are called." Amyn said. "If you look to the highest peak, you'll see a large groove."

"I see it!" Alexander said excitedly. "It looks like a U-shape at the top of the mountain."

Amyn nodded, "that is the Dragon's Quadrant…if you could see it for yourself, it's truly magnificent. There is a long, solid brass quadrant carved into the mountain itself. The Dragon's have been using it to measure the stars for millennia."

"Dragons were astronomers?" Charlotte asked.

"Yes…" Amyn's silver eye seemed to glow as he spoke. "And mathematicians and scientists as I told you before…they are also tremendous artists. They helped build the City of Gibh."

The siblings frowned in unison, clearly confused.

"The city of the Skeags…a place of such immense antiquity that it precedes the existence of man." Amyn stepped carefully over a small sapling which was struggling to find purchase against a boulder. "You see, after the Days of Fire, the Skeags retreated into their secluded realm and have never been seen since…"

"Why?" Alexander asked.

"Because they grew tired of the world and its fleeting, transitory nature…the Skeags, like their Draconic ancestors, are eternal and as such are not concerned with mundane affairs."

"Have you ever seen it?" Charlotte asked from behind them.

Amyn and Alexander glanced back in unison.

"The City of Gibh…" she asked almost bashfully.

Amyn nodded slowly, "I have…only once…"

"And…" Charlotte's eyes widened with expectancy.

Amyn turned back to the rolling hills, "I saw more than I can tell…suffice to say…it defies adequate description and words will never do it justice."

They continued on in silence. A pod of grackles soared overhead, rising and falling like a dark wave. They circled the travellers and then darted off towards the forest.

Charlotte let her thoughts wander along the green hills. It was a sight of such splendour that she almost forgot the stiffness in her joints. Having grown up in the capital, she had never had the opportunity to connect with the natural world. Being in the forest and seeing the white stag had been a spiritual experience for her, one which made her question many of the assumptions she had once held about life. The world suddenly seemed exciting and mysterious again.

She chanced another question, "will the Star Goddess return?"

Amyn gave a sigh as though the thought pained him, "I believe she will…"

"Because the Alderamin prophets say so?"

"No…because *I* say so…"

There was a harsh edge to the old man's tone which the children hadn't heard before. They walked on and didn't ask any further questions.

Charlotte was mildly disturbed by the dark anger she had heard in Amyn's voice. For a moment, she had been genuinely afraid. It was as though the veil around the old man had briefly lifted and revealed something which had been hidden underneath. Something ancient and terrible. A pulsing power which seemed as though it was held in check only by the old man's refusal to unleash it. It was a moment Charlotte would long remember and it was undeniable proof that their guide had not deceived them. He was exactly who he had claimed he was.

*But he's more than that…*she thought. *He's far greater than he seems to be…and far more dangerous.*

A Change of Seasons

"A lingering shadow blanketed the lands after the Ardhians arrived. Their first settlements were beacons of light in a dark world and they went forth fearlessly. They made extraordinary strides and for over a hundred years, Danyr led a crusade against the Giants. With the might of the four Great Relics at His disposal, He was utterly unstoppable. As He went, He planted the seeds of colonies which would later emerge as today's great cities. Mightiest among them was Arinönde due to its ideal location and rich natural resources. The Lawmaker, Drachmuin, inscribed his commandments on pillars in every colony. Those pillars still stand to this day."

-excerpt from 'The First Founding' by Salam Alheera

Approaching with a coterie of armed guards, Princess Rionéolas made her way up the steps of the Bright Cathedral. The building's splendour was unsurpassed in all of Arinönde and it shone with golden radiance against the sun. The cathedral had been built on the highest ground in the city and stood like a sentinel above the surrounding buildings. In its sheer magnificence, it dwarfed even the castle which the Princess had always believed was an intentional sign of subtle dominance.

She felt nervous as the she made her way towards the great, baroque doors. Several High-Rectors were there to greet her and their long, flowing red robes shone resplendently. At their forefront was Renard Cartusian, greatest among his fellows.

Cartusian bowed as the Princess approached, "Majesty…your visit has been highly anticipated."

The Princess glanced up from under her hood, "has it?"

"Oh yes…" Cartusian rose and smiled broadly. "And I understand that you wish to use the Sanctum…"

The Princess frowned. Beneath her cloak, she clutched the Red Book tightly to herself.

Cartusian beckoned her to come forward, “we shall give you the grand tour, Majesty…it’s my understanding that you have never visited us before. Your Father, too, has never come…”

“My Father is a busy man,” the Princess said softly.

Cartusian smiled and nodded, “of course, of course, Majesty…the ruling of a kingdom surely takes a great deal of energy. However, if you would mention to your Father that he should at the very *least* receive the sacraments…”

“I will mention it.”

Cartusian sighed with relief, “very good…right this way, Majesty.”

Two servants in brown robes pushed open the great doors and the splendour of the cathedral shone forth in all of its radiance. For a moment, the Princess was frozen with awe. She had never witnessed such a display of architectural ingenuity.

Cartusian noticed the reverence in her eyes and smiled, “magnificent, isn’t it…built nearly two hundred years ago by the masons of the Stellar Guild. It could last for another thousand years due to the mastery of its execution.” He pointed to the great, stained-glass windows which surrounded the enormous hall. “These windows were executed by a master whose name we do not know to this day. In fact, we don’t even know how he accomplished the feat of colouring the windows to such an exacting level of perfection.”

The Princess glanced at the luminescent windows. She could see the power of alchemy present in their execution, but she dared not point it out. To do so would have been dangerous, even for her.

“Ahhh…and here we have a statue of the Light Father blessing Danyr.” Cartusian gestured towards a magnificent marble sculpture. It was of a kingly personage with a halo and long beard kneeling before the sagely figure of the Light Father.

The Princess had seen many representations of the Mage Emperor and this was by far the most impressive. Danyr appeared to be gazing down with a frown on his face as though he wrestled with a great inner storm which would soon be unleashed upon the lands. The crusades of Danyr were common knowledge to most educated people in the empire, although the Princess had long suspected that much of what they were taught had been distorted.

"Ahh..." Cartusian's mellifluous voice echoed through the vast hall. "We come to it at last..."

The Princess looked up and gasped. Before her was a great staircase leading upwards towards a light of such splendour that nothing could be seen beyond it.

"Glorious, isn't it?" Cartusian said. "The Sanctum Sanctorum."

"Some power is at work here..." the Princess said.

Cartusian nodded, "it is a conduit of magical energy. The most potent of its kind. This cathedral was built over a sacred site and it is this site which powers it."

The Princess knew of ley-lines and geomantic energies, but to have such things confirmed so casually by the High-Rector made her wonder just how much more was being concealed. She glanced to the stairway with trepidation, the power emanating from beyond was palpable.

"Do not fear, Majesty..." Cartusian said. "You alone have been granted permission."

She glanced towards the High-Rector and nodded, "...thank you, Cartusian."

The Rector bowed and gestured towards the light.

The Princess looked to her escort and they nodded solemnly. This was something she would have to undertake alone. She turned back to the great staircase, removed her hood, and walked forward into the blinding brightness.

Ascending the great stairs was far more difficult than she imagined. The brightness had a tangible *presence* to it which seemed to weigh down upon her. Beneath her robes, the Red Book seemed to be pulsing as though infused with the energies of this place.

At last, she came to it: the Sanctum Sanctorum.

She stood in awe as she gazed upon the sheer magnificence of it. A luminescent, *living* light which pulsed in a rhythmic motion. She knew instinctively that this light possessed an unfathomable amount of information which she could access on a whim. It was a truly heady moment for her and it made the vast collection in her personal library seem meagre by comparison.

She steadied her breathing and focused her mind. This was not the time to indulge in idle thought and she needed every ounce of her will for what she was about to do. She closed her eyes and spread her arms out wide.

*Focus...focus...*she intoned in her mind repeatedly like a mantra.

She formed the image of the wizard in her mind's eye and suddenly, her consciousness was soaring over vast plains and fields. The transition was so sudden that she was momentarily taken aback but she quickly regained her footing and managed to steady her nerves.

Here she was, standing in an endless green field before three individuals, two of which were staring at her in shock.

"Who…who *is* that?" Alexander's voice was shaking.

Amyn frowned for the briefest moment then spoke, "…Princess."

Princess Rionéolas' eyes widened, "you…you can *see* me?"

Charlotte gasped and her face was very pale.

Amyn cocked his head to the side, "you went to the Sanctum, I see…it's the only way you could teleport yourself here."

The Princess frowned, "teleport? No…I…I'm supposed to be astral projecting…" but even as she spoke, she could feel the warm breeze on her skin and the ground beneath her feet.

Amyn crossed his arms, "that may have been your intention, but the Sanctum is far more powerful than that."

The Princess clasped her hands together and the undeniable feeling of physicality made a sudden, ferocious panic surge through her. She shouldn't be here right now.

Amyn sensed her disquiet immediately, "fear not, Princess…you're in no danger."

She met his steady gaze with her own, "can I get back?" The words had an undercurrent of desperation in them.

"If you're a particularly skilled magical practitioner, then yes…" Amyn said.

The words struck a nerve and the Princess began to clench and unclench her hands, as though attempting to muster a great effort.

Amyn and the siblings looked on silently until the Princess at last collapsed to her knees, a look of despair on her face.

Amyn's silver eye shone in the midday sun, "your Father sent you to track us."

A look of fear crossed the Princesses' face but she did not deny it. She knew better than to try to lie to this man, "yes…they're after you."
"Who?" Alexander asked.
The Princesses' emerald eyes regarded him for a moment and he felt a strange sensation of vulnerability, as though she were looking into his very being.
"Everyone…" she said softly.

"My Lord, we have word that the Hexekar are closing in on the wizard…" Mannon, one of Mabinogan's commanders said gruffly.
Mabinogan smiled, "they will take no action against him…the King himself has forbidden it. He wants *us* to bring him in."
Mannon frowned, "but *why*, my Lord?"
"They don't want to dirty their hands…" Mabinogan said with more than a little contempt. "They can't risk offending the power of Anturac…if they apprehend a pure-blooded Ardhian on foreign soil and word gets out, they will have no choice but to extradite him…however, if we lowly Barbarians bring him in…then they can lay the blame on us."
Mannon nodded slowly but the blankness of his stare showed that he had failed to comprehend the situation.
"Think of it in this way, Mannon…" Mabinogan made a sweeping gesture through the air with his powerful hands, as though painting a picture. "No province in the empire can stand against the might of Anturac…they allow a significant degree of autonomy, but they will not tolerate one of their own being incarcerated by *any* vassal state, no matter how esteemed…" he grinned broadly. "Now, this is where the politics come in…and the King is playing it very cleverly although not so clever that he hasn't assumed that we of the Móg Flagen are anything more than blithering idiots. He imagines himself subtle enough to pull the wool over our eyes…"
Mannon nodded slowly.
"Regardless…the fact remains simple: the King is attempting to come out on top. He will have us bring him the Ardhian wizard and then, when Anturac comes calling, he will point his finger our way. In between, he hopes to have just enough time to glean

whatever secrets he can from the so called 'heretic' and can easily feign ignorance later."

Mannon's eyes widened, "and what will become of us…my Lord?"

Mabinogan smiled but there was a bitter undercurrent to it, "dust, Mannon…Anturac will grind us to dust. There won't be a single one of our people left…" he looked up and his dark eyes shone. "Which is why we are going to make the first move…we will strike Arinönde within the week…we won't need a large force, just a capable one."

"Ingenious, my Lord…" Mannon said with admiration.

"In the meantime, gather our best shamans…I want them to predict the fortunes of the coming war and combine their abilities to give us any advantage we can muster." Mabinogan commanded.

"Yes, Lord…" Mannon bowed and departed.

Alone again, the Lord of the Móg Flagen sat quietly with his own thoughts. He had come to the understanding long ago that such an enemy as Arinönde could not be reasoned with but nor could they be underestimated. The great walls which surrounded the city were nearly impenetrable to siege.

But now, thanks to the King's single-minded obsession…we'll be able to walk through the front door.

His booming laugh echoed across the camp and into the hills beyond.

PART II

THEY OF THE NIGHT

A Different Kind

"The Black City of Metanoia, which lies at the heart of the Enclaves of Night, cannot be adequately described for no mortal has ever gazed upon it and lived. The Vampyre strongholds, which once stretched as far as the Easten Seas in the old days, are now confined to an area only slightly larger than Arinönde. Structures of great antiquity have been found which do not match any architectural achievement known to man. It is presumed that a very different solar cycle once existed, one which allowed night to reign supreme for six months of the year. It was this which allowed the Vampyre nations to spread so thoroughly. Alas, they now lie confined to their respective domain and are held at bay by the Eldann. It is something that every mortal man should be forever thankful for."

-writings of an anonymous scribe

Viran moved quickly along the black corridors of the palace. He was in no mood to stop and chat with the courtiers that lined his path and he kept a brisk pace in order to avoid them.

The Empress had requested his presence.

Such a summons meant only one thing: something drastic had occurred as Viran was never called forth merely to engage in idle matters. As general of the Vampyre armies and a member of the Black Court, his attentions were always directed towards some sort of crisis. Recently, he had been stewarding the war against the hated Eldann and he was slightly annoyed that he was being summoned during so critical a juncture.

Regardless, he obeyed without question. One did *not* ignore a direct summons from the Empress without the direst of consequences.

He glanced out of one of the arched windows as he went and saw the vast landscape of the Enclaves of Night. The Enclaves were enormous, magically wrought domes which blanketed out the hated sunlight and allowed eternal night to reign supreme over the Vampyre lands. The general smiled briefly before he at last reached his destination: the wrought iron doors of the Empresses' throne room.

He nodded to the guards stationed on either side and they turned in unison to open the great door. Its ancient gears creaked as it slid along, at last coming to a stop and revealing the immensity which lay beyond.

The room was vast, perhaps more so than any building in the Enclaves. The huge, domed ceiling seemed to reach up into the heavens themselves and was adorned with frescoes depicting the history and culture of the Vampyre race. A long, blood-red carpet ran from the entrance to the throne itself and was illuminated by the gentle glow of torchlight. An endless procession of the Empresses' personal guardsmen lined the path; their faces locked in a stony gaze.

Viran made his way towards the throne, glancing up at the ancient frescoes. He was well versed enough in the history of his people to understand some of what he was seeing. The Battle of Black Ridge, a pivotal turning point in Vampyre history when they had beaten the hated Eldann back and won a vital strategic stronghold, was depicted with stunning accuracy. At the center of the fresco was a Vampyre in red armour leading the charge which had turned the tides of the battle and later the war itself. Viran smiled as he looked at this depiction of himself. The battle was still one of his crowning moments despite the fact that it had happened nearly a thousand years ago.

At last, he reached the throne and bowed low to his Sovereign.

Freya Draconnis, Empress of the Vampyre race, regarded her greatest general with an affectionate nod and bid him rise.

"Viran…" the Empresses' voice seemed to echo from beyond eternity.

"Highness…" Viran rose to his feet and met the Empresses' cold gaze. She was a being of divine perfection and one of the last of the First, the original progenitors of their race. "You summoned me…"

"Yes…" the Empress leaned forward. "Have you been kept abreast of recent events?"

Viran frowned, "no, Highness…not unless you mean the recent Eldann raids on one of our forts."

The Empress waved her hand in a dismissive motion, "no, those parasites are of no concern to me…I'm speaking about the *human* kingdoms…"

Viran rubbed his chin softly, "have they crossed our borders?"

"No…they are not that foolish…but our spies tell us that they are in possession of a rather singular map."

"What kind of map, Highness?"

The Empress leaned back in her throne and smiled. Her great, feathered wings were folded elegantly behind her back, "a map which leads to the Great Relics…"

Viran gasped, "the relics of the Light Spire…"

The Empress nodded slowly.

Viran lowered his eyes, "Highness…have the humans possessed this map the entire time?"

"Yes…to think that it was originally in *our* possession only adds insult to injury…" the Empress sighed deeply. "Our race is but a shadow of what it once was…but I intend to change that."

Viran bowed once more, "Majesty…direct me as you will and I shall retrieve the map…"

The Empress smiled once more. Her general's loyalty never ceased to impress her, "no need, general…we cannot make any sudden moves as our enemies will use every opportunity to counter them." Her glowing eyes narrowed. "Besides…the matter is more complicated than that…an Ardhian wizard is in possession of it."

Viran gasped, "an *Ardhian*? Majesty, forgive me, but there hasn't been a pure-blooded Ardhian on the Continent in ages uncounted."

The Empress nearly laughed at her general's naivete. The Ardhians had been venturing across the Continent since the days of their arrival on it, they had merely done so discreetly, "regardless…only an Ardhian can read their archaic language and thus we must allow the wizard to uncover the path for us…no doubt the humans have already conceived of this idea."

"Majesty…" the general's voice had more than a little hesitation in it. "If you know this…then surely the Eldann do as well."

The Empress nodded slowly, "oh, most certainly…which is exactly why I have summoned you…you are to attack the Eldann fort at Sigisford immediately."

Viran's eyes widened, "are our troops prepared?"

"They were prepared four days ago, but you are the first to know their purpose."

Viran bowed, "it shall be done Highness…" he turned to leave, then stopped himself. "Majesty…if the Ardhian *is* after the Relics…"

"Leave this strategy to *me*, general…there are too many political webs involved. If we do not tread lightly, then we will wake the a great, sleeping spider…"

Viran nodded, the uncertainty vanishing from his eyes, "by your will, Highness…Draganathan be praised." He turned and walked briskly from the throne room.

The Empress watched him go and as the doors shut behind him, she contemplated what the future held. She, like all of the First, was gifted with considerable powers of foresight. She could map the future in her mind, but only to a degree.

What she saw coming disturbed her to no end.

Her contacts within the Order had kept her well informed of their plans. She chuckled to herself as she thought of the frailty and weakness of humanity. How easily she had managed to infiltrate their ranks and to corrupt their vision to her own purposes.

The humans will do anything for a chance at immortality… she thought with a grin.

Some among them, the most capable, *would* be made Vampyres so that they could give their skills to the greater cause. The rest, however, would be discarded as any tool was when it had worn out its usefulness.

Her thoughts turned to the Ardhian.

Who are you? Renegade…

She had known many of the mightiest among them personally. Had even taken the greatest of them as a lover and a consort to propagate the Royal Bloodline. There were only a few Ardhians left who would have the skill and audacity to pull off such a stunt.

And surely with the full support of Anturac...

She was not so naïve as to imagine that the wizard was acting alone. This was a carefully planned operation and it was all being guided from the Ardhian throne. Danyr *himself* had likely authorized it.

But to what end? To retrieve the Great Relics? You had the Relics in your possession once before...it was you who hid them after all...

The Mage Emperor was no fool. She had fought alongside him in countless battles and had even saved his life several times. He had repaid her in a way which had bound their kingdoms together and ensured a long-lasting peace despite the tensions with the Eldann.

*I wonder...Danyr...*she thought with pursed lips. *If you were to look upon your son again..., would you even know him?*

She pushed these thoughts away. She needed her mind to be focused and ready when the time came. She could see the writing on the wall already: the long peace was about to end and a new age was dawning.

The Elders of the Vampyre Council convened. Among them were some of the most illustrious figures in the Enclaves. Mighty Draynim of the House of Eternal Night and Hexir of the House of the Illimitable Void chaired the meeting.

The Elders rose as one, "Draganathan be praised…" they said in unison. "May the Lord of the Deep guide our steps…" when they had finished, they took their seats.

Draynim alone remained standing, "brothers, sisters, you all know why you've been summoned."

The Elders nodded grimly.

"It seems…" Draynim made a sweeping gesture across the dais. "That the Empress has deemed it a necessity that we declare war on the Eldann once more."

"Her Majesty doesn't make mistakes…" Lora, a fiery Vampyress from the Cathian Mountains said. "How many times has she led us to victory?"

Draynim raised his hand as though warding off a vengeful spirit, "I meant no offense…Countess…I merely wished to hear your opinion on the situation."

Hexir rose, "we stand by the Empress…" he lowered his pale eyes for a moment. "However, we do have our doubts…this attack will destabilize the region and perhaps the rest of the empire as well."

"I wasn't aware we were *included* in the empire…" an Elder said sardonically.

Hexir turned to him, "the Empresses' son ensures the peace with Anturac…we are bound to them by blood."

"By a *half-breed*, you mean…"

Hexir fixed the Elder with a baleful gaze, "and what are *you* Draugmir? Do you imagine yourself one of the *Ancient* Vampyres? Are you one of the *First*? None of us can claim that right save the Empress and two others who have secluded themselves away from the Enclaves for centuries." He arched his back and gazed around the room contemptuously. "I suppose that makes *all* of us half-breeds. In fact, the prince is more of a full-blood than any of us!"

There was a minor uproar as the offended Elder rose from his seat with fangs bared. After a brief scuffle, order was restored and the Council seated.

Hexir frowned, "now…the Council *must* give the Empress our full support…however reluctant we may be." He turned to the left of the auditorium where the scuffle had erupted. "If we do not, we will stand alone when the deluge comes."

"The deluge is here already!" a voice near the back called out. "The kingdoms of Man have begun sowing the seeds of their own downfall…*we* should be there to pick up the pieces."

"Need I remind you…" Hexir said sternly. "That the kingdoms of Man have been most generous to us…they have provided ample sustenance to our Enclaves over the centuries…are we to give *that* up on a whim?"

He was referring to a secret agreement, one which ensured a steady supply of colonists to the outlying Vampyre lands. Ignorant and defenseless, the villages were allowed to develop before being harvested by the Vampyres and carried off screaming to sustain the Enclaves of Night. The cycle had repeated itself countless times and it had stayed the Vampyre Lords from venturing into the human kingdoms to the north.

The Council grumbled briefly. Hexir could tell that they had grown decadent over the millennia and he despised them for it.

Only Viran could lay claim to being a worthy successor to their mighty ancestors.

Draynim spoke, his raspy voice echoing through the chamber, "it is decided then, we will go to war with the Eldann once more…whatever the Empresses' designs, we will follow them without question."

"Here, here!" some of the Elders cheered.

A few among their number grumbled with obvious dissatisfaction, but there was little they could do. The majority had spoken.

Draynim descended the dais and clasped arms with Hexir. They nodded briefly to one another before releasing their grip.

"I assume we know what the Empress is doing." Hexir said softly.

Draynim nodded, "of course…her wisdom far exceeds ours."

"Still…this entire venture stinks of desperation."

Hexir laughed, "not desperation, old friend…but *decisiveness*. The Empress is moving on instinct to ensure that we are not left behind in this grand game…and what a game it is."

Draynim smiled slightly and put his hand to his chin, "perhaps you're right…in which case, we should ensure that the entire region doesn't destabilize…"

"The Enclaves will follow our lead…" Hexir smirked. "They have no other choice."

Dislocation

"The religions of our lands are as varied as they are sophisticated. The Drya'Din, or Sea People, worship the primordial waters which existed before Creation. The Eldann have Aryavartha, their fiery solar deity and keeper of the eternal flame. The Vampyres and several fringe cults worship Draganathan...the God From Outside and Father of the Deep. Most interesting, though, were the Dragons. According to scant accounts, they worshipped the Cosmic Egg which gave rise to all life. This view seems to have several facets in common with the Drya'Din and makes one wonder if the two have a connection which remains hidden."

-'The Beliefs of the Races' by Adamis Shavan

The Princess appeared to be on the verge of hysterics but she was holding herself together admirably. Her hands shook and she glanced around with a look of continual anxiety.

Amyn's soft voice drew her back to reality, "as I said, Princess, you have come here bodily."

"But *how*? It still makes no sense to me..." the Princess was shaking.

"It will, in time."

She turned her emerald eyes towards Amyn, "you...you disguised yourself as my cat...you stole the orb from my Father's Vault."

The siblings glanced at the two of them with a confused look on their faces.

Amyn crossed his arms, "the orb was never your Father's to keep, but in truth, it was his great-great-grandfather who *stole* it from a sacred Ardhian site…I merely took back what was rightfully ours."

"You won't get to where you're going…" there was a hint of spite in the Princesses' tone, as though she still harboured the hurt of being deceived. "My Father has organized every able-bodied man in the empire to find you. The shores of the Southern Sea are still far off and Anturac is even farther."

Amyn smiled, "this entire thing is far bigger than your *Father*, my dear, and what makes you think I'm going to Anturac?"

For a moment, the Princess appeared stumped, "you're…you're *not* going to Anturac?"

Amyn shook his head slowly, "you're behind, my dear, and barely catching up…as I said, this is bigger than Arinönde and its petty grudges. Suffice to say, you are now in *my* keeping, as you will not survive much longer without my protection."

The Princess frowned, as though the very thought of putting herself under the wing of this man offended her, "I don't need you…I can turn myself in to the Hexekar…"

Now Amyn *did* laugh and it had a cruel edge to it, "is that the *best* your Father can do? I see the Bright Church has taken over the operation right under his nose." He shook his head like a disappointed schoolmaster. "To think that I held Animrens in higher esteem than that. A pity that he had to prove me wrong…"

The words stung the Princess visibly and the siblings were taken aback by the sudden callousness of their guide.

The old man spoke slowly to ensure his point would find its mark, "you may turn yourself into the Hexekar if you wish, Princess, but you don't fully understand the kind of men you're dealing with. Though the Bright Church is centered in Arinönde, they do not answer to your Father nor do they fall under his sphere of influence. They are a separate entity entirely and thus, would have no problem making a young Princess disappear."

The Princess gasped and her eyes widened.

Amyn nodded, "one less Animrens to claim the throne means that when the King dies, the Church can claim the royal diadem for themselves and appoint an heir of their choosing," the silver orb of his eye fixed on her. "It's amazing…how few people notice a *cat*."

The last word was like an icepick in the core of the Princesses' being. It shook the final shreds of false bravado she had mustered and she collapsed to the ground, sobbing.

Alexander rushed forward to comfort her and she gripped him tightly, her tears staining the front of his tattered shirt.

Charlotte seemed frozen in place and Amyn was as unreadable as stone.

After a few moments of silence, the old man sighed deeply, "it is to Nin-Ghasta that we will go…you're welcome to join us if you wish, Majesty."

Charlotte glared at Amyn, "how can you be so cold…"

The old man turned to her slowly, his silver orb seemed to shine with a fiery light, "do not saddle me with your petty emotions…as I said before, you are free to join me, or to go your own way."

Charlotte's eyes widened in disbelief. For a moment, she didn't recognize this man. Gone was the kindly demeanour, replaced by a dark, forbidding presence which chilled her to the bone. She lowered her eyes, conceding defeat before the old man's indomitable will.

Amyn turned to Alexander and the Princess, "the final stretch lies before us…once we pass Valleyhold," he looked towards Charlotte. "Provided we aren't intercepted along the way by the numerous mercenary forces at our heels." He turned and began walking without looking back.

Alexander released the Princess and helped her to her feet.

She looked at him for a moment as though seeing him for the first time and smiled slightly, "thank you…" she said softly.

Charlotte noticed the redness in her brother's cheeks and was deeply amused. When the Princess turned to her, she bowed slightly, "Majesty…is it *really* you? *The* Princess Rionéolas Animrens?"

The Princesses' melancholy demeanour suddenly vanished and she laughed with great mirth. To Alexander it sounded like music.

"I suppose I am… but I'm a long way from home…" the Princess glanced towards Amyn who was walking off into the distance. "It seems our guide is leaving us…"

Alexander crossed his arms, "he's unpredictable but he's kept us out of danger so far…"

The Princess turned to him, “oh my, in all the confusion…I didn’t even ask you your names.”

Charlotte stepped forward, “I’m Charlotte, and that’s Alexander.”

The boy frowned and his shoulders sagged. Charlotte’s eyes widened when she realized that she hadn’t let him introduce himself. She had been so used to taking the lead since they had been on their own that she had forgotten to stop herself. Her brother was growing up fast and she was having trouble learning to accept it.

She had also seen the way he had looked at the Princess and she at him.

Alexander stared off into the distance, “well, we’d better run after him…he may be old, but he’s no slouch.”

The Princess smiled, “alright…I suppose I could use a little change of scenery…the castle walls make for a bland sight.”

The three of them chuckled and raced after Amyn who was walking towards the dying light of the setting sun.

Gur-Naga knelt and pressed his fingers into the cold dirt. The tracks were fresh, perhaps no more than three hours old. They were getting close to their quarry. They had covered nearly two days worth of travel in one, stopping only briefly to eat and drink near the River Sassa. Unlike the Hexekar with their bulky supplies, the barbarian warriors of the Móg Flagen travelled light. They took only what was absolutely necessary for swift travel and relied on the land to provide for their needs.

Mabinogan would be pleased when they returned with the wizard in hand and it was the prospect of his approval that spurred them forward.

Gur-Naga, one of the most experienced trackers, signalled to his brethren the direction of travel. Their quarry was moving towards Valleyhold and had even been foolish enough to pass through the Great Forest to do so. Gur-Naga had avoided this route and taken several hidden backroads across uncharted terrain. The wizard must be very desperate indeed to pass through the Forest as even the Móg Flagen dared not go there. There were too many powerful spirits to contend with to say nothing of almighty Druim himself.

But what if he's not desperate...what if we're dealing with a dangerous adept...

These were deep thoughts, especially for Gur-Naga and he pushed them away. He feared no man living especially not a *wizard* of any kind. All of the wizards he had encountered had been members of the Bright Church and they had been cowardly and weak to contend with. Magic, and its use among the Móg Flagen, was reserved for the shamans of the tribe and even they, revered as they were, were no match for a sword.

They pushed forward. This would be an easy catch.

Night was fast approaching. They would snatch the wizard while he slept and dispose of whoever was with him quickly. After that, they would have an easy return to camp and even the Hexekar would grant them passage. Mabinogan would praise their efforts and reward them handsomely.

It all seemed too good to be true.

The Beastmen and the outcasts would at last claim their rightful place as heirs to the land that was once theirs. Too long had the outsiders reigned over them, condemning them to a life of squalor on cold steppes and fringe territories.

No more.

Gur-Naga signalled to his troop to move forward. Their next stop would be at the camp of their prey.

As night fell, the fire roared with a splendid crackle. The Princess pulled her cloak tightly around herself and huddled next to Alexander and Charlotte. Amyn sat across from them, aloofly smoking his pipe.

Alexander turned to the Princess, "don't worry, we'll get you back home."

Charlotte nearly put her head in her hands. She could tell that her brother was smitten, but what chance did he think he had with a *princess*?

Princess Rionéolas smiled indulgently, "thank you...but I don't know if home is where I want to be right now..."

"You'd rather be *here*?" Charlotte could barely contain her disdain. "I'm sure the castle is far cozier than a dirt ground in the middle of nowhere."

"Valleyhold is hardly nowhere..." Alexander said.

Charlotte sighed. Her brother's defense of their new companion irked her to no end. A princess she may have been, but she was a *long* way from home and here, in these plain clothes and next to this fire, she seemed as ordinary as anyone else.

The Princess regarded Charlotte for a moment, perhaps sensing her hostility, "growing up in the castle isn't all it's cracked up to be…you'd imagine that it's nothing but luxury and freedom, but this is far from the truth. There are boundaries and codes of conduct that *must* be followed at all times…that's not even touching on the political intrigue."

"I saw it myself…" Amyn said from across the fire and his voice shocked the others to attention. They had forgotten he was even there.

The Princess leaned forward and frowned, "yes…you had a bird's eye view to everything…you were hiding among us like a *snake*."

Amyn blew several smoke rings but his expression remained unchanged, "you feel betrayed, Princess, I understand that…but I *did* appreciate your kindness while I was there…" he stared off into the distance. "You would be a better ruler than your father."

"My Father is a great man…" the Princesses' voice was shaky with anger.

Amyn nodded, "a great man can have his flaws as well, Princess…"

"And what about *your* flaws…"

Amyn emptied the ash from his pipe, "oh, I'm not excluding myself from that…"

The Princess crossed her arms as though the answer dissatisfied her, "and what will you stand to gain from all of this? The orb will lead you to the Great Relics…is *that* what you're after?"

Amyn's eyes widened, "how did you know about the Relics?"

The Princess laughed haughtily as though she had scored a great victory, "every child in Arinönde knows about the Relics…every myth ever conceived mentions them at least once…but to think that they're actually *real* and that you're mad enough to believe you can find them just makes this journey of yours all the more imbecilic."

Alexander and Charlotte were stunned by the Princesses' outburst. They sensed she was raging against more than just

Amyn. It was as though she had identified him with every figure of authority that had ever held her back.

Amyn sighed and his face appeared almost sad, "well…I suppose you're right."

The Princess leaned back and her eyes widened, "…*right*?"

"That is exactly what I'm after…the Great Relics were used by Danyr and Drachmuin to clear a path through the Old World and forge the new. But they were too powerful for anyone to wield forever, even ones so mighty as them, and so they were sealed away. I seek them now to right an old wrong…" he glared at them for a moment with the threatening silver of his eye. "What that is will be *my* business and mine alone…"

The group nodded cautiously and even the Princess seemed to have lost some of her fire.

She cocked her head to the side, "is that why my Father is after you? He wants the Relics?"

Amyn chuckled and there was more than a hint of malice in it, "your father has no idea the Relics exist. He's after me for my magic…he thinks I will be the key to renewing the Royal Art that has been lost to your people for generations. The Bright Church has hoarded the knowledge in their libraries and killed the last true practitioners of it. Your people have been spiritually impoverished for at *least* five hundred years."

His words hung heavy in the din.

Alexander raised his head slightly, "if you really *are* a magician…why haven't we seen any of your tricks?"

"*Tricks?*" Amyn practically spat the words. "Is that what you believe real magic is? I tell you boy, my high opinion of you begins to dwindle by the hour."

The youth winced at the barb, but he could see a hint of mischievous light in the old man's eyes.

Amyn's bushy eyebrows frowned, "do not be deceived by your indoctrination, my lad…there are far greater depths to magic than mere tricks…do you suppose we made it this far by chance? What with the entirety of the empire at our heels."

The Princess reached into the folds of her cloak, hesitated for a moment, then withdrew her hand. In it was a slender, blood-red volume which seemed to emanate a palpable, unearthly power, "what about *this*?" she shook the volume back and forth gently. "Does this have real magic in it?"

For the first time, Amyn's eyes widened with visible shock, "*where* did you get that?"

The Princess smiled slightly, "the castle has a secret library…one which none except the Chaplains are allowed access to…" she looked up and met his gaze. "You must have missed it in your wanderings."

Amyn leaned back, "that book is *dangerous*…even for one such as yourself."

"Bah…" the Princess rested the volume on her lap. "I've glanced through it…it hardly seems threatening."

Amyn gasped, "glanced through it and *understood* it?"

The Princess nodded nonchalantly.

"Princess…the only people who can understand that tome are those with Ardhian blood…" the old man stopped himself mid-sentence. He seemed to be measuring his words carefully. "Your family must be descended from some of the first kings of old. It would explain the flaming red hair, for it is a common Ardhian trait."

The Princesses' eyes widened, "…you mean to say…I have *Ardhian* blood?"

"What else would explain your magical prowess?" Amyn smiled, as though he were suddenly speaking to an equal. "Ours is a gift from the Great Flame…the Arcalypsis Flame."

"I've read of this Flame…" the Princess clutched the aged volume to herself tightly.

Amyn's eyes shone in the twilight, "and you long to know more…as all beings do," he leaned forward. "Follow me then…and I will show you more than you could ever imagine."

They sat in silence for a moment as the flames crackled.

Alexander frowned and looked up at Amyn, "…what is the Arcalypsis Flame, exactly?"

The Blood Tides

"The great, baleful red star or Blood Star, which the Vampyres call Ghanghoul, is a harbinger of misery and desolation in every age. The court astronomers of Arinönde, while an illustrious brotherhood, are by no means the first to chronicle the rise and fall of this heavenly body. There are extensive records which exist on many of the ancient ruins which litter the lands. While many great minds have tried to fathom their true meaning, there are a few who claim that the archaic symbols carved into their surfaces are in fact star maps. On many of these maps, the Blood Star is always depicted with a cross through it which was meant to represent calamity and destructive change."

-'The Ardhian Lands' by Wolter Keers

The attack on Sigisford was swift and brutal. Viran brought forth the best of his infantrymen for the lightning assault which he executed with characteristic precision. The Eldann were caught completely off-guard and their forces were scattered. The surprise and ruthlessness which greeted them had not been seen since the start of the Long Peace and it left no doubt as to the stake which the Vampyre's had placed in their Empresses' guidance.

Reports came back to the Enclaves through the Vision Crystals which every Vampyre carried and they relished the news of their hated adversaries fleeing in terror. Among the Elders, the news was received solemnly, for they knew what it portended: war with the Eldann would now resume and the might of Anturac would likely intervene.

The Empress, whose vision far exceeded those of her subjects, remained unmoved. She had foreseen much of what was to come and now prepared a special task-force for a mission which was far more important than any which had preceded it.

The great doors to the throne room opened slowly, creaking with ancient gears as they did so. Striding forward was the heir to the kingdom, the young Prince Carrinon himself. As he approached his Mother's throne, his pace slowed and she was able to look upon her progeny with a keen gaze. His features were angular but possessed of the innate nobility of his bloodline, for he came from the principal stock of two great races. He had his Mother's dark, wolfish eyes and jet-black hair but his face was that of his Father from the aquiline nose to the pronounced cheekbones.

Wearing his dark sash and silver armour, the Prince smiled as he approached the throne, "Mother…" he said softly.

"My son…" the Empress nodded graciously and rose to embrace him. They held each other tightly for a moment and then released. "You have heard the news…"

"War has begun…" the Prince's eyes glowed with excitement. "The Eldann will not take kindly to our intrusion."

"Nor should they…" the Empress turned and seated herself on the throne once more. "But this war is merely a diversion from a far greater task…one upon which our very existence hinges."

"Is that why you summoned me, Mother?"

The Empress nodded slightly, "you will lead a group into the Dragon's Teeth Mountains to seek out my brethren…"

"The *First*…" the reverence in the Prince's voice was palpable.

"Yes…the three of us are the last…I will need them by my side when the time comes."

The Prince's eyes betrayed anxiety for the first time, "what have you seen, Mother?"

The Empress appeared uncomfortable, as though speaking her visions aloud would bring them to fruition, "…our world is ending…everything we have ever known is about to change. We must make the first move to ensure our continued survival."

The Prince shifted on his feet, "…and…Father?"

The Empresses' eyes softened, "your Father moves in his own way…rest assured, he is five steps ahead of us."

"Then we must move quickly..." the Prince bowed. "You honor me, Mother, with this task...I will *not* fail you."

"I know..." the Empress ran her slender fingers along the arm of the throne. "You will go with three others who have already been notified."

The Prince looked up, unsurprised by his Mother's potent foresight, and smiled slightly, "who?"

"You will see..."

"When do we depart?"

"At sundown...one of the Elders will brief you."

The Prince bowed once more, "thank you, Mother..." he turned swiftly to leave.

"Carrinon..." the Empresses' voice called out softly.

The Prince turned slowly.

"...tread carefully."

He smiled and nodded before departing.

The Empress leaned back in her throne and shifted her great wings to the side. Vampyres were not a people given to fits of sentimentality, but there was a fierce sense of loyalty among the bloodlines which went back generations.

She nearly laughed to herself. Who was she fooling? She was a mother who was worried about her son and the future which lay before him. It was at moments such as this that she realized that the chasm between Vampyres and humans was not so great as she had once imagined.

Prince Carrinon moved swiftly around his personal quarters. He grabbed only what was absolutely necessary for his journey. A Vampyre always preferred to travel hard and light rather than well-stocked and easy. He took a wool blanket, his sword, some dried blood-mix, and a small golden locket which lay on his dresser. He eyed the locket for a moment as he held it in the palm of his hand. It shone in the perpetual twilight before he raised it and tied it around his neck.

Departing, he was immediately greeted outside of his room by Cerbenus.

The Elder bowed slightly, "my Prince..."

Carrinon nodded, "...Cerbenus."

"The others await..."

The Prince frowned, "who?"

"Duric, Lariana, and Murien…"

The Prince sighed with mild disgust, "they could find no one else?"

"No one so pliable…they will follow you without question."

This was another ploy by his Mother to ensure his safety. The Prince knew that she was wary of plots against his life, "I could have travelled alone…"

Elder Cerbenus smiled slightly, "of course, Highness…however, you don't know your way through the Grey Gulf. Murien has traversed it many times."

"Then why do I need the other two?" the Prince felt his blood beginning to boil.

Elder Cerbenus bowed his head lower, "the High Families insisted on it…it is a move for status with the Empress…you know how politics go."

"Wonderful…"

The Prince was furious.

The political machinations of Vampyres went back centuries. With their eternal lifespan, there was an indefinite amount of time to plot and scheme. Some plans would come to fruition after years of careful preparation and the Vampyre Elders in particular were notorious for their long-held grudges.

The Prince had little choice, "are they prepared?"

"They await only your arrival, sire."

Carrinon nodded and continued on his way with the Elder close behind. He didn't relish the idea of being grouped with companions for this journey, but what choice did he have? The Council must be placated, as always. He began to wonder if his Mother wasn't losing her grip on power.

My Father would never allow such insolence…

He clutched the golden locket around his neck and walked on in silence.

At last, he and Cerbenus came to a great, intricately wrought iron door. The door opened to them with surprising swiftness and they made their way into a small, dimly illuminated hallway.

The three Vampyres who were waiting for them bowed as the Prince and the Elder approached. They were garbed in long, woolen cloaks and simple clothing fit for the road ahead.

The Prince regarded them for a moment. They were each from one of the High Families and their Enclave was represented by the various insignia they wore.

There was nothing extraordinary about any of them.

Despite their illustrious lineages, these were as far from purebloods as you could get. Their families had likely been turned from humans several centuries ago.

The Prince snorted contemptuously, “is everything prepared?”

Duric bowed, “sire, we await only your instruction…”

Lariana leaned towards Murien while eyeing the Prince up and down, “he’s not as tall as I imagined…”

Prince Carrinon turned to her for a moment and frowned before glancing towards Elder Cerbenus, “where exactly is it that we are headed?”

“The journey will be perilous in the beginning, my Prince…you must pass the Grey Gulf and make your way to the Dragon’s Teeth.”

“The Grey Gulf…” Murien said softly. “Dangerous place…”

The Elder turned to him, “which is exactly why *you* shall be directing this team. You’ve travelled there before.”

Murien nodded but he remained silent.

Carrinon couldn’t believe he was being paired with these ingrates. He turned back to the Elder, “why does my Mother not simply reach out to her brethren telepathically?”

Cerbenus smiled, “she has…young Prince…one has responded to the call but the other is in hibernation. He has entered the astral realm and can only be awakened in person.”

“Convenient…” Lariana said.

Carrinon turned to her, “and what skills do *you* bring to the table?”

Lariana lowered her eyes for a moment, “dedication, sire…you won’t find one more skilled in hand-to-hand combat…”

“Bah!” Carrinon sneered. “You are proficient in the ways of *Man* I see…you’ve lost touch with your Vampyre roots…” he let his cat-like eyes settle on her. “If you were ever in touch with them to begin with.”

The barb stung visibly and much of the hauteur of the young Vampyress vanished swiftly.

Carrinon looked at the other two, “and how old are you? Is there someone here with some merit behind them, or am I among mere children?”

There was a heavy silence for a moment, then Duric spoke, “I’m three hundred years old…my Lord.”

The Prince threw back his head and laughed, “my point is proven…”

Elder Cerbenus, seeing that the Prince was threatening to sink the expedition before it had even begun, intervened, “sire, I can assure you I have vetted each of these volunteers *personally*. Do not let their youth deceive you, for their skill far surpasses any warrior in our ranks.”

The Prince sighed and turned to Murien. When he spoke, his tone had softened considerably, “you have passed through the Grey Gulf.”

Murien nodded, “yes, sire.”

“We make our way there then…you will lead us. Remember that we will be travelling by daylight as well. The sun poses no threat to me, but you will be under considerable duress.”

“Fear not, sire…” Lariana pointed to their cloaks. “Made with the finest fabrics from one of my family’s alchemists. It will provide protection from the hated light of day…”

The Prince smiled slightly, “then let us be off this instant.” He turned to Elder Cerbenus and took his hand in a tight grasp. “When we return, it will be with one of my Mother’s brethren.”

The Elder smiled and nodded, “be well, young Prince…may the might of Draganathan guide your steps.”

Carrinon nodded and turned without a word.

The rest of the group eyed him for a moment, then, realizing that he was departing, hurried after him.

Elder Cerbenus watched them go with crossed arms. He took a deep breath and tried to ponder what the future held for his people. His foresight was nowhere near that of the Empress, but he could sense the cloud of doom which hung ominously in the distance. Now was not the time for half-measures nor for timidity.

The war with the Eldann was a predictable thing and didn’t trouble him in the least. They had fought that hated foe for generations uncounted. What worried him was what the Empress had seen coming. A looming shadow which he couldn’t perceive, but so great was the threat that not only would she break the Long Peace, but she would risk the life of her only son as well.

Dark times lie ahead...the Elder thought grimly and he was deeply disturbed that he couldn't see beyond the coming shadow.

When Two Paths Meet

"Those who know, speak not, and those who speak, know not."

-Ancient aphorism

Gur-Naga saw the dying embers of the campfire clinging to life, sending out small gasps of smoke into the chill night air. He turned and signalled to his brethren to begin surrounding their target. The Beastmen grunted softly as they brandished their weapons.

Gur-Naga had placed special emphasis on the fact that the wizard was to be taken alive and could not perish under any circumstances. As he squinted into the night, he saw that there were three others sleeping around the fire. He grinned and thumbed his dagger gently.

As the group closed in, they got a better look at their prey: two young women and a boy. He was momentarily confused as he had been informed that the wizard was travelling with only two companions. He quickly brushed these thoughts aside as they were little more than children but this didn't concern the Móg Flagen. They were not of the *Unterwilt* and therefore, the laws of combat did not apply to them.

In other words, they were fair game.

The ring began to tighten. Gur-Naga spotted the wizard immediately and pointed him out to the others. They nodded in unison and began to move in. As they approached, their footsteps barely audible on the soft ground, Gur-Naga suddenly had the sinking feeling that one amongst their quarry was awake. If that was the case, they best move quickly.

Gur-Naga took the lead, moving past the others and brandishing his dagger. He eyed one of the supine bodies on the ground and raised his hand to strike a deathblow. For a moment, his gaze wandered from the prone form on the ground to a spot just beyond the dying embers.

He froze. A singular, silver orb was shining from the darkness.

As he squinted into the shadows, he was stunned to realize that it was an eye which was gazing at him. He felt suddenly exposed as though his innermost secrets were being perused by this strange being. He thought he heard voices in his head. He dropped the knife and gripped his temples, falling to his knees and letting out a scream.

The other Móg Flagen looked over in shock at the sight of their leader who was now lying prostrate on the cold ground.

The commotion awoke the three youths who appeared disoriented and confused. They fumbled across the ground, trying to find their feet.

The old man, who could only have been the wizard they had pursued, rose to his feet slowly, the silver orb of his eye shining malevolently in the darkness, "you should know better…" his voice was like a thousand icepicks and it shook his hardened pursuers to the core. "You have no business intervening in Ardhian affairs…"

The Móg Flagen stepped back, almost unconsciously, fear visible on their faces. At last, one of them gave out a war cry and rallied forward with his axe raised. Soon, the others broke free from the spell and followed suit.

The commotion awoke the siblings and the Princess and they all screamed in unison at the terrifying sight of flailing Beastmen around them.

The wizard raised his arms, incantations from some elder age flowing from his tongue. The dying fire suddenly came to life, dancing up into the air and moving like a sinuous snake in concentric circles. The wizard made a circular motion through the air with his hands and the fire lashed out in all directions. The Barbarian warriors were met with a wall of impenetrable flame and it devoured them like a hungry beast.

Chaos now reigned supreme.

The Móg Flagen were fighting to find a way to approach their quarry, but each step they took was countered by fire. Gur-Naga still screamed on the ground and his comrades tried to reach him but found themselves unable to approach.

Amyn's voice, roaring like a growing tempest, shook the rocks free from their foundations and sent them soaring into the air. It was a sight which struck terror into the Beastmen and reverted them into a primal state of flight. Their discipline now completely eroded, the Flagen were in full retreat.

Gur-Naga lay unconscious on the ground and his men abandoned him without looking back.

As the last of the pursuers retreated, Amyn lowered his arms. As he did so, it was as though a bubble around the camp had burst and the encircling fire and rocks dissipated and fell to the ground.

Alexander, Charlotte, and the Princess looked on stunned. They seemed to be incapable of movement as though frozen in place by a fear they could scarcely comprehend.

Amyn turned to them and they averted their gaze, too afraid to meet that terrible orb directly, "it is over…" the wizard said softly. He glanced towards Gur-Naga who was taking shallow breaths as he gradually regained consciousness.

Amyn spat on the ground and walked over to the prone form. He cocked his head slightly, then lifted his right leg and stepped on the man's chest. Gur-Naga gasped as though he were being held by a force far greater than an old man's foot.

Alexander approached slowly, examining their assailant. The man, if he could be called that, was tall and broad shouldered. Tribal tattoos ran down his powerful arms and a pair of goat horns adorned the top of his head. He looked more like a beast which was trapped in a man's form and yet, for all of his apparent might, he lay helpless beneath the force of Amyn's foot.

"If your people had remembered how to speak the tongue of the animals, you would've heard the birds warning me of your presence before you even set foot in camp…" Amyn's voice had an undercurrent of threat in it. "You're not from one of the local tribes…"

"And you're not a mere wizard…" Gur-Naga snarled.

Amyn smiled cruelly, "you're Móg Flagen, aren't you?"

Gur-Naga refused to answer but his eyes indicated that Amyn was correct.

"The markings on the arm…" Amyn pointed to Gur-Naga's bicep. "A dead giveaway…the image of a boar consuming a snake…the symbol of the Unterwilt."

"You seem…to know much…*wizard…*" every word Gur-Naga spoke required tremendous effort.

"Your people have forgotten the Old Ways, clearly…if they had remembered, they never would have set foot here."

Gur-Naga managed a slight smile. His teeth were stained red with blood, "you may have driven us off this time…but we will never stop hunting you."

Amyn frowned, "your pursuit will leave you running in circles."

"How far do you think *you* can run?" Gur-Naga gasped and took a deep intake of breath. "The entire…empire…pursues you."

"The empire is in its last days…only ash and fire await it."

"What would…you know…of ash and fire…" the Barbarian coughed up a wad of blood.

Amyn leaned closer, the force of his presence alone seeming to hold Gur-Naga in place, "I was there when *fire* rained from the skies…I was there when creatures beyond your comprehension emerged from the Tartarian planes. I have witnessed the entropy of time itself as it came undone and have crossed the unfathomable leagues of the Abyss."

Gur-Naga's eyes widened with growing fear.

Amyn smiled slightly, "but death is not to be your lot today…instead…I curse you to wander these lands like the beasts you descend from…turning and turning until nothing human of you remains and your people themselves put you down like the dog you are."

"No…" Gur-Naga could barely speak. "…please."

Alexander and the others were shaking with fear. Amyn turned to them and the pitiable sight of their terror appeared to soften him.

He glanced back at Gur-Naga, "or…you can return and tell your Chieftain to abandon this petty pursuit."

"I…I cannot…" Gur-Naga was nearly frantic. "I cannot return…in failure…it will bring death to me regardless…"

Amyn's silver eye glowed, "go to him, and repeat what I am about to tell you…it will spare your life."

Gur-Naga seemed to contemplate this for a moment, then nodded slowly.

Amyn spoke once more, but this time, his voice was inaudible to all save Gur-Naga. The siblings and the Princess strained to hear, but it was as though an invisible barrier had come down. All they could decipher were muffled phrases.

Gur-Naga's eyes widened as comprehension filled them. He nodded slightly once more and Amyn released his foot. The Barbarian sighed as though the air were returning to his lungs, then leaned over and coughed harshly into the grass.

Amyn stepped away and stood with his arms folded.

Gur-Naga struggled to his feet, taking deep intakes of breath. He turned to the wizard, lowering his eyes against that terrible gaze, then limped away towards the hills. After a few minutes, he was a dark shadow against the horizon.

Amyn turned to the siblings and sighed deeply.

"What was *that*?" Alexander asked, his voice still shaking.

Princess Rionéolas seemed too stunned to speak. After a few moments, she composed herself, "I...have never seen...magic like that."

"Nor will you again, if I have it my way..." Amyn said. "I've said before that magic of any kind is not for mere *show*..."

"Forget that then..." Charlotte alone seemed to be able to retain her senses. "Let's keep going."

Alexander gave her a look of disbelief as though she had somehow missed what had just unfolded before their eyes.

Amyn seemed to smile slightly and pointed to Charlotte, "ahh...now this is someone who understands the true nature of magic. It is not something to be boasted about nor discussed, it simply *is*."

Alexander and the Princess seemed confused.

Charlotte nodded towards the wizard in acknowledgment but remained silent.

"That was more than just magic..." Alexander's voice trembled slightly. "I...I don't know what that was."

"No one in the Bright Seminary, nor the highest adepts of the Bright Church, would be capable of a feat like that..." Princess Rionéolas said.

Amyn frowned, "nor are they capable of *shapeshifting*..."

There was an awkward silence again, then they all noticed that the sky had begun to lighten. Day was fast approaching, although the terrifying events of the night had seemed to occur only moments ago.

The siblings began to gather their things without a word and the Princess took a swig from the pouch of water Amyn had given her, "this water is incredible…" she said after taking a gulp.

"It's from the Great Forest…" Amyn said. "A blessing of Druim. It will quench your thirst with a mere mouthful…perfect for long journeys."

The Princess smiled and wiped her mouth with her sleeve. Her instructors at the castle would've been mortified at the thought that she had adopted peasant mannerisms. In fact, they were probably wondering where she was at this moment. She didn't doubt that her Father would have the best Royal Guardsmen scouring the province trying to find her. No doubt the High-Rector would be able to explain what had happened.

She abandoned these thoughts as they served no purpose. She turned her mind towards their destination, "this Tower…you said it belonged to Drachmuin."

Amyn lifted his satchel and nodded briskly.

"He's the writer of this book… is he not?" The Princess gestured to her robes where the ancient tome lay hidden.

Amyn pointed towards the horizon as if to indicate that they should get moving. As they began to walk, he spoke, "Drachmuin was the Lawgiver, although he and the other Serpent Priests have been dwarfed by the reputation of Danyr."

Alexander was walking briskly alongside them, his interest clearly piqued, "did Drachmuin actually *live* in this Tower?"

"Yes… it was his place of study for many years."

"He was a hermit?" Alexander asked.

Amyn shook his head, "no, no, boy…he was a scholar and scientist. He studied the phenomena of this world with an acute eye."

"Did you know him?"

"Intimately, yes…"

Alexander nodded and turned his eyes back to the ground. The fullness of daylight was now upon them and they could see something cresting the horizon in the distance. It towered over the landscape like a brooding sentinel.

Amyn pointed towards it, "behold, the Tower."

The youths gazed on in awe. Even at this distance, they could see the sinister magnitude of it.

The Princesses' jaw was practically hanging open, "why have I never known of this… I've studied every map in the castle and this Tower is not listed among any of them."

"Because…" Amyn said softly. "It is a forbidden place…none who have ventured there have ever returned and the empire's attempts to dismantle it have met with failure. It is protected by an elder magic beyond your comprehension."

Charlotte turned to the old man, "and…*we're* supposed to just walk in there?"

Amyn nodded as though that alone would suffice.

Charlotte was not satisfied, "you're leading us to our deaths, then…"

"No…I'm leading you to a new life."

"A new life?" Charlotte clenched her fists. "Who are *you* to decide what's best for us? You've led us on a wild goose chase since we met you…always blurting out riddles and half-truths and I'm sick of it." Her hands began to shake as though the tempest inside of her was threatening to overwhelm her.

Amyn looked at her for a long time, then spoke softly, "you've been through much, child…and I will not fault you for feeling the way that you do. But ask yourself: what do you have to go back to?" The question hung in the air for a moment, then the old man continued. "If you had stayed in Ainshyre, you'd now be dead…sacrificed on an altar by a power-mad cult. If you try to find sanctuary in another town and start over, you will be put to work in one of the mills or factories. Parentless children do not often get a free pass in this life and the obstacles which greet them are immense beyond comprehension. I've told you from the start that you are not prisoners and can leave my side at any time..." he gave Charlotte a hard look.

Her shoulders sagged in defeat. Her head fell forward and she struggled to hold back tears.

Amyn moved towards her and put a gentle hand on her shoulder. She did not resist him. He gazed into her eyes and his own silver eye began to shine gently, "you are part of something bigger than you know…" his voice became very quiet. "I too have lost everything dear to me…perhaps I see myself reflected in you."

Charlotte nodded slightly and her face softened as though his words had found their mark.

Amyn turned and continued onwards.

Princess Rionéolas approached Charlotte tentatively, "may I give you a hug?"

Charlotte burst out laughing, "you're an *Animrens*, a member of the Royal Family…and you're *asking* to give me a hug?"

The Princess smiled and leaned forward to embrace her. They held one another for a moment and when they released, Charlotte had a visible aura of peace around her.

"Come on," the Princess said, smiling. "Let's follow that crusty old dog. Besides, I'm excited to see the Tower up close."

"Excited?" Alexander said as they began to pick up their pace. "Didn't Amyn say that no one who has ventured there has ever returned?"

The Princess nodded, "did you *see* what he did to those Barbarians? If anyone can get into that Tower, it's him…besides…" she clutched her robes where the Red Book lay hidden. "I want to see the dwelling of one of the original Serpent Priests…if we *can* get in…it'll be a historic moment."

Alexander shook his head in disbelief. Despite his uncertainty, he was excited too.

An Unlikely Grouping

"The Old Gods, long forgotten by the common man, are linked to primeval myths too ancient to comprehend. Their temples have been cast down and their idols defaced. Likely, it was fear that drove the first settlers to remove these haunted images and destroy the dark tribes who worshipped them. Their names have been lost to history, but what little is known of them tells that they presided over a time of great devastation, a time before the first man ever gained sentience. They had a name then, which is one of the few pieces of lore surrounding them that remains: they were called An'Deir. What the term means, we do not yet know, but no one can speak it aloud without a feeling of dread engulfing them."

-"What Came Before" by Ather

Prince Carrinon kept a steady pace ahead of the others. He had no desire to mingle with them and even less desire to hear the grating sound of their voices, *"Mother..."* he communicated into the Void. *"Why did you bind me to these fools?"*

A voice, unmistakable in its power, filtered back to him, *"they have skills you will need, my son...you have always been capable, but it is also wise to accept help."*

The Prince snarled to himself but did not communicate further. His Mother was right as usual.

"Your Highness! Your Highness...daylight will be approaching." Murien called from behind him.

"Then ready *your* protection..." the Prince growled.

Pathetic...he thought. *Useless half-breeds*...

Despite what some may think, he did not see himself as anything less than the standard bearer of his glorious Ancestors.

The fact that he had Ardhian blood only added to his sense of self-righteousness. No one had ever had the gall to call *him* a half-breed…certainly not to his face.

But he knew there were rumours. Rumours that his Ardhian blood had tainted the purity within him. Despite his outward bravado, these rumours hurt him deeply. He was proud of his heritage on *both* sides and saw himself as the first of a new and glorious race. His Vampyre ancestors had shaped the world to their liking, creating technologies that made the human kingdoms appear primitive by comparison.

The war with the Eldann was purely a staging ground for warriors to sharpen their skills.

He alone among his kind had visited Anturac in his youth. Three times he had set foot upon the hallowed ground of his Father's domain and he had been astounded by what he had seen: a city that appeared to be made of gold, a palace made of crystal, silver engines of unfathomable technological sophistication moving effortlessly through the sky.

During those visits, he and his Father had wandered through the great gardens of the Crystal Palace, admiring the splendour around them. Sometimes they had walked in silence, sometimes his Father had spoken to him and the young Prince had absorbed every word.

"Did you know, my son, that our world was once even more advanced than what you see here?"

The Prince's eyes had widened, *"more advanced? What's more advanced than this?"*

His Father had laughed, *"there is much for you to learn and your immortality will ensure that you've plenty of time to learn it..."* he had stopped speaking and looked wistfully into the distance.

Carrinon knew his Father's thoughts were reaching out to his Mother.

In Anturac's Great Library, Carrinon read books of such antiquity that they had to be protected with ancient spells of preservation. He studied astronomical charts and ancient Ardhian relics which had been kept safe since before the Days of Fire.

The Prince had always had a keen mind for astronomy in particular, which he and his Father considered to be the 'Queen of the Arts'. His Father had an enormous telescope in his personal study and the young Prince had spent days at a time gazing at the sky. His Father had told him that the greatest astronomers in the known world were the Alderamin. The Prince had long wished to meet these elusive sages for himself but had never queried his Father about where they could be found.

And so, the days had passed in the Capitol and when at last he had returned to his Mother's side, he had eagerly anticipated his return to his Father's land.

Alas, after his third visit, that day had never come.

For nearly five hundred years the Prince had petitioned his Father to return and been roundly denied each time. He felt heartbroken and betrayed by what he saw as obvious neglect.

"Your Father moves at his own pace..." his Mother had said. *"This, my son, is the price of immortality...time itself becomes meaningless."*

The young Prince had sneered at this explanation, but as he had matured to the fullness of adulthood (he would age no further) he had begun to understand what it meant. Indeed, five hundred years may have seemed an eternity to him when he was a boy, but as a man, it could pass in a blink. He began to see the world through his parents' eyes for the first time and understood that his Father had not been neglecting him, he had merely been seeing reality from a different plane of existence.

All of these thoughts ran through his head as he walked on.

The path was quickly becoming mired by jagged rocks and enormous chasms. The Prince and the others, blessed with their preternatural skills, avoided these pitfalls easily.

Lariana, able to teleport brief distances, utilized this ability to the full while mocking the others, "come on, slowpokes!" She cackled as she took the lead.

Carrinon looked at her with disdain.

"You're going the wrong way!" Murien called out.

Lariana stopped and glanced around at the fog-filled desolation, "this place is so dreary…"

"It's the *Grey* Gulf…" Murien's voice had more than a hint of sarcasm in it. "What did you expect?"

Duric walked on silently. He alone among the three seemed tolerable to Carrinon. He had the bearing of a warrior and, half-blood or not, a warrior could be relied upon.

Carrinon slowed his pace to match Duric's until he was side-by-side with the young Vampyre, "what regiment did you serve in?"

Duric looked up with surprise, as though he hadn't noticed Carrinon's presence, "uhh…the Seven Wings, sire…"

"It doesn't take the gift of telepathy to see that you've fought before." Carrinon said with a smile. "Against the Eldann, yes?"

"Yes, sire…" Duric seemed uncomfortable, as though he wasn't sure where this line of questioning would lead.

"Fear not…" Carrinon's mellifluous voice was deceptively calming. "I may need your skills on this journey…the other two," he gestured ahead to Lariana and Murien. "Will only slow us down."

"Forgive me, sire…" Duric at last managed to meet the Prince's gaze. "But they're my friends…and while my loyalty will always be to the Throne…I will never abandon them."

Carrinon cocked his head with more than a hint of surprise. There was a finality in Duric's tone which left no room for debate. The lad was truly loyal, regardless of the consequences to his own being.

Carrinon was more than a little impressed.

"Very well…" the Prince said. "We shall all finish this journey together, come what may."

Duric nodded. He had heard what he wanted. "What will happen once we reach the Dragon's Teeth, sire?"

Carrinon turned his gaze back to the path, "we will awaken one of the First."

"The *First*? As in, the First Vampyres? The same as the Empress?"

"The same, yes."

Duric's breathing began to quicken, "we will…we will *meet* one in person?"

Carrinon frowned, "I believe that was implied, yes…"

"Who are they? I mean…I've heard legends of the First, but I believed the Empress to be the last."

Carrinon nearly laughed at the youth's naiveté, "there are three pure-blooded Vampyres left in the world. My Mother, Apophanis, and Maledict. Apophanis was my Mother's tutor…Maledict is her brother."

"Your *uncle*?" Duric was practically panting.

The Prince gave him a look of such contempt that the youth turned away quickly and remained silent, although Carrinon could see that there were innumerable questions waiting to burst forth.

The Prince indulged the youth's curiosity a moment longer, "after the Days of Fire when my Father and the Ardhians arrived, they were met by a hostile land. Giants roamed the world and all manner of creatures that have now passed into myth encroached upon their encampments." He stopped speaking for a moment, as though reliving the images of his Mother's story once more for the first time. "The Ardhians were nearly wiped out…it was the Vampyres that saved them."

Duric gasped and his eyes widened, "I thought the Ardhians fought their own way forward through sheer ingenuity."

Now the Prince *did* laugh, "not a chance…they were on the brink of destruction when my Mother and the Ten arrived at their encampment. You see, back then, there were ten Masters remaining. Ten pure-blooded Vampyres…do you have any idea the power of such a group? They could level mountains and shatter the skies if they had wished. Instead, they offered the Ardhians a deal: replenish their numbers and they would help them create a new home. The deal was sealed with the union of my parents and my eventual birth."

Duric looked ahead to Lariana and Murien. They were engaged in some kind of idle conversation which was probably inane and of little consequence and here he was learning the secret history of his race, "why don't we know this story? Why has it been suppressed?"

Carrinon gave him a hard look, "because…time corrupts all things. The original Ardhian bloodline has been diluted through the generations of interbreeding with the Lost Tribes. And so, the once immortal lifespan of that hallowed people has dissipated. Now, if you look on the common man, they have forgotten their illustrious lineage and choose instead to believe that Danyr and his people were some greater beings which descended from on high to save them." The Prince sighed for a moment, then continued. "Now…what would you say the average lifespan is of a mortal? Sixty years? Seventy?"

"I'd imagine about that, sire…"

"Bah!" the Prince practically spat. "Now, we use them for little more than cattle…they are an amusement to our kind, nothing more. You see…the intermingling of the races created several unexpected consequences. The half-blooded Vampyre offspring couldn't survive in direct sunlight and they had a thirst for blood which required constant satiation. Thus, the divide continued to grow until it has reached its current state of decadence.

"The First never drank blood, nor did they fear the sun…they were free in a way that you cannot possibly comprehend. They were the true Guardians of this world."

Duric nodded absently, his mind was ablaze with a thousand thoughts, "what happened to the other Eight?"

Carrinon smiled slightly, "some stayed…but they will only reveal themselves when the time is right. Others journeyed between the stars…"

"What!?" Duric's voice carried up to the other two and they turned to see what the commotion was about.

"You alright there, sire?" Lariana called back. "Don't let his calm exterior fool you, Duric can be excitable sometimes."

Murien chuckled and they turned to resume their previous discussion.

Duric gave them an irritated look then turned back to the Prince, his voice a low whisper, "there's so much we don't know…"

The Prince now spoke directly into the youth's mind, *"and you will know nothing more for now…too much knowledge, too soon, can be dangerous."*

Duric's jaw shook with the jarring effect of the Prince's telepathic communion. His hands twitched slightly for a moment, then he managed to steady himself. He looked as though he was about to speak, but then lapsed into silence. The power of revelation seemed to weigh heavily on him.

The Prince smiled to himself. The youth had handled what he had been told well. He was beginning to think that perhaps his Mother's wisdom had prevailed once more in her choosing of his companions. He just wished he had her foresight so that he could see what it was she was planning for him.

The seemingly endless vastness of the Gulf was beginning to wear on the group's nerves. Murien and Carrinon alone seemed to be immune to the growing despair which began to creep in.

"We've been walking for hours…" Lariana complained. "Is there no end to this foggy nonsense?"

"It hasn't been as long as you think…" Murien said. "And we'll be travelling for another day before we breach the Gulf."

Lariana rolled her eyes, "wonderful…"

Duric remained silent and seemed to be lost in contemplation.

Carrinon turned towards Murien, "did my Mother go to your families personally?"

It was a strange question and Murien seemed confused, but he did not hesitate to answer, "yes, sire…She did."

"Ahh…" the Prince nodded and smiled. "Did she say *why* she had chosen you to accompany me?"

Murien and Lariana shook their heads.

"No…" Murien said softly. "But we were honored by Her presence…we did not hesitate to say yes, we know that the Empresses' designs are unfathomable and wise beyond our comprehension."

Carrinon frowned. It was exactly the response he had expected and he was profoundly disappointed. His Mother was wise, to be sure, no one in the Enclaves would dispute that. What bothered him was the fanatical acceptance of her will by the multitudes. He knew it bothered *her* as well, but she was a pragmatist and she understood that the people needed a figurehead to turn to. Gone were the days of the Ancients who were free-thinking and independent. They would never have tolerated a Messiah of any kind no matter how esteemed.

The Vampyre race had fallen far indeed.

Still, Carrinon was not prepared to give up his enquiry, "so…you have no idea why you were chosen… none of you have any particular gifts or skills?"

"Besides the ability to teleport?" Lariana said with mild sarcasm.

The Prince smiled. In the palace, he was used to the obsequious gestures of his courtiers. This kind of honest interaction was refreshing.

Murien leapt gracefully over a boulder, "I have a talent for finding my way…do you know how many have wandered into the Grey Gulf and never been seen again?"

Lariana frowned, "oh come now, how many *human* caravans have passed through here unmolested?"

Murien seemed to consider this, "…a few…I suppose."

"Regardless…" Duric spoke up and his voice drew the attention of the others. "Murien knows the quickest way through. You could wander for days, even weeks in this place. Sure, even humans have found their way out, but for every two that made it, five vanished."

There was silence for a moment and Murien seemed to glow under the compliments of his peer.

The Prince was slowly beginning to understand why his Mother had chosen this group. It wasn't anything to do with special ability nor magical prowess, nor perhaps even intellect. Instead, there was an undercurrent of loyalty among these three. They were prepared to defend one another and they were steadfast in their devotion.

Such traits were scarce in the Enclaves and could not be bought.

*Well done, Mother…*the Prince thought. His admiration for her only grew with the passing of the ages.

"The sun is already above us…" Lariana said, practically snarling at the sky. "I can feel it…though the fog shrouds the worst of its effects."

"Your cloaks will protect you…" the Prince said calmly.

Lariana shot him a nervous glance, "yes…but to tread in open sunlight will be a new experience for me."

"Do not fear it…" Carrinon's voice was uncharacteristically soothing. "The power of the cloaks will repel even the most virulent effects of sunlight. Who knows…" he smiled slightly. "You may even come to *enjoy* the daylight."

All three of the young Vampyres laughed.

"Next you'll tell us that we should embrace humanity with open arms and start eating pigs…" Murien quipped.

A strange sound echoed through the canyons of the Grey Gulf, one which had not been heard in many years. The Prince was laughing and it bounced off the rocks like music on the wind.

Cast to the Wind

"Antaryan, the Lord of Cosmic Fire, is worshipped heavily in the desolate wastes of the Black Mara Desert. His cult has endured for millennia and the lore surrounding Him was passed down in oral traditions before being recorded in the temples. A long line of ancient Hierophants acted as guardians over the worship of the Deity and kept the rituals of His sanctum. The Hierophants' rule was one of prosperity and peace for many long ages, until a sinister corruption wormed its way into their ranks. Legends say that Antaryan, furious at the degeneracy of His people, seared the kingdom in a great conflagration which consumed the order of Hierophants and burned their corruption to the wind like ash."

-translation of the ancient tablets of Mal

Valleyhold, with its charming scenery and gentle church spires, was as bland and forgettable as any other town they had passed through. There was a serene simplicity to it which barely left an impression on the youths. Their eyes were, instead, fixed upon the great spire in the sky which seemed to loom over them the closer they got to it.

Their approach towards it seemed rapid and unhindered. Time itself appeared to have allied with them and it wasn't long before they found themselves in Nin-Ghasta, the final threshold before the Tower itself.

Unlike Valleyhold and countless other towns, Nin-Ghasta had a dreary aura surrounding it. The gambrel roofs of the town seemed to be crumbling and there was a palpable aura of despair.

"Nice place..." Alexander said with both sarcasm and shock.

"Keep your wits about you..." Amyn cautioned. "The people of Nin-Ghasta do not look kindly upon outsiders." He turned to the Princess, "you'll want to keep a low profile...I doubt anyone here will recognize you, but if they should, it will draw unwanted attention."

Princess Rionéolas crossed her arms and frowned, "my Father likely has the entire kingdom looking for me...what *more* unwanted attention could we attract?"

Amyn made a shooing motion, "regardless...be wary. The Tower is close at hand."

Charlotte craned her neck to the high bluffs overlooking the town and the black spire which lay at the top, "I can see that...it must be quite the view from up there."

"Come..." Amyn gestured towards a path which ran through the town.

As they approached, a large wooden sign, nearly half-decayed, blew lazily in the wind.

"What does it say?" Charlotte asked.

Alexander craned his neck to see, "it says: 'Nin-Ghasta'. Then it says something else which I can't make out...it looks as though it were scratched away."

"Charming..." the Princess said. She glanced up towards the Tower. From this distance it was still imposing with its polished, black stone. "No wonder this place is falling apart...they have to live in the shadow of *that*."

They moved down the path towards the town at a steady pace. On either side of them, buildings loomed silently, all of which appeared to be abandoned.

Charlotte couldn't shake the same feeling of dread that she had in Ainshyre and memories of that blighted place came rushing back to her in quick succession. She shuddered involuntarily at the thought that they had nearly perished there and still couldn't understand why uncle Adair had tried to sacrifice them to whatever god he and his fellow villagers worshipped.

She pushed these thoughts away as they approached. They were with Amyn and after what she had seen him do to the Barbarians, she had absolutely no fear that they would be harmed.

Walking down the main drag, they at last saw signs of life, mostly drunks weaving in and out of the pubs which seemed to be the only thriving businesses in town. Several of them leered wearily at the youths as they passed, some looking as though they might leap forward to grab them but the sight of Amyn stayed their hand. They seemed to regard him with a kind of primal fear, as though the drink had dulled their rational senses enough for them to sense the old man's true power.

The Princess pulled her hood tighter over her face, trying desperately to hide from the staring reprobates.

Soon, the drunks lost interest and stumbled back into the pub to drink away whatever unnamed sorrows they harboured.

"We're not staying here for the night…are we?"

There was more than a hint fright in Alexander's voice.

Amyn shook his head, "we are nearly at the Tower itself…we will not dally here a moment longer than we have to."

The youths sighed in unison. Their relief was palpable.

As they proceeded along the path, they passed a shaggy old man who was seated on a wooden bench with what was clearly a bottle of alcohol in his hand. He swigged from it as easily as he would if it were water and turned his head to the approaching group.

"Ahhh…tourists come to see our lovely town." His voice was like gravel.

"It is lovely…" Charlotte said against her better judgement.

"So it is…" the old man wiped his face and flashed a toothless grin. "Come to see our biggest attraction 'ave you?" He pointed upwards to the looming Tower. "Been there since long before I was born…and it'll be there long after I die."

Charlotte stopped for a moment, "the Tower of Drachmuin. Is that what you call it?"

The old man nodded, "aye…t'was built by the wizard *himself* many ages ago…we have lived in its shadow ever since."

"Charlotte…" Amyn said impatiently as he stood waiting.

Charlotte ignored him for a moment longer, "why do your people not move away?"

The old man laughed and then coughed, it was a pitiable sound, "because…none of us 'ave the will anymore. The power is too great. It governs all things…we are its willing slaves…"

Amyn turned and continued walking.

Charlotte put a gentle hand on the old man's shoulder. The plight of Nin-Ghasta at last began to make sense to her, "we will find a way inside…perhaps, a way to free you all."

The old man met her gaze with his watery blue eyes and she thought she saw something close to terror in them, "none 'ave survived…none who venture forth come back…we do not speak of it…if your path binds you to it, then go forth…but do not throw yer life away."

Charlotte withdrew her hand and the old man's head collapsed forward. He seemed to be lingering on the edges of consciousness.

Amyn was already making his way up the cobblestone path but Alexander and the Princess stood by, waiting.

"Come on, Charlotte…" Alexander said softly.

Charlotte backed away from the old man and glanced at the dilapidated decay which surrounded them, "this was a mistake…" she craned her neck towards the enormous bluff upon which the black spire stood. "We should never have come here…"

"And where *else* would we go?" Alexander asked plaintively. "We have nothing and no one to take us in…"

"Not true…" there was a rising anger in Charlotte's voice. "We have other great-aunts and uncles who would house us."

"After our encounter with uncle Adair…I don't trust them anymore."

"Uncle Adair was *twisted…*" Charlotte snapped. "We can't paint the others with the same brush."

"Where is Aymn?" the voice belonged to the Princess.

They stood dazed for a moment, then began to search with growing desperation.

"I don't see him…" Alexander said, his voice barely concealing the fright which was welling up inside of him.

"Damn him…" Charlotte cursed. "He's abandoned us for the Tower."

"Why would he do that?" Alexander seemed to be genuinely hurt.

Charlotte's eyes were as hard as stone, "we're not going to wait to find out…come on." She bolted up the path without another word.

The Princess and Alexander took off behind her, trying to keep up. When they turned the bend, the cobblestone path disappeared and was replaced by blackened, jutting rocks.

Charlotte squinted ahead, she could still make out the pathway which wound round the mountainside, although it was now far more treacherous. She turned to the others, "come on…"

Tentatively, they proceeded forward and the air around them seemed to change instantly. It was as though they were stepping through a hidden divide into another realm. The sky seemed to darken and growl as though it too was possessed of evil intent.

The youths jumped over fallen rocks and avoided the sharp edges of the bluff as they went. The top of the promontory seemed to be a lifetime away and they realized only now how tired they were. They couldn't remember the last time they had eaten and their nerves were frayed to their limits.

Charlotte, alone among them, seemed to be imbued with strength and vigour, as though her growing hatred for the man who had abandoned them spurred her on.

The Princess nearly slipped on a jagged outcropping and Alexander's hand swooped down with lightning speed to steady her.

She looked into his dark eyes for a moment with relief, "...thank you."

The boy smiled slightly and, in that moment, small traces of the man he would eventually become shone through. His face had a nobility to it which the Princess had noticed briefly when they had first met. She steadied herself and looked up the path, "come on, we're losing her."

Alexander nodded and together, they continued their treacherous journey. What awaited them at the top of the cliff, they knew not. The journey upwards seemed interminable and it was inconceivable that an old man could travel so quickly up such a steep incline.

But he's not an old man... Alexander reminded himself. *That's just a guise. One of many...*

The boy cursed himself for being foolish enough to place this man on a pedestal. He had begun to hero-worship him without even realizing it and it bothered him deeply. Here was another individual who had used them to his own ends and then discarded them.

It makes no sense...why have us along in the first place?

"Alexander! You're falling behind..." Charlotte called out.

The boy looked up in surprise and realized he had been lost in his own thoughts. He hurried to keep up with the others.

The Princess had slowed her pace and smiled at him when he came up next to her, "I'm beginning to think I'm out of my depth…" she said softly. "Father always told me the world was a cruel and merciless place…my tutors said the same…" her eyes seemed to mist with emotion. "…I never believed them."

Alexander walked on quietly. He sought desperately for the right words, "well…there's good and bad in everything, isn't there?"

The Princess looked up and nodded slightly.

"I mean…" the boy seemed to fumble over his words for a moment before regaining his footing. "Yeah…there's been a lot of bad that's happened to us…we lost our family and our great-uncle tried to kill us. And sure, our guide has abandoned us in this barren wasteland…but…" he looked up and met her emerald eyes. "We met *you*, didn't we? So, it can't be all bad."

The Princesses' face lit up, "I'm glad to have met you too, Alexander."

"Come on, guys!" Charlotte was now well ahead of them and the impatience in her voice was palpable. "It'll be night before we reach the top!"

The Princess and Alexander glanced at one another briefly and couldn't help but laugh.

Gur-Naga made his way into the encampment looking like a feral animal. His clothes were in tatters and his eyes were wild with anxiety. His brothers barely recognized him.

He headed straight to the center of camp and found his master's tent. The Guardsmen stepped aside as he blundered forward. Pulling aside the flap, Gur-Naga approached the small fire in the center of the enclosure with obvious tentativeness.

"You return empty-handed…" a voice said from the shadows.

Gur-Naga bowed, "my Lord…forgive me…the wizard was far too powerful."

"You are the only one to return…" Mabinogan said softly. "The others?"

Gur-Naga lifted his head slowly; there were tears in his eyes as he remembered the charred bodies of the comrades he had found on his journey back. They had retreated from the wizard's wrath and he had expected to meet them along the way, but alas, it seemed that none of them had been unscathed, "gone…my Lord…" He remembered then what the wizard had told him. The words that were meant to save his life. "Lord…the wizard did give me a piece of information which you may find valuable…"

Mabinogan crossed his powerful arms and frowned.

Gur-Naga sighed nervously, "he said: Anturac will not intervene."

Unexpectedly, his sovereign laughed heartily and Gur-Naga could scarcely hide the complete confusion on his face.

Mabinogan rose from his seat and for the first time, Gur-Naga noticed that there were other chiefs present in the darkness around him.

The Lord of the Móg Flagen's eyes glowed in the twilight, "they must recognize the decadence of Arinönde at last. They see that Animrens is a fool and desire a *true* King to sit on the throne." He gestured around him to the chiefs. "While you were tracking the wizard, the War Council has assembled…" he pointed towards a regal figure who was seated behind him. "Korazon…explain the recent developments."

Korazon rose slowly, his pale white hair tied into a taut pony-tail, "the Princess has vanished…all of Arinönde is in chaos. The King is blaming the wizard for her abduction and has dispatched ten regiments to seize him."

Gur-Naga rose slowly, his eyes wide, "*ten regiments*? But that would be-"

"The entirety of their standing army…" Mabinogan said with obvious relish. "In his haste to procure his missing daughter, the King has thrown caution to the wind. He is prepared to violate national borders if need be…but in doing so, he has left himself defenseless."

There were grunts of approval around the fire from the other chiefs.

Mabinogan turned and addressed them, "we have been wise to gather our forces when we did…our preparations are already made, and in a stroke of good fortune, the King has left the capital defenseless…" he closed his hand into a fist. "It will be *ours* for the taking."

Korazon bowed to his Lord, "I have assembled the outlying tribes, as you asked, master…give me the honor of leading the surprise attack on the capital."

Mabinogan smiled slightly and put a hand on Korazon's shoulder, "consider it done, my old friend..." he turned to Gur-Naga. "You shall accompany him."

"But...my Lord..." Gur-Naga stuttered. "I have *failed* to procure the wizard..."

"And it's very good that you did...for had you succeeded...the entirety of the Royal Guard would be headed *here*..."

There were chuckles around the fire.

Mabinogan turned to Korazon, "assemble every able-bodied being...we leave for the capital immediately."

Korazon bowed and departed without a word.

Mabinogan turned to Gur-Naga and grinned broadly, "fortune favours the bold."

"My Lord..." Gur-Naga seemed to be in a state of shock. "*Did* the wizard take the Princess?"

"Does it matter?" Mabinogan sneered. "He has proven to be a worthy scapegoat nonetheless..."

"When we attacked their camp, there were three others besides the wizard himself..." Gur-Naga's voice was barely a whisper. "Two of them were the children he was travelling with, but there was a third girl as well..."

Mabinogan studied his servant closely, "travelling companions, perhaps, but I doubt that the Princess was among them. It's more likely she has rebelled against her Father's rule and run away." He turned towards the flap of his tent with a low chuckle. "I can't say I blame her..."

The other chiefs were beginning to leave. There was a sense of irresistible excitement in the air and Gur-Naga couldn't help but be caught up in it. Despite his shame over his failure and the exhaustion of his long travel, it appeared that Loch had favoured him after all. Instead of being punished, he would now be witness to a new chapter in the history of his people.

One which would be written with the blood of their hated oppressors.

The Desolate Gaze

"Every pantheon has its tricksters and troublemakers, and the An'Deir are no different. There are many entities of considerable power in the wider universe of which we know very little. Perhaps chief among these is one which has apparently made itself known to our peoples from time immemorial. The N'Dantin Dreamers call it Beliyal, or the Green Man. To the Alderamin, it is Tsal-Mawat which translates as the Angel of the Abyss, but to all other accounts the being is referred to as Nihiloculus, the Desolate Gaze. Little is known of this entity save that madness and woe seem to follow it wherever it goes. We have, however, no direct accounts of its appearance, which lends more credence to the idea that the creature is merely a creation of myth. Nevertheless, the being is associated with the turning of cosmic cycles and has only ever been seen during times of great upheaval and terrible change."

-"What Came Before" by Ather

The Vampyres had reached a clearing and it seemed as though the fog was beginning to lift at last. In the distance, there was still a grey, monotonous view of endless cliffs and low-lying clouds. Spectral phantoms danced through the sky above and there was a sense of foreboding, despite the fact that the fog was less dense.

Murien took a deep breath of the clear air and sighed as the trail became clear to him, "this way…" he gestured and the group followed.

Carrinon eyed the rock formations as they continued along and wondered what stories they told. How many travellers had been through these treacherous lands and been lost to the fog? Hundreds? Thousands? The figures mattered little to him, but the implications were immense: the Enclaves had been built next to the Gulf for strategic purposes.

No doubt, his Mother and the other Ancients had seen the Gulf as the perfect barrier to their western borders. No army could possibly pass through it and only the most adept of travellers would have any luck finding their way.

It was an ingenious move.

But then again, he had come to expect nothing less from his illustrious forebears. The thought that he was now assigned to recruit one of them made his heart quicken.

His Mother had told him stories of his uncle and Apophanis. They, like all of the First, had roamed this land like gods. Their power was unfathomable to mere mortals and it made sense that they should be summoned at this critical juncture. History was about to turn once more in one of its sublime motions and the established order was soon to be upended.

These were unusual thoughts, even for the Prince, whose mind could fathom the subtlest philosophical concepts with ease.

"Look…" Murien pointed ahead. "Does anyone else see that?"

"See what?" Lariana pushed him aside and shot her gaze back and forth.

Murien gave himself a shake, "I thought I saw something."

"Maybe you need rest…" Duric quipped with a smile.

Murien gave him a playful push on the shoulder, "I'll rest when I'm dead…"

That brought a laugh from all of them and it echoed through the canyons and reverberated back to them with renewed force. The sound made them stop in their tracks.

Someone else's laughter had been mingled with their own.

"This place is eerie…" Lariana said. "Let's keep moving."

Duric nodded, appearing nervous for the first time, "…agreed."

They made their way along, climbing an enormous, jagged rock and leaping down twenty feet with effortless grace. None among them could shake the feeling that they were being watched intently.

The Prince, in particular, seemed to be on edge, "there's something out there…" he said at last, giving voice to all of their fears. "I can *feel* it."

"Look! There it is!" Murien pointed ahead of them into the distance.

The others tried to follow the direction of his hand and were momentarily confused, until they at last saw it: a red orb, rimmed in green, floating above the rocks far ahead of them. It seemed to be an interminable distance away and yet they could make it out clearly.

"What *is* that?" Duric asked, his voice less shaky than before.

"No idea…" Murien said as he continued to walk on.

"Look…" Lariana pointed to the right. "Another one…"

They turned and spotted the second orb immediately. It seemed to come in and out of focus but there was no question that it was moving. It began floating ominously towards the other orb until they were suddenly side-by-side.

"It…it looks like a pair of eyes." Murien said softly. "Eyes from beyond."

"Let's get out of here…" the Prince said. Yet even as he spoke, he found himself unable to move.

Panic struck the group as they attempted to will themselves onward but remained rooted in place. Duric and Lariana gave a mighty effort to lift their own legs but they may as well have been cast in stone.

The Prince looked upon those terrible red eyes, rimmed in solid green. He saw now, without a shadow of a doubt, that they *were* eyes and behind them was a countenance too vast and too terrible for his mind to comprehend. Reality seemed to vanish around him until he was held helpless in that malign gaze for what felt like an eternity. The eyes, the gaze from beyond, regarded him and his fellow travellers with a combination of baleful contempt and haughty amusement.

"We…we shouldn't be here…" Murien kept saying. "I can't look away."

The entirety of the landscape seemed to be consumed in green light. There was nowhere to run, nowhere to hide, and no chance of escape. They were caught in the sight of a being they couldn't fathom and which felt as far beyond them as they were beyond insects.

The baleful gaze regarded them a moment longer, then turned.

The Vampyres at last found their feet and bolted. Luckily, they all turned and ran in the same direction, otherwise they would have been split up and irretrievably lost. They ran as though the Hounds of Hell themselves were upon them. They ran until they felt the first stirrings of exhaustion and when they could run no more, they collapsed in a clearing.

Murien's eyes were wide. He began to shake uncontrollably, foam running down the corners of his mouth.

"Murien!" Lariana gripped his shoulders tightly and tried to steady him.

"Move!" the Prince commanded as he knelt forward and gripped Murien's head tightly, massaging his temples. The Prince closed his eyes and tried to root out whatever sickness had taken hold on the young Vampyre's mind. He felt a profound sense of nausea for a moment, then plunged forward with the last ounces of his psychic powers.

Murien's convulsions ceased and his body went limp.

The Prince released him and stood up slowly.

Lariana and Duric rushed to their friend's side, practically sobbing as though already mourning his death.

Suddenly, Murien opened his eyes, "what's going on?"

The others leapt back with sudden fright.

"You were just shaking for two minutes…we thought you were dying!" Lariana wailed.

Murien shrugged nonchalantly, "I remember none of it…" he raised his arms and they pulled him to his feet. He brushed himself off and smiled, "where to now? We're not on the usual path anymore."

The Prince gripped Murien by the shoulders and looked intently into his eyes, "you don't remember what just happened?"

Murien frowned, "are you alright? We've been walking and then I must have slipped, or something."

The Prince continued to stare into his eyes, "you have no recollection of anything? No break in consciousness from the moment we left the path?"

Murien stared on blankly, "sire…what's going on?"

"Nothing…" the Prince said. He turned to the other two and gave them a meaningful look. "We'll not bring it up again..."

Lariana and Duric nodded with wide-eyed comprehension and kept their mouths shut.

"Well…no bother…" Murien glanced around to get his bearings. "We can get back to the path if we go-"

"The path is barred..." the Prince said coldly. "We cannot go back that way."
Murien looked at Carrinon as though he had lost his mind, "alright then...there's another way. Let me see if I can find it." He closed his eyes and raised his head high, breathing in through his nose. "That way..." he gestured ahead.
Carrinon glanced briefly at the others and saw the same anxiety written on their faces. They were entrusting themselves to someone who had just suffered a complete nervous breakdown. What if their guide's abilities were not what he had made them out to be and they were destined to wander these cursed hills for eternity?
But there was something...wasn't there...
Carrinon pushed these thoughts away. He did a quick back and forth across the craggy ridges to ensure that the green orbs had vanished. To his relief, they were nowhere in sight. Whatever had stalked them was gone. The others seemed to have driven the moment from their mind and he dared not speak of it aloud lest he draw the entity back to them.
Memories flooded him. He sat with his Mother in her study. *"There are things..."* she had said. *"That you are not yet ready to learn. Suffice to say that we share this world with beings beyond our comprehension. Some are benevolent...others are not."* She had leaned closer to him as though some outside force may hear. *"In our language, the original Vampyre tongue which is never spoken anymore, we referred to them...the Outer Ones...as An'Deir."*
His thoughts came rushing back to the present and he shuddered at their implications. For now, there was little time to dwell on them. What choice did they have but to follow their guide onward.
"How much longer before we're out of this hellish place?" Lariana could scarcely hide her unease.
Murien, alone among them, seemed to be perfectly calm, "not long, another few leagues at most."
Carrinon turned to Duric and spoke directly into his mind, *"watch him...we don't yet know the full extent of his breakdown, nor how it has affected him..."*
Duric seemed momentarily shocked to hear the Prince's voice in his head, then his back stiffened and he nodded grimly.

They advanced further into the endless grey. It seemed as though they were merely wandering in some sort of purgatory. A purgatory from which they would never escape.

The Tower of the Dark Wizard

"The Tower of Drachmuin is one of the great wonders of our world. It has long been studied, from the exterior of course, for none have been able to penetrate it. What mysteries the Tower holds may forever remain undiscovered by the eyes of Man. There was a concerted effort by King Aldusious Animrens, father of the present King, to destroy the edifice. To his dismay, it could not be so much as scratched despite the tremendous effort on the part of the Royal Guard. The black stone remains inviolable and perhaps most curious of all is the fact that the Tower has no direct entrance. Terrifying gargoyles and monstrous forms surround it and these creatures have been the source of persistent folklore among the locals. The statues, they say with absolute conviction, are alive and sometimes they swoop down into the valleys below to drag those foolish enough to venture forth from their homes at night to their doom. One can't help but laugh at this peasant superstition."

-'The Tower: An Analysis' by Professor Hardy

Onwards they climbed, an interminable distance it must have seemed. The great wall of rock to their left had become a permanent feature of the ascent while to their right, a great chasm falling downwards greeted them.

The Princess and Alexander were struggling to keep pace with Charlotte, whose fury hadn't abated one iota. It was as though she were possessed by a kind of madness which propelled her forward, heedless of any dangers which may appear.

Alexander's legs felt like jelly. His breath was visible as the air began to chill and it seemed as though they were encircled by great, grey clouds.

As the Tower at last came into view, the three of them stopped and stared on in awe. What they were beholding was beyond their wildest dreams: a tall, black spire made of gleaming stone which seemed to pulse and thrum with eldritch energy.

For a moment, the group hesitated to go further, such was the horror which the sight evoked. Charlotte began to understand at last what the old man had meant when he had told her that the people of Nin-Ghasta lived under the thrall of this infernal building. She briefly forgot why she was here and what she had been angry about. Every fiber of her being wanted to turn back and the crushing sense of dread she felt began to overwhelm her senses.

It was Alexander who broke her from her trance, “come on…we’re almost there.”

Charlotte shook her head, “maybe we shouldn’t…”

“We didn’t come this far to turn back now…where *else* will we go?”

She smiled at her little brother for a moment and nodded slightly, “you’re right.” She turned back towards the Tower. “Let’s go.”

The Princess stood close to Alexander as they approached and was practically huddled beside him.

He turned to her, “alright?”

She nodded, then glanced nervously back to the infernal spire.

Alexander gripped her hand tightly, smiled, then led her on.

As they cleared the edge of the bluff, the details of the Tower became clearer to them: it appeared to be surrounded by a chasm which ran for miles into an unseeable abyss. A long stone bridge snaked across the endless depths and enormous, forbidding statues lined the bridge’s length. The statues were of winged creatures too terrible to look upon for long. Their eyes seemed to glow with a yellow hue in the gloom and their open mouths were splayed with sharp teeth and a lashing tongue.

“Horrible…” the Princess said softly as they approached. “What *are* those things.”

Alexander got a better look at the statues the closer they came, “I don’t know…but I’ve never seen anything like them.”

“Me either…” Charlotte said softly. “This place wasn’t meant to be trodden on by mortals.”

“That obvious?” Alexander quipped.

Charlotte scowled at him for a moment then chuckled.

As they approached the great bridge, the air around them became very still.

"Feels like the thin place Amyn told us about…" Alexander said.

"Everything Amyn told us was a lie…" Charlotte spat contemptuously. "We need to question his motivations now that he's abandoned us."

Alexander became silent and lowered his head slightly.

Charlotte found herself welling up with sympathy for her brother. He had put his trust in so many: their father, their great-uncle, Amyn. All of them had betrayed that trust to a tee and she found renewed strength in her growing anger. "Come on…let's cross."

For a moment, Charlotte pulled away from the group and ventured ahead. It seemed as though the wind had suddenly ceased and there was only a kind of blank, unforgiving silence which surrounded them.

Princess Rionéolas tried to stare ahead, avoiding the terrible gaze of the stone creatures. A few times, against her better judgement, she glanced up and met those eerie yellow eyes. She could have sworn that they were following her. She did a double take and to her utter dismay, they *were* following her.

"Alexander…" she whispered, terror rising in her voice.

"What? What is it?" the boy asked. He noticed the pallor of her face and he gripped her shoulders tightly, drawing her gaze away from the statues. "Don't look at them…"

The Princesses' breathing was becoming rapid, but she nodded slightly and began to regain her self-control. Every ounce of her wanted to get off this bridge and be as far away from this wretched place as possible. Soon, she found her feet once more and they continued on.

Charlotte was once again well ahead of them, her head turned down to avoid the sight of the statues.

After an interminable period of time, they came at last to what should have been the entrance. They had imagined a large, ornate door would greet them, but instead there was only black brick.

Charlotte pressed her hands against the cold stone, "there *must* be an entrance…"

Alexander sighed, "sister…give it up…we can't get in."

The three of them held onto each other as exhaustion finally gripped them. They were on the edge of collapse and felt a growing sense of hopelessness.

"Wait…" the Princess said softly. She reached into the folds of her robes and pulled out the ancient, blood-red tome. "Maybe there's something in here…it was written by the very wizard whose Tower we seek entrance to."

Alexander smiled, "it's our best hope…"

The Princess thumbed through the book at lightning speed. Alexander caught glimpses of magical illustrations and arcane circles. He felt a growing excitement and dread at the sight of the spidery writing. He could *feel* the antiquity of the book and wondered with a growing curiosity about its contents. Now, however, was hardly the time to peruse such a volume.

"Here…" the Princess stopped at one of the pages and her eyes scanned it furiously. A moment later, she closed the book and placed it back within the folds of her robe. She approached the gate and stared at it intently.

Alexander and Charlotte looked at one another in confusion.

The Princess continued to stare at the gate, then she closed her eyes and took several deep breaths. Lifting her hand slowly, she touched the cold stone and began to run her fingers along its surface.

To the astonishment of the siblings, a golden line formed and followed wherever the Princess touched. Soon, she had formed a large circle which gleamed resplendently before them. She lifted her hand, placed it near the center of the circle and began to form a triangle. She placed two more triangles on the left and right of the circle and connected them with various lines. When she was finished and stepped away, she had created what appeared to be a mathematically proportional glyph. She smiled broadly at her glowing handiwork.

A moment later, there was a creaking sound, and the bricks began to shift. To the astonishment of the group, the once impenetrable gateway now opened before them. The bricks seemed to melt away as though they had never been there at all and when the last of them had vanished, a yawning blackness was all that remained.

Tentatively, the Princess stepped forward. She could feel the rush of cool air emanating from the gate and knew that they would now be able to move unhindered into the Tower.

She turned to the others, smiled slightly, and entered the gateway without a word. A moment later she had vanished into the darkness.

Alexander and Charlotte looked at each other in astonishment, turned back to the gate, and proceeded into the gaping maw of the Tower.

For a moment, they wandered in a kind of visceral blackness. It was as though they had been sucked into a primordial void and a brief, primal panic set in. It didn't last, however, as they suddenly found themselves in a long, dim hallway illuminated by torches.

The Princess was standing in front of them with arms crossed and a smile on her face, "I wasn't sure if that glyph would work…" she glanced around at the gloom for a moment then turned and pointed to the stone steps at the end of the hallway. "That way, I would guess."

Alexander and Charlotte nodded but proceeded with caution. They still had an uneasy feeling about this place.

"We didn't see Amyn on the way in…" Charlotte said bitterly. "Which must mean *he* is here as well."

"Keep your wits about you…" the Princess said.

The stairs began to spiral as they ascended, and they saw various rooms go by as they went. Some were small and empty; others were filled with various magical treasures which the youths could not identify. On one of the main floors, they saw what was obviously a vast library which stretched from floor to ceiling. The Princess gasped at the sight, and it took a considerable amount of her will not to venture forth and thumb through the tomes. A large, ornate stone statue of a Dragon stood in the center of the room, its wings spread, and its arms lifted to the heavens.

"Incredible…" Alexander said.

"Let's keep moving…" Charlotte turned and proceeded up the stairs.

Their ascent, much like the climb up the bluffs, seemed to take an eternity. All throughout, they did not encounter a single soul. The silence around them was eery.

The Princess turned, “do you think Amyn is at the summit?”

Charlotte frowned, “I would wager he is…”

Alexander scratched his head softly, “why did he want to get to this place so badly? He said we were coming here for transportation…but that hardly makes sense.”

“Nothing Amyn did or said made sense, Alexander.” Charlotte’s voice had taken on a note of condescension. “He was a trickster and a conman…nothing more.”

“But we *saw* his magical powers…when those Barbarians attacked.”

“We saw what we wanted to see…” Charlotte increased her pace which seemed to be an indication that she was done discussing the matter.

Finally, the stairs opened up to another vast room, this one with an enormous telescope at its center and astronomical charts on the walls. Dark wooden tables surrounded the observatory, and they were covered in books and scraps of paper.

Princess Rionéolas marvelled at the telescope. It was at least ten times larger than the one in her Father’s castle. She imagined that looking through it would reveal the very secrets of the cosmos itself and she made her way towards it almost unconsciously.

Charlotte moved towards one of the many desks which was strewn with various books and papers. How long had all of this sat here untouched? A century? Two? It mattered not. She realized that some of the scrolls before her were ancient. They were clearly made of papyrus and had already begun to crumble.

She found herself fascinated for the first time since their arrival. There was history here, undoubtedly. Perhaps the ancient wizard had a hidden treasure and that was why Amyn was so desperate to seek this place out.

As she glanced through the papers, she turned and saw Alexander and the Princess looking through the enormous telescope. She couldn’t help but smile at the excited rise and fall of their voices. It reminded her of a time when she hadn’t been jaded and broken by life. A time she longed desperately to return to, although she knew it to be impossible.

One of the papers caught her eye. She reached forward and picked it up to examine it. She could see that the ink was fresh, far fresher than any of the others.

This must have been written recently...but how? If no one has ever been here?

The thought made her look around instinctively as though she would catch some voyeur watching them from one of the doorways. Alas, she saw nothing and returned her eyes to the paper. It appeared to be a letter of some sort, written in an elegant, spidery hand:

Dearest Brother,

I can only say that your prophetic vision has proven once again to be infallible. The Plan moves ahead on schedule. We cannot allow the various nations to catch wind of it, lest all be permanently lost.

It has been nearly two centuries since you last wrote, and receiving your letter filled my heart with joy. Time may have separated us...but it can never break our bond. Our people have been a shadow of themselves for many ages, but soon, we will see our sun rise again.

I have enclosed in this letter the names of several ancient burial grounds which you may visit to draw forth any help or advice you may need. I know that you are a far more capable necromancer than I, but it would not hurt for you to have aid from some of the ancestors during these turbulent times.

I myself shall remain hidden, for the time being. I am making my own preparations and have paid my associates to assemble a large number of fresh corpses. As you know, the war we started in Savan has provided more than enough material.

I will keep you posted as things develop. For now, these are exciting times. I think you can agree that we have never been closer to breaking the bonds that ensnare this world. We must be wary, however, lest the ***Others*** *learn of recent developments. To have even one of them become wise to what is occurring could jeopardize not just the planet, but the entire solar system. Our brothers in Anturac are growing nervous as they believe we may already be too late. The Alderamin have relayed that several of the star clusters in the Polar Hemisphere have vanished and a strange anomaly appears to be moving in our direction.*

I pray that this is not so. Nevertheless, we will survive...we always have.

Praise the Arcalypsis Flame! Praise the Forefather!

Your friend, eternally,

Azan Al'Marif

Charlotte dropped the letter. Her hands were shaking. She couldn't comprehend what she had just read but it shook her to the core. She looked over at the Princess and Alexander and they seemed to be oblivious.

She turned back to the desk, and, against her better judgement, picked up another piece of paper and examined it. This too appeared to be written in a similarly elegant manner although the paper was more akin to parchment and far older than the previous one.

Fellow Serpent,

It has come to my attention that you have asked for more resources in your research of the Light Spire. I can assure you that anything you need will be provided. I would offer you the finest study we could muster here in Anturac, but I know you would refuse it. You have always worked best on your own terms, and I will continue to respect that.

I saw my son just this last week. He is very nearly a man now and to see him embrace that is most gratifying to me. He still asks for you as he has always been fond of you. I often wish he were not so far away, yet there is little I can do at the moment...

As your research progresses, please do keep me up to date. And do feel free to come to Anturac one of these days. Your companionship has always been cherished.

Danyr

Charlotte stood ramrod straight. She felt a potent presence behind her. Turning slowly, she squinted into the shadows which seemed to be encroaching almost imperceptibly. She glanced to her right to see if the Princess and Alexander could feel it too but they betrayed no signs of any anxiety and were still absorbed in trying to fathom the enormous telescope.

As she stared into the darkness she saw, to her horror, that there were eyes staring back. The dark figure stepped forward now, the shadows dispersing around him as he approached. He was dressed in a long, black robe with a long red scarf which was draped over his shoulders. On his head was a black, brimless conical hat and his snow-white beard was trimmed and pointed making him look every bit like one of the wizards of legend. Despite his attire, the silver orb of his eye was unmistakeable.

"Greetings…" Amyn said softly.

His arrival had been so unexpected that it jolted the Princess and Alexander from their reverie and they both let out a mild shriek of shock.

"I expected you would find your way in Princess…" Amyn said with a slight smile. "But time is short, it seems."

"You abandoned us…" Charlotte had found the lost threads of her earlier anger and clung to them desperately in an attempt to suppress her growing fear.

"You abandoned yourselves… you cling to life like shades and live a hollow existence. You kept me amused on my journey, but I am not forced to abide by *your* timetable." Amyn said cruelly. His voice had an unmistakeable air of authority in it. No longer a charming old traveller, here and now he had taken on the forbidding aura of a being out of legend. "You have found your way into my Tower…I suppose that makes you my honoured guests." He turned to the enormous, arched window near the telescope. "The festivities are about to begin."

"*Your* Tower?" the Princess asked. "It has lain abandoned for centuries uncounted, and now you will merely claim it as your own?"

Amyn laughed and it echoed down the long corridors on either side of him, "you poor creature…" his eyes seemed to blaze with a hidden fire. "You should consider yourselves fortunate that I told my guardians to stay their hand when you arrived. Their hunger knows no bounds."

The youths stood, stunned. Their jaws were agape.

They were convinced that their guide had gone truly mad. Had this entire journey merely been the pull of an insane old man's delusions of grandeur? Had he sought to adorn the ancient wizard's vestments and seize his Tower in the hopes that some hidden power would be granted to him?

The youths did not have the time to solve the conundrum as a tremendous rumbling sound echoed up from the valleys below. The Princess rushed to the window and shielded her eyes at the sight of the blinding brightness which greeted her.

Just beyond the threshold of Nin-Ghasta, something was beginning to materialize.

"What *is* that?" Alexander squinted into the white brilliance.

The Princess gasped, "it looks like a Tesseract…"

Alexander turned towards her and frowned, the confusion on his face was obvious. He looked back out the window and saw, to his horror, that figures were emerging from the light. Thousands of what appeared to be knights on horseback brandishing golden spears wreathed in lightning. They looked like the ancient gods of myth.

"Arinönde…" the wizard spat with contempt.

The Princess turned to him, wide-eyed, "*how*…that's impossible…"

The wizard laughed, "yes, the Sanctum Sanctorum is a device of unparalleled power, hidden in plain sight. They needed you to use it so that you could find me, Princess…"

"I…I don't understand."

The wizard reached out, "give me that locket."

The Princess clutched the gold chain at her chest, "…it…it was my Mother's."

"I care not who it belonged to…show it to me."

The power of his voice was such that she could not resist even if she had wanted to. She reached dreamily for the locket and slowly lifted it from her neck before handing it over.

The wizard examined it for a few moments, then gave it back to her, "it's a tracking device."

The Princess was slack-jawed with disbelief.

The wizard smiled cruelly, "your Father is a cunning man, Princess. He would use his own daughter as bait…" he turned away and began moving towards the stairs. "No matter…they will not make it to the Tower before we depart."

"Depart?" Charlotte asked, her voice quivering. She had remained uncharacteristically silent during the earlier exchange.

The wizard kept his back turned and refused to answer. A moment later he ascended the stairs and was gone.

The youths turned and looked out the great window. The regiments of Arinönde, the great lion emblem of that mighty kingdom adorning every banner, were moving steadily towards Nin-Ghasta in tight formations.

The Princess reached over and gripped Alexander's hand tightly. The revelations which had fallen from the wizard's mouth were almost too much to bear.

From near the summit of his Tower, he looked on with disgust. The forces of Arinönde must be truly arrogant to think they could assail him here. It mattered not; they were already too late.

He moved out onto the balcony and turned to one of the gargoyles that was perched to his right. Leaning forward, he whispered, "…go."

The creature's eyes illuminated with a yellow phosphorescence. Its stony skin grew darker, as though it had been called forth from some lightless abyss and was now taking on physical form. It stood tall on the balcony, spread its wings, and let out a shriek. Far below, the call was answered in kind by its fellows. Soon, hundreds of dark bodies had taken to the air and were soaring up to greet the host of Arinönde.

"It was a worthy attempt, Animrens…" the wizard said softly. "But you're still ten steps behind."

He turned and moved towards the enormous, golden machine at the far corner of the room. He ran his fingers along one of the levers and pulled it gently in tandem with several others. The Tower began to rumble from its foundations and the wizard returned once more to the window.

Far below, his servants had engaged in a bloody skirmish with the knights of Arinönde. They threw their opponents aside like ragdolls and lifted others into the air before dropping them to their deaths.

There was another fierce rumble and the rocks around the bluffs began to give way. The arcane machinery beneath the Tower started to churn for the first time in uncounted centuries.

Slowly, inexorably, the Tower began to rise.

Beyond the Barrier

"The destruction of lesser civilizations should occur as a matter of course. They have proven their inability to adapt to the current climate and thus, their continued existence is an insult to their superiors. Humanity is one such race. Their decline appears to be imminent which is no concern of ours. They have always been little more than cattle to us and when they are gone, they will be swiftly replaced."

-Excerpt from the Vampyre Annals

The deplorable fog began to lift at last and the group gave a collective sigh of relief at the sight. They had wandered for a claustrophobic eternity in that despair-filled region and were glad to be rid of it. The sun was now cresting the horizon and the welcome bliss of darkness was beginning to embrace the land.

Lariana removed the hood of her cloak. The sun was now a deep red and its hated rays would no longer affect her. She breathed in the cool air and smiled broadly at the coming of Mother Night.

"Are we free from that treacherous gaol?" the Prince asked with more than a hint of irritation.

Murien nodded, "indeed, sire…we breach the Gulf at last."

"Excellent…" the Prince stood tall with his arms crossed and gazed into the distance. He could see a jagged collection of mountains off to his right and he pointed towards them, "that's it…yes? The Dragon's Teeth?"

"Yes sire…" Murien said softly.

The Prince, with his excellent vision, eyed the region carefully. He could make out various paths even at this distance which would prove treacherous to their ascent and he made a mental note to avoid them as they progressed.

Duric, never given to excessive speech, mumbled something to himself.

The Prince turned to him, "yes…we have a ways to go yet and there will be little time to stop."

Duric's eyes widened when he realized he had been overheard and he nodded slightly, visibly embarrassed.

The four of them took another glance at the vista spread out before them. The stars were beginning to spill out across the sky and the mountains became a jagged, black outline against the horizon. The dim lights of sleepy villages dotted the landscape and the smoke of distant chimneys was visible even at this distance.

Carrinon put his hand up to the sky and measured the polar star with his fingers. It told him they were at least half a week's journey from their destination. Every Vampyre from birth could read the stars as easily as they could read any map and they were rivalled only by the Alderamin in their astronomical abilities.

Carrinon didn't need to tell the others his calculations as they had already done it themselves. "We could stop in one of those villages for food if any of you are hungry…" the Prince pointed casually to the nearest plume of smoke.

Lariana licked her lips, "I'm famished…"

Duric and Murien nodded in unison.

Carrinon smiled, "it's settled then…we shan't stay long for I don't wish to rouse unwanted attention."

They walked towards the village like wraiths in the darkness, barely making a sound as they went.

Redgin Cairn was drunk. So drunk, in fact, that he could barely make out the shape of his own feet when he glanced down at them. He laughed to himself and spat on the floor absent mindedly.

"Hey!" the tavern owner growled. "This isn't no pig pen!"

"Aye, aye…" Cairn waved the man off and lifted the rest of his drink to his lips. Downing it in one swift motion, he slammed the cup on the bar counter.

"If ye weren't such a good customer, Cairn, I'd have had your hide ages ago…" the tavern owner said angrily.

"S'pose you did…" Cairn slurred. "This place would be out of business."

There was a roar of laughter behind them as a group of men cheered to Cairn and downed their drinks. They were friends of his, of course, for Cairn knew just about everyone in not only the village of Loch-Gammond but in all of the neighboring ones as well. He was the elected mayor of the region and it was his job to ensure that he met every person he could to ensure his success in the coming year's election.

Cairn had served six terms as mayor in all, the longest of anyone yet, and he intended to make it a seventh. Given his proclivity for passing out silver coins to children on the street and the enormous amount of volunteer work he performed, it appeared as though he would be a shoo in. The other contenders were barely laudable by comparison.

While performing his mayoral duties, Cairn doubled as the village drunk. He was known to frequent taverns across the province and his more virulent detractors claimed that if he spent as much time performing the functions of his office as he did knee-deep in pubs, the provinces wouldn't be on the verge of a financial crisis.

Still, Cairn was popular with the common folk and that was all that mattered.

He tipped the tavern owner and said goodbye to his cronies as he stumbled towards the door.

"See ya the 'morrow, Cairn!"

"Aye…hold down the fort 'til then…" he practically mumbled.

As he pushed the door open, the night air was cool on his face and momentarily sobered him up. He doubted that his wife was still awake at this hour and his two children were likely asleep as well, although Eleanora seemed to be stricken with nightmares as of late.

The sky was clear and the stars shone in the fullness of their splendour. He gasped for a moment at the sight. How many times had he seen these same stars and paid them no heed? Yet tonight, they seemed to have a life of their own and appeared to demand his attention.

He said a silent prayer of thanks to the Light Father for the blessing of the sight and then began the long slog home. It wasn't that his house was far away, it was the fact that the excessive consumption of alcohol made his steps laborious and distracted. Soon, he reached the village square which had a small fountain at its center and a plaque dedicated to those who had died in the Savan Wars.

The Wars had taken a terrible toll on the entire region and there seemed to be fewer young men these days because of them. The Savan region lay to the West, just above Nin-Ghasta. There was some sort of political assassination which had taken place there and it had triggered a war with the neighboring provinces. Savan had blamed both Arinönde and Dunholde for the murder and had taken what they deemed appropriate action against them. In the initial skirmish, three regiments of Savan troops had snuck across the border into Dunholde and burned the first town they had come across.

It was in this turbulent political climate that Cairn hoped to ride his campaign to success. He intended to give people a reprieve from the constant anxiety of war by endorsing grander celebrations and more national holidays. It may have seemed counter-productive to the more militaristic stance of his competitors, but he knew it was exactly what was needed.

He contemplated this prospect as he continued towards home. He was nearly there, another block and-

Is that blood?

He stared into a black pool ahead of him. The moonlight barely seemed to touch it but he could tell intuitively that it was indeed blood. A lot of it.

He felt a chill run up his spine and suddenly found himself stone cold sober. It was as though he had been jolted back to reality by an unexpected instinct for self-preservation.

Could the puddle be human blood? Impossible…surely a stray dog or a wolf had wandered into the village and taken its fill of some of the chickens. Most people in Loch-Gammond kept animals on their small plots and it was not uncommon to see chickens wandering aimlessly about the cobblestone streets.

All of this, of course, was idle speculation. He didn't wish to remain to find out what the source of this attack was, for it could

only be a large animal of some sort. He turned slowly, all of his senses hyper-focused and alert.

Just as he was about to make a run for it, he saw a figure approaching him from the shadows. His back stiffened and his fists flew up, but as quickly as he had raised them, he lowered them back down.

A young woman was approaching.

She could not have been more than twenty and her face, pallid as it was, had the youthful exuberance and joy that all young women seemed to have at that age. Her clothing was of a make he had never seen before: dark, elegant, and flowing with unnatural grace. He also noticed what appeared to be chainmail beneath her shirt, as though she were lightly girded for battle. He was relieved to see that she carried no weapons and the sight of her set him at ease almost instantly.

"Fine night…is it not?" the girl said softly.

Cairn nodded, "aye…little late for you to be out I should say…you must be from another village as I've not seen ye before." He could feel his drunkenness beginning to take hold of him again.

"Just passing through…" the girl said, her eyes glowing preternaturally in the darkness. Cairn couldn't tell if it was from the moonlight or some drunken hallucination.

He noticed that she had walked right past the puddle of blood as though it wasn't even there. It made him wonder if he was seeing things. It appeared likely that he was, "well, Miss…are you staying local? Perhaps I can walk you home…"

"That would be lovely…" she purred.

Cairn felt a sudden jolt of longing surge through him. The girl was indeed beautiful and something in her eyes told him that she was wiser than she appeared. He was usually quite faithful to his beloved wife, but if the opportunity for a dalliance on the side presented itself, he had never been one to turn it down.

"You know…" he slurred in spite of his best efforts to maintain his composure. "I'm the mayor round these parts."

The girl grinned wolfishly, "is that right? So, you're a man of importance, then…"

Cairn beamed, "aye, I am…I can make sure a young lass like you is well looked after…" he leaned in. "Very well looked after."

She put a hand on his face gently and smiled. She didn't seem to be intimidated by him at all.

"By the Light, child…" Cairn shuddered at her touch. "You're as cold as the grave!"

Her eyes seemed to change in that moment, taking on a blood-red hue. When she smiled, he noticed that her teeth were sharp and pointed. It was as though he were gazing into the face of some creature from the abyss.

Cairn took a step back involuntarily, his face a mask of horror.

"Don't worry Mr. Mayor…" the girl said in a kind of sing-song mockery. "I'll make sure you're *well* looked after."

He felt something then. A hot spurt running down the front of his shirt. He had barely registered the sudden sensation and when he reached up, he noticed that his throat was gushing. It had been cut so swiftly and with such deft precision that he hadn't even felt it. He staggered to the right and fell, his face smashing into the pavement. In his last moments his mind swirled with both drunken disbelief and the cold realization that he was moments from death. A minute later, the life left his eyes.

Lariana cocked her head to the side and leapt forward, lapping up the blood greedily.

"Save some for us…" Duric said from behind her. He moved swiftly to her side and turned the man over. Eyeing the lifeless form, he dove forward for the open throat and drained the still warm body of what little blood remained.

Carrinon and Murien appeared from the shadows.

"Satiated?" Carrinon asked coyly.

Lariana and Duric looked up at him and nodded.

"Good…I don't think anyone else noticed…" Carrinon crossed his arms. "The villagers will have enough gossip for the rest of the year now."

"'Mayoral candidate kills family of five' will be the preface of their conversations I imagine." Murien said with a grin.

"Place his body near the house…lay a knife at his side." Carrinon commanded, pointing towards the small hut that he and Murien had just exited.

The others nodded and moved quickly.

"Duric…" Carrinon gestured to the house once more. "There is still some warmth in those bodies if you wish to take your fill…"

Duric beamed hungrily, "thank you, sire…"

He bolted towards the house with demonic speed and disappeared into the darkness within.

Carrinon watched him go and felt a tug of contemptuous despair rise in his chest. His Mother had told him that the First were uncorrupted by the bloodlust of their lesser children. It was the mingling of the races which had caused the unforeseen ailment to arise. Indeed, his Mother did not need any sustenance whatsoever, although she could partake in food if she wished when the desire struck. He imagined the other First were the same.

It made him pine for a time when his race had been pristine. Perhaps there would be a cure one day for this insufferable sickness. Indeed, he needed very little blood to survive (a privilege of his much purer Vampyre heritage) but he needed it nonetheless and it irked him to no end. So long as the Vampyres depended on blood, they would depend upon humanity. True, they could gather sustenance from other sources with great ease, but none of them were as abundantly available as the blood of humans.

*Perhaps the First Elders will have an answer... a way to reverse this curse...*he thought bitterly.

Once, the Vampyres had been gods. Now, they were little more than glorified predators eking out an existence on the margins rather than ruling from the summit.

The Mouth of B'aal

"The policies of Aldusious Animrens were sometimes draconic in nature, although always fair. His reign was marked by peace and a few military victories against the Beastmen. His power was such that all through his reign, petty crime practically vanished entirely. This may have been due to the King's proclivity to have would-be offenders executed on the spot. After his death, his kingdom passed to his son who has emulated the Father in many ways, save that he is less hardened and more practical. During Aldus' reign, the banking clans thrived and found a foothold once more. His time as King has been fairly prosperous, although his detractors claim that he has merely ridden off his Father's coattails and done little innovation himself."

-Treatise on the Great Kingdoms

The Princess lost her footing and would have plunged out of the window if Alexander hadn't gripped her hand and pulled her back.

The Tower was moving. It had seemed like their imaginations at first, but now it was undeniable.

Far below, jagged rocks and boulders the size of houses were crashing down the bluffs and the town of Nin-Ghasta was being decimated by the debris.

Charlotte gasped at the horrific sight. She saw one of the gargoyle creatures pick a knight and horse off the ground with ease and toss them contemptuously to the side. The beast roared at the sky in triumph and its great, black wings began to beat.

The front line of the knights of Arinönde had been decimated by the black-winged creatures and the beasts now headed back to the Tower en masse. The sky was darkened at their approach and the horrified youths felt a surge of terror at the sight of them.

Surely the creatures would cast all three of them from the broken cliffs surrounding the Tower when they returned.

This, however, was not the case.

The beasts circled the black Tower as it rose, their voices a howling cacophony. Their Master had returned and this was their celebratory welcome for him.

"We're getting higher…" Alexander said as he began to back away from the window.

The Princess turned to him, "yes…there's too much debris below to see Nin-Ghasta anymore."

"Nin-Ghasta is gone…" Charlotte's tone was harsh. "Amyn has seen to that."

Alexander shook his head as though he refused to acknowledge the gravity of the situation.

The Princess clutched the Red Book within the folds of her robe and felt it throbbing with an unearthly power.

"He revealed as much to us…" Alexander said. "There's no denying it: this is *his* Tower and it obeys *his* will…"

Charlotte ran a hand through her matted hair, "I…I read a letter over there…" she pointed to the cluttered table to their right. "It confirms as much…Amyn…has been working with Anturac."

The Princesses' eyes widened, "to what end? That could only mean that the hand of Danyr *Himself* is guiding him…"

Charlotte made her way towards the table with a kind of sad resignation. She perused some of the papers and lifted one in particular towards the Princess.

Rionéolas' eyes scanned the spidery writing intently and her mouth fell open, "…this confirms it…a letter from the Mage Emperor."

"Let me see!" Alexander practically snatched the letter from her hand. "Unbelievable…I always thought Danyr was a myth…I mean…I thought He *might* be a historical personage…"

Charlotte put her hands to her temples and rubbed them gently, "this could still all be part of some old man's delusion…"

Alexander turned to her, unimpressed, "would some old man be able to levitate this Tower off the ground?"

Charlotte sighed, "…I suppose you're right." She glanced back out the window and saw that they were now very high. The clouds were practically cresting the Tower and the gargoyles still surrounded it in a kind of ritual circumnavigation.

The three youths eyed the long staircase behind them. Holding their collective breaths, they made their way towards it tentatively, wondering what kind of madness they would find as they ascended.

The stairs seemed to lead on interminably, but whether it was by design or the fact that all three of them were terrified out of their wits, they soon found themselves in a large room which appeared to be either the summit of the Tower or very close to it.

Immediately, they spotted the wizard with his long black robe. His back was turned to them and he appeared to be gazing at a magnificent vista into limitless sky, "your Father's kingdom will fall, Princess…" the wizard said with a dry voice. "Already, his enemies move to seize their opportunity."

The Princess took two steps forward, anger rising in her, "what do you know of it?"

She could almost feel the wizard smile although she couldn't see his face, "I know more than you think…"

"You will take us home…" the Princess commanded, though her voice lacked the authority she wished it had.

The wizard turned and faced them. They barely recognized him in his conical hat and long cloak. His eyes shone with a terrible light and his skin appeared more pallid, "I will do no such thing…I am moving in the *opposite* direction."

Charlotte clenched her fists, "let us off this thing…*now*."

The wizard laughed. It was a hollow, harsh sound, "you think you can command *me*, do you?"

Charlotte's eyes flitted towards the other two and she saw her own fear reflected there.

"You are my honored guests…" the wizard turned back to the window. "Pray that I don't alter your status…"

Alexander, mustering what courage he could find, spoke in a low voice, "where…where are we going?"

"The Mouth of B'aal…" was the cryptic answer he received. "In the Eastern Desert."

The others cowered backwards, then a strong gust drew their attention towards the window. Glancing downwards, they were horrified to see the dizzying height to which they had ascended. The black-winged host were beginning to descend around the

Tower and started to perch on various outcroppings. The ground around the Tower had remained attached to it and large obelisks of jagged stone jutted outwards forming a sinister wall around the black spire.

"Thinking of jumping?" the wizard asked with a half-smile.

Alexander turned to him and clenched his fists, "you're keeping us prisoner."

The wizard cackled gleefully, "you are more than welcome to attempt escape…" he moved towards them slowly. "But be honest with yourselves, you have *never* wanted the life that exists down there. Each of you has aspired to something larger, something with greater significance."

The three youths stood, spellbound, as the wizard spoke. His mellifluous voice burrowing his honeyed words into their minds.

"You each long to be what you *aren't*…don't you?" He turned to the Princess. "You long to escape the yoke of your Father and to make a name for yourself beyond his shadow…" the wizard cocked his head slightly. "But I wonder, Princess…if you have the courage to take such a leap of faith."

The Princess remained silent, her lips quivering ever so slightly.

"And you…" the wizard's silver orb settled on Alexander. "You have talent, my boy…*real* talent. There is no denying that. The only thing that hinders you is the circumstances you were born into. A sad fact, but a harsh one nonetheless. You've always sensed there was more than the drudgery and meagreness which has surrounded you. You have a natural thirst for esoteric knowledge and a mind subtle enough to grasp it. Had you been born in Ardhia, you would no doubt have been selected for the Priesthood."

The boy's eyes widened, then he lowered them to the floor.

The wizard's eyes at last fell on Charlotte.

She bit her lip, "I won't be taken in by your manipulations…"

"Ahh…the heart of a warrior." The wizard folded his arms and smiled. "You present a strong front because you feel you *have* to…but I know what lies beneath that façade: a girl who has been battered against the rocks too many times to count and now seeks to protect herself by taking on the role of both mother *and* father to herself and her brother."

Charlotte's mouth fell open as the words found their mark.

"Close to the truth, aren't I?" The wizard said softly. "But I don't think you want that for yourself…do you? You'd much rather be like the Princess and live a life of security in the castle…" the wizard ran his hand gently through his white beard. "It must irk you to see the Princess so desperate to escape her circumstances…perhaps it confirms one of your deepest fears: that there is nothing in this world which can bring you happiness and all of your desires will only lead you back to where you started…"

The three of them stood, stunned, as though under some sort of spell.

The wizard turned his back to them, "you can make yourselves at home, if you wish…there is an amply stocked pantry on the lower levels." He turned to them slightly so that only the glowing orb of his eye was visible. "But do not deceive yourselves…you *chose* to come here and thus; you have placed your destinies in *my* hands." He turned away from them. "Now, I have business to attend to…" he moved slowly towards the stairs and vanished into the shadows beyond.

Charlotte turned to the others, her face was white, "what do we do?"

"What *can* we do?" The Princess said softly. "We're trapped on this floating fortress with nowhere to go and we're dealing with a man who has powers beyond our comprehension…"

"Where did he say we were going?" Alexander asked.

"To the Mouth of B'aal…" the Princess turned and looked out the window. "I've read some old lore on it…the Eastern Desert is a perilous place."

"Why go there then?" Charlotte could barely contain her irritation. "Why drag us to some forsaken land like that?"

The Princesses' voice was very quiet, "the Great Relics…" She began to pace back and forth. "He told us himself he was after them. They were said to have been forged from the Light Spire *itself*. They had the power to shape aspects of reality and to do other wondrous things which we can't even imagine. Danyr *Himself* wielded them at one time. But the Relics were too powerful, even for the Mage Emperor to hold onto forever, and so, he hid them."

Charlotte sighed, "so…is that what is hidden in the Eastern Desert?"

The Princess shrugged, "I don't know…but I did hear my Father discussing the matter with one of his counselors. He said that the orb which had been stolen was an ancient Ardhian artifact…" she leaned in close to them. "A *map*, to be precise…" she lifted the Red Book out from the folds of her robe. "They're mentioned in here as well…" she glanced cautiously towards the darkness of the stairs, thinking she would see that silver orb staring back at them, and was relieved to see only shadows. "This book was written by Drachmuin…if that *is* the man who holds us captive…then perhaps there are more clues hidden in it."

"Doubtful…" Alexander said. "If it possessed knowledge which he didn't want you to have…he wouldn't have let you keep it."

The Princess nodded, "true enough…but perhaps it can help us get inside his mind…perhaps we can glean a weakness from it."

Charlotte threw her arms up, "this is ridiculous…he's covered his tracks too carefully…"

The Princess smiled slightly, "yes…he has…but he is *not* all-powerful nor all-knowing. He *has* made mistakes. When he was hiding among us as a cat, he was very nearly caught when he stole the orb. Besides…" she gestured towards the book. "If there's something in here that can give us leverage against him, we'll have to read *between* the lines…"

"You read all you want…" Charlotte turned away angrily. "I need some sleep…" she made her way towards a corner of the room and collapsed against the wall. Mere moments later, she appeared to have lapsed into unconsciousness.

Alexander looked at the Princess with exhausted eyes. He appeared utterly defeated.

Rionéolas felt her former optimism beginning to wane. Her shoulders sagged forward and she sighed deeply.

Alexander put a hand on her arm gently, "we need rest…maybe even some food from the pantry."

"What if it's poisoned?"

Alexander laughed, "well…if he wanted us dead, I doubt he would go to so much trouble."

The Princess smiled slightly, "I suppose you're right…" she eyed the stairs cautiously. "Let's see what the old man has stored…"

The Feet of the Dragon

"The Elder Dragon, Maledon, mightiest and most powerful of his kind. Equaled in greatness only by Snógle. It was Maledon who designed the legendary Dragon's Quadrant and who fought alongside the Ardhians during the Days of Fire. He alone has wisdom enough to see the way forward. He alone is worshipped as the Dragon God."

-Words carved into Sabura Cave

"Magnificent...aren't they?" Carrinon said softly.

"The Dragon's Teeth..." Lariana craned her neck and stared at the jagged spires which towered above. "How are we ever going to scale these abominations?"

Carrinon smiled, "with a bit of luck and will, no doubt."

Duric knelt and placed his pack on the cold earth. The sun would soon be coming up on the horizon and he was keen to ward off its killing rays with his cloak.

The others, sensing the arrival of hated daylight, did the same.

Carrinon, alone among them, stood in defiance of the Lord of Light.

Murien donned his cloak. "There will be few villages from here on out...it's a good thing we gorged ourselves at the last one."

"Yes..." Carrinon said softly. "We will be rationing our supplies and will have to ensure that we time our arrival in each village appropriately." He turned to Murien. "How many households do you estimate exist on the mountains themselves?"

Murien put his hand to his chin as though straining under the weight of the question, "I would guess...perhaps...half a dozen. Likely all either hermits, prospectors, or mountain men..."

"*Mountain* men…" Lariana practically spat. "Their blood will likely taste like saltwater."

Duric chuckled, "no one said the trip would be easy…you're welcome to turn back now."

Lariana gave him a look of such utter disdain that he averted his eyes from her.

They took a moment to gather themselves, then proceeded on. The verdant fields began to give way to the same jagged stone they had encountered in the dismal maze of the Grey Gulf.

"These mountains have some sort of field around them…can you feel it?" Lariana asked softly.

Carrinon nodded, "undoubtedly. There is a powerful vibrational current here…it's very subtle though."

"Gives me the jitters." Murien said.

The sun was now bathing the land with its soft rays and the Vampyres squinted against it. Walking in daylight was still a jarring experience for the youths and they marvelled at the mystical power of the cloaks they wore.

Duric pointed along the mountain peaks. There were three in all, each rising like a jagged fortress towards the heavens, "we could spend weeks in these mountains…it might be a good idea to take stock of where we're heading."

Carrinon stopped and lifted his head high, eyeing the peaks, "yes…you're probably right. The First could be anywhere here and he is unlikely to make his presence known to just anyone." He put his hands on his hips. "Which is why we will continue on until *he* finds us…"

There was a moment of silence, then Lariana spoke, "*that's* the plan? Wander in these mountains and hope that the First takes notice?"

The Prince turned and stared at her for a moment. He was unused to such open defiance and it threw him off-guard, "have you got a better idea?"

Lariana didn't hesitate, "yes…we *draw* him out."

The Prince laughed contemptuously, "very good…and how exactly do you plan to do that?"

Lariana's eyes narrowed, "how do you draw out a sleeping animal? You begin to mark their territory as your own."

The Prince frowned with disgust. He was offended that this *half-breed* would have the gall to compare the most illustrious members of their race to animals.

Lariana didn't bother to wait for a response, "you said there are settlers on these mountains, yes?"

The Prince held back his anger and nodded.

"Then we start killing as many as we can…"

Murien and Duric's mouths dropped open.

Carrinon moved towards Lariana menacingly but she held her ground. Soon they were eye to eye. "Have you gone mad?" His voice was barely controlled. "You think indiscriminate killing will draw the attention of the First?"

Lariana's mouth creased with a slight smile, "…yes."

The Prince threw his arms up, "unbelievable…"

"She may have a point, sire…" Duric said softly.

The Prince turned to him, "is that so?"

"Yes…the people on the mountains are surely a superstitious lot. They may be sparse in their settlements but if we imbue them with enough terror, the ruckus they'll make-"

"This is absurd…" the Prince spat. He looked at Murien as though seeking his support.

Murien shrugged, "I can't think of anything else…"

Lariana grinned and crossed her arms, "the humans have always been like simple children. They can be used for sustenance, or they can be used for *our* purpose. We will drive them through the mountains like frightened sheep and their terror *will* provoke a response."

The Prince crossed his arms, "you realize that the First don't feed on blood. What good will herds of frightened humans be to him?"

Lariana waved him off as though he were an uncomprehending child, "I'm not concerned about the physical backlash…I'm concerned about the *psychic* one. If the other First are anything like Her Majesty, then they are powerful psychic beings. Far more powerful than the average Vampyre…" she turned back to the mountains with a look of exultation on her face. "Push the humans through…make them feel terror like never before…and the First *will* pick up on it."

The Prince despised her utterly in that moment. Not because she was wrong, but because she was *right*. Worse, the idea was nothing short of genius.

"Very well…" Carrinon said, subtly admitting his defeat. "We will proceed…"

The air became more chill as they made their ascent. They were now able to glance back and see the valley below all the way towards the haze of the Grey Gulf. The village of Loch-Gammond was in a tumult and wagons were coming and going in droves.

Lariana smiled to herself at the pitiful sight. Human beings were so weak, so utterly predictable. She despised the human blood that ran through her own veins, as all Vampyres did. She could scarcely acknowledge that she had come from such degeneracy.

As they proceeded on, the Prince motioned for them to stop, "let us set up camp here, for now…"

"Is that wise, sire?" Duric asked. "We've only begun our ascent."

The Prince breathed deeply of the chill air, "the mountains will be easier for us to scale at night. Besides…" he turned to Lariana. "Human beings are more frightened in darkness."

She smiled slightly and nodded.

"Very well…I'll scout the area and see if there are any good caves for us to sleep in." Murien bolted up one of the rocks effortlessly and vanished.

Lariana sat down on a boulder and ran her hands along the cold stone, "is it true that *Dragons* used to inhabit this place?"

"Yes…" the Prince said. "Hence the name: Dragon's Teeth."

"There's no need to be snide, sire…it was just a simple question."

The Prince clenched his jaw in a futile attempt to control his anger, "this is the problem with the younger generation…no respect."

Lariana smiled, unfazed, "sire…have you ever been with a female?"

The question was so unexpected that the Prince was momentarily stunned to silence.

Duric hid his face to stifle his laughter.

"Of course I have!" the Prince was practically shouting and his voice echoed back to him. He paused for a moment, then continued. "At my age, I have seen all there is to see of the world and its delights." He gave her a hard look. "It has left much to be desired."

There was a moment of silence then the soft laughter of the Vampyress echoed through the canyons surrounding them. The Prince looked on in utter confusion as Lariana bowled over and clutched her sides.

"I'm glad you find that amusing…" the Prince said coldly.

"Oh…forgive me, sire…" Lariana wiped the tears from her eyes. "It's just the way you said it…you've clearly never met a woman who could lighten you up!"

The Prince folded his arms, "this inane conversation is a waste of time."

At that moment, Murien returned, breathing heavily, "found one…a good cave, just over this ridge."

Lariana turned to him, "good timing…the Prince was just telling us about his love life."

Murien's eyes widened and his face revealed total confusion, "well, there's plenty of time for that later…we'll get settled in the cave first." He turned and vanished beyond the rocks.

The Prince could scarcely hold back his irritation. Once again, he questioned his Mother's wisdom in this endeavour. Placing him amongst these three fools had been a clear mistake and the endless banter was costing them valuable time. Now, more than ever, he longed to find the First. To bathe in the awe-inspiring power of one untainted by this corrupt world would be a balm to his soul. Perhaps the mere presence of one of those august personages would cleanse him of his doubts.

"Come on, sire, we're moving…" Duric said softly.

Carrinon gasped for a moment as he remembered where he was, then nodded as he began to walk forward.

The group leapt over the rock wall and immediately spotted the cave that Murien had selected: a small, dark alcove which was nearly camouflaged against the sheer cliff face. It was the perfect spot for them to camp and await the coming of night.

As they approached the cave, the group noticed a slight rumbling vibration beneath their feet. Pebbles and stones began to roll down the cliffs as a great tremor beckoned them forward.

"What is happening?" Lariana asked, her demeanour now one of slight fear.

Carrinon looked up at the sky and squinted, "something is coming."

At that moment, they were deafened by a great roar. It seemed to shake the very foundations of the mountains themselves. All four Vampyres clasped their heads in shock and screamed at the sheer force of the sound.

A moment later, the roar ceased and a great beating of wings could be heard.

Duric looked towards Carrinon in horror, "that…that's not."

Carrinon's eyes widened, "*…Dragon.*"

Suddenly, the sky above darkened as a great shape came into view. Soaring with unfathomable power and grace over the peaks, it moved steadily above them like a dark titan from the Age of Myth.

The Vampyres instinctively sought cover in the cave, but it soon became clear that the Dragon had no interest in them. It circled the highest peak, then dipped down and vanished behind the mountains.

"By Draganathan…" Lariana whispered. "I've never seen one up close."

"I have…" Carrinon said softly. "My Father used to ride Snógle during the Days of Fire…"

"*Snógle…*" Duric's voice trembled. "Mightiest among his kind."

"*That* honour goes to Maledon, but Snógle is very close behind. He was a fearless creature, enormous in size and he and my Father share an unbreakable bond to this day…" Carrinon couldn't hide the wistful longing in his voice. "I had hoped…to be able to find my *own* Dragon one day."

Murien frowned, "I wasn't aware Vampyres and Dragons had *any* connection. I had only ever heard of them as fearsome beasts which devoured the living and the dead alike."

Carrinon smirked, "you know nothing of our true history…and you can blame the Elders for that. They have obfuscated reality to the point that it is unrecognizable…" he ran his hand along the cold stone wall. "My Mother has allowed it…not because she couldn't stop it…but because she can see that we have fallen far from our original purity. We are not worthy of our ancient heritage."

"And this is for *her* to decide?" Lariana's voice brimmed with irritation. "What gives her that right?"

Carrinon fixed her with a glare of such ferocity that she immediately bowed her head, "forgive me, sire…I spoke out of turn."

Carrinon nodded slightly, satisfied by her sudden contrition, "you have no idea the degree of politics our race has succumbed to…this is why we *must* reach the First. When they are joined with my Mother they will be a force of such unstoppable might that they will set aright all the wrongs of our kind."

"And yet…" Duric said. "They hide on these mountains when they could be helping our people."

"They help our people in ways you cannot fathom…" Carrinon said. "Their bodies are in a state of hibernation, but their mighty minds and spirits soar forth through the Aether. They commune with the others who have gone to greater planes of existence to seek a new world for us, keep cosmic forces at bay which would otherwise threaten our very existence, and preserve the true heritage of the Vampyre race."

Duric sighed, "forget my earlier comment, then."

Carrinon smiled, "this venture may seem pointless to you, but you need to broaden the scope of your vision. You need to see things in Deep Time."

Lariana nodded slowly as though she understood, then pointed upwards, "I thought the term 'Dragon's Teeth' was merely a name…you failed to mention that there were *actual* Dragons *still* living on it."

"I thought that was implied…" Carrinon said. "Regardless, we will camp here and then continue on with the plan."

"Good…" Murien said softly as he pulled the hood of his cloak further down his face. "I could use a rest…"

A Desperate Plight

"The Ardhian Laws run counter to our own. We should not submit ourselves to these distant conquerors so blithely without considering what it is they want from us. For all we know...the last of the true Ardhian's could be long dead and it is merely a conclave of puppeteers who remain to pull our strings."

-'A Plea to the Nations' speech by Rector Cartusian in the Great House

The way forward was no longer clear to the Princess. She and Alexander had found plenty of food in the wizards' pantry. They had been discovered hours later by Charlotte, fast asleep on the pantry floor. She had smiled and helped herself to some food before leaving them be.

When the Princess had awoken, she felt refreshed but filled with despair. The full force of their plight now crashed down upon her like a great avalanche. There was nothing in her reservoir of experiences which could prepare her for this.

The wizard had not been seen since he had left them. The youths knew that he was in the uppermost level of the Tower, yet they refused to venture up the long flight to see him, such was the terror he evoked.

In the observatory, the youths gathered together as the Princess pored through the Red Book, desperately seeking something that would give them the upper hand against their captor.

Alexander couldn't help but marvel at the Princesses' rapid retention of information as the pages flew by.

"Here's a brief history of the Tower itself!" the Princesses' excitement bubbled over. "Perhaps there's a means of escape."

"Doubtful..." Charlotte said coldly. "I stand by my earlier point: there is no escape, otherwise he would have us in chains in a dungeon."

Alexander's eyes fell to the floor. There were times when he despised his sister's pessimism. Nevertheless, she was right. It seemed that they were pitted against a foe who was their superior in every way. He had outwitted entire kingdoms and his magical prowess was unmatched.

The sound of the pages fluttering by drew Alexander from his reverie. He shot his hand out at lightning speed causing the Princess to gasp, "what is that?"

The Princess looked down at Alexander's hand which rested over a symbol of some sort. It was clearly the classical magical circle, but with a series of arcane glyphs surrounding it, "I...I don't know. I've never seen anything like it."

Alexander leaned in closer and frowned, "it says something about a gateway...could it open a way for us to escape?"

"It's difficult to say... there are many perils to performing such an operation, and besides..." the Princess glanced back towards the dark stairs. "I doubt *he* will allow it...the amount of energy required would be immense and he would sense it immediately."

"Damn him..." Charlotte muttered. "Damn him..."

Alexander put a gentle hand on his sister's shoulder but she pushed it away and moved towards the window.

"There *must* be a way..." she said to herself. She turned back to the Princess, "you seem to know him better than we do..."

The Princess frowned and recoiled at the words, as though stung.

"Why does he keep us here?" Charlotte continued. "Does it give him some sort of twisted satisfaction?"

"No...not quite..." a gentle voice behind them said.

They all gasped and turned in unison to see their captor, regal in his black robes, standing in the shadows.

The wizard ran his hand through his white beard, "you imagine that if I simply released you here...you would survive?" He laughed and it was a harsh sound. "You damn fools...they say youth is wasted on the young and they're right!"

As he spoke, Charlotte moved slowly to the right. She saw a golden candelabra on one of the tables and began to make her way towards it.

The wizard continued, "I suppose I can understand the Princesses' plight, but the two of *you*?" He looked at the siblings disdainfully. "You have *nothing*…nothing in this world to go back to…no one on the outside waiting for you."

Unable to contain her fury any longer, Charlotte moved with lightning speed. She scooped the candelabra from the table and charged forward with a cry of such rage that time seemed to stand still. For a moment, it looked as though she would close the distance between herself and the wizard and bring the candelabra down on his head.

Alas, it was not to be.

Moving with a suddenness that was uncanny, the wizard turned, saw her advance, and blasted her with a wave of white lightning.

Charlotte fell to the ground immediately, writhing in agony. Her blood-curdling screams of helplessness induced an immediate reaction from her brother.

"Stop!" Alexander shrieked as he bolted forward on instinct.

The wizard turned and engulfed the boy in the same incandescent tendrils as his sister. The two of them writhed in agony for what seemed an eternity until at last the brightness around them vanished.

"That was foolish…" the wizard said softly, seemingly unperturbed by what had occurred. "I would *not* recommend it again…"

Charlotte stared up at the ceiling vacantly, her breaths were shallow.

Alexander forced himself up but his arms and legs felt like jelly, "you bastard! You've killed her!"

"Hardly…" the wizard said coldly. "But I *could* have if I had wished…"

The Princess knelt and held Alexander close, "are you alright?"

The boy nodded but the pain on his face was visible.

The Princess helped him to his feet and together they shambled over to Charlotte, who was still in shock on the floor.

"The effects will wear off…" the wizard said with an almost paternal note of affection. "But be warned…try such a stunt again, and I will *not* hesitate to kill you."

"*Monster*…" the Princess spat. "Your very existence *sullies* the Ardhian people."

The wizard laughed once more, "child…do not berate me with petty insults. I remember your most distant ancestors when they were strong and proud…" he gave her a look of total disdain. "How pitiful they have become."

The Princess winced at the barb but held her ground, "they may be pitiful to you, but at least they've created something rather than *destroying* their own land and the lands of others in search of cosmic knowledge."

The wizard nodded slightly and smiled as though he were mildly impressed, "you've been reading my book, I see…" he nodded towards the folds of her robe. Suddenly his face darkened. "What would *you* know about cosmic knowledge. You have no idea the forces you contend with when you speak of such things. You can pillage that little book for all the ideas you want, but I can assure you, you will find *nothing* which will serve you." He turned and began to ascend the dark stairway once more. "Do not mistake my hospitality for licence to do as you wish…" he vanished into the shadows, his silver eye lingering for a moment in the darkness and then disappearing.

"What…what happened?" Charlotte asked as she sat up.

"Thank the Light Father…" Alexander said softly with tears in his eyes. "I thought you were going to die."

"How long have I been out?"

"A few hours…"

She glanced towards the darkened stairs, "and… *him*?"

Alexander lowered his eyes, "gone…he said he'll kill you if you attempt to do that again."

Charlotte sighed deeply. Her bravado was gone, replaced by a look of such total defeat that Alexander couldn't bear to see it.

The Princess ran a gentle hand through Charlotte's hair, "I'm glad you're alright…" she glanced at Alexander. "What he says is true…our gaoler won't hesitate to kill us."

Charlotte's head slumped forward slightly, "then…what choice do we have but to go with him…" she pulled herself up with the help of the others. When she at last stood, she stared out the great window into the endless sky beyond. "Besides…he's right."

"He's *right*?" Alexander couldn't believe what he was hearing.

Charlotte turned to him, "what do we have left in this world? A few distant relatives that we've never even seen?" Her eyes began to mist with tears. "Our own great-uncle tried to kill us…maybe we're no better than stray dogs."

They sat silently for a moment. It felt as though the weight of the world was on their shoulders.

At last, the Princess spoke, "I don't see it that way at all…"

The siblings looked up slowly.

"Being in the castle, I've never had friends…oh, my Father has servants galore, of course: Rectors and cooks, guardsmen and cleaners. But I've never bonded with any of them. Not like I have with you two…" her eyes began to mist with tears. "You are *not* stray dogs…you are *friends*…and when this is over, I'll make sure you never want for anything ever again."

Alexander and Charlotte's eyes were wide with shock and surprise. Then, spontaneously, they leaned forward and hugged the Princess tightly. They held one another like that for quite some time before letting go.

The Princess rubbed the tears from her cheeks, "we're going to get out of here…we *must* believe it."

Charlotte nodded slowly and smiled, "I misjudged you…Highness…I always imagined that because of the station you were born into, that you would be weak." She lowered her head with visible shame. "I was so wrong…perhaps it's the other way round…perhaps *I* was weak…and your strength has ennobled me."

The Princess put a hand on Charlotte's shoulder, "we must work together…our division is what *he* wants…if we stand united, we can outsmart him."

Alexander stood and brushed the dust from his knees, "well, we better think fast…the air is changing out there."

The Princess frowned slightly, then rose to her feet, "you're right…it's getting warmer."

"Didn't he say we were headed East?" Charlotte asked.

The Princess nodded, "the Eastern Desert…but we couldn't possibly be moving that quickly. It defies every law of physics."

Alexander couldn't help but laugh, "much like this floating Tower…"

Charlotte began to walk towards the great window and the others followed. The air was rushing by and they appeared to be moving steadily, but not at a rate that was excessive. They chanced a glance beneath them and were stunned to see that the pastures of Nin-Ghasta had been replaced by verdant forests.

"Impossible…" the Princess muttered.

Alexander turned to her, "what's impossible?"

"If we *are* headed East, then we must be well over Matis-Manna. What I can recall from my studies of geography tells me that it is only these woods which separate us from the Black Desert."

The three of them moved away from the window.

"Black Desert?" Alexander could scarcely hide his curiosity.

The Princess nodded, "we will pass over the Channa Mountains first…" she turned her emerald eyes towards him. "They call it the Black Desert because the sand is so dark it looks black. The old legends say that Antaryan, son of the Light Father, was so disgusted by the old desert Priesthood that he burned their civilization to the ground, hence the term."

"Fascinating…" Alexander leaned back slightly. "We never learned any of this when I was in school…"

The Princess smiled, "there is much that isn't taught nowadays…I was fortunate because my Father's library contained many out-of-print volumes…" her eyes took on a faraway look. "He must be worried sick about me."

Charlotte put a gentle hand on the Princesses' shoulder, "we'll find our way back to him…"

The Princess clenched her fists, "what if what our captor said was true: that my Father *was* using me as bait."

"I don't believe that…" Alexander said softly. "What parent would do such a thing?"

The Princess met his eyes once more and he recoiled at the coldness in them, "you don't know my Father, Alexander…I love him dearly and he can be the greatest man in the world, but as I've grown, I've seen another side to him. He has a cruel, ruthless part of his being that all monarchs *must* have in order to rule their kingdoms." She gazed down at the floor. "It just hurts…is all…it *hurts*."

Guiding the Herd

"She will one day return to us in full splendour. Her divine light, once the guiding force of our people, shall be renewed. Let no one deny this prophecy for the stars themselves decree it!"

-Asmael, Alderamin Prophet of the Starlight Epoch

The plan had worked even better than they could have hoped. The first settlement they encountered had dispersed before their fury like wild animals fleeing a great fire. There were perhaps five families stampeding through the mountains and they accumulated further numbers as they went.

The harrowing tale of a remorseless assault by dark creatures of the night had taken root quickly and the superstitious mountain folk had not hesitated to pack their belongings and leave their homes. They were far more resourceful than those in the villages and cities and far more inclined to heed their own intuition.

And their intuition told them one thing: run.

So run they did. Some of the men had made the foolish mistake of attempting to face the menace head on and none had returned. Soon, there was a veritable caravan of people the likes of which had never been seen on the Dragon's Teeth.

From one of the high peaks, Carrinon looked down with his arms folded and smiled. Lariana's plan was working magically. He could *feel* the sheer terror of the humans as they fled and it excited the predator in him. He had to restrain the temptation to plunge forward and slaughter them en masse. He could have easily annihilated these primitive creatures but it would have undermined their purpose.

The Prince turned to Duric who was looking on behind him, "now, we wait…"

"How long, sire?"

"However long it takes…the First will surely reveal himself soon enough." The Prince eyed the fleeing caravans. "The psychic energy of these pathetic wretches is being magnified by the magnetic pull of the mountains. It's as though the Dragon's Teeth are acting as a conduit."

Sure enough, the ripples of psychic energy were so potent that they had an almost tangible quality to them. Carrinon knew that Duric and the others were not sensitive enough to see these waves as he could but they could feel their presence.

Lariana strode next to them, "not a bad idea, eh?"

Carrinon nodded grimly, "yes…well done."

"Why thank you, sire."

Carrinon turned, "Murien, go forth and keep harassing the caravan, we don't want these psychic waves to dissipate just yet."

Murien nodded, "with pleasure, sire…" he leapt like a great cat and vanished over the edge of the cliffs into the darkness.

"I'm going with him." Lariana said.

Carrinon frowned, "there is no need…one of us will suffice."

"Still…it's *my* plan…"

Carrinon sighed as though he were nearing the end of his patience, "very well…but don't kill too many of them…we need to keep enough of them alive to form a psychic beacon."

Lariana smiled, "well, obviously!" She turned and leapt forward into the abyss.

Carrinon sighed deeply, "…insolent children."

Duric's soft laughter could be heard behind him, "they haven't changed in all the centuries I've known them."

Carrinon turned to him, "how long *have* you known them?"

Duric's feline eyes took on a wistful hue, "as long as I can remember…our families were friends before we were born."

Carrinon nodded slightly. He understood the way political relations formed bonds in the Vampyre community. Politics seemed to define everything in their society, from the highest Prefect to the lowest serf. Political machinations were rife, for what else could they do to keep the endless roll of eternity amusing?

Carrinon imagined once again that if they could channel all of the energy that they used for intrigue towards a higher goal as their illustrious ancestors had, they would already have equaled them in greatness.

"Sire?" Duric asked softly.

The Prince shook his head and snapped out of his reverie.

Duric smiled slightly, "the humans are moving quickly…we best try to keep up to them."

Carrinon nodded, "Agreed…" he looked off into the distance. "Do you think this will *actually* succeed?"

Duric chuckled, "I have no idea, sire. But I know that those humans are making a bloody ruckus across these mountains," his eyes glimmered. "It's loud enough to wake even the dead."

Carrinon smiled, "Good…" he turned back to the mountains. "Let's go."

The Prince leaped with effortless grace down the endless crags and boulders which lined the lower canyons and Duric followed swiftly. As they went, bounding impossibly through the columns of rock, they caught sight of Lariana and Murien. They were standing side-by-side and looking over a sheer rockface.

Lariana turned slowly as the Prince and Duric arrived, "Glad you could make it…" she grinned. "We've been picking off the stragglers one by one but the main bulk of the human mass is moving haphazardly. They're staying in tight formations in an attempt to ward us off."

Carrinon looked out and saw where the humans had camped far below them, "we must harry them until we wake the First."

"*Will* the First intervene?" Murien asked tentatively. "It seems unlikely that he would care about such pathetic wretches."

Carrinon gave him a hard look, "it's not the *wretches* that he cares about…it's the wave of psychic and emotional energy being released. It's probably more excitement than these mountains have seen in years."

"Undoubtedly…" Lariana said softly. She extended her arm and pointed down towards a group of human hunters who were moving slowly as though attempting to avoid being seen. She laughed at the sight of them, "pathetic…isn't it? We've been so successful that they don't even know what hunts them. They likely still think it's some sort of mythical mountain creature."

Murien smiled, "I forgot how potent human superstition can be…"

"Regardless…" Carrinon said. "We must continue to chip away at them." He glanced around cautiously, "and keep your senses alert for Dragons…"

The others shuddered at the dreaded word.

Murien felt suddenly exposed on this high ridge, as though a great shadow could swoop down from the skies at any moment to snatch them up.

"How do those humans live in these mountains?" Lariana's voice was so low it was almost a whisper. "Among *Dragons…*"

Carrinon crossed his arms, "you can thank my Father for that…his alliance with the great Dragons of old has held firm to this day. The descendants of Ardhia have benefitted greatly from it." He nodded towards the encampment below. "Perhaps we have been too harsh in our judgement of these mountain folk…they are descended from a great race and it is all the more reason why their terror will be useful to us. The Ardhians were natural magicians and I'm certain that their power has trickled down to these people…albeit in a greatly diluted form."

Lariana brushed her hair daintily from her eyes, "regardless…I feel a fresh hunger arising in me. Perhaps I'll enjoy one of those hunters. Their courage will be a magnificent salt for the blood." She grinned wolfishly and leapt from the cliff, vanishing into the dark below.

Murien watched her go, "she can't sit still, that one."

Carrinon spat on the cold ground, "yes, patience was never a strong suit among the young ones."

Murien winced slightly at the barb. He knew it had been intended for his ears. While he respected the Prince for his prowess and status, he despised him for his condescension.

Carrinon turned to him, "that offended you, did it?"

Murien's eyes widened, "no…no sire…not at all…"

Carrinon frowned, "if you cannot be forthright with me, then get out of my sight and return to my Mother's stronghold."

Murien felt utterly exposed. He had forgotten that the Prince possessed the gift of telepathy, "sire…forgive me…"

"It offended you…" Carrinon said bluntly.

"It…it did…sire."

"Good…" the Prince smiled. "Glad to see I'm not stuck with a group of prideless degenerates." His cold eyes fell on Murien and held him there, "I don't *want* you to be honest with me…I *expect* it. Learn to take pride in yourself and your heritage. If you wish to call yourself my companion, then you best tolerate nothing less…"

Murien's back straightened and he sighed, "yes sire…I shall do that." His demeanor seemed to transform and a glow of confidence appeared to shine from his countenance.

"And you?" the Prince turned to Duric. "Will you also hide yourself in shadow when you disagree with my decisions?"

Duric smiled, "no sire…you can count on an honest appraisal from me…"

Carrinon nodded, "our time together has shown me one thing: our people have indeed fallen far from their birthright. It is my hope that the First will help us restore that. You must never forget the greatness that dwells within you…"

Murien nodded and his eyes glistened with tears. Carrinon was either an inspiring leader of the highest order, or a master manipulator. Either way, Murien would have gladly fought for him in that moment.

Died for him even.

When Lariana at last returned, her mouth was stained red with blood. She ascended the cliff effortlessly and began to wipe her face with a dark cloth which she produced from one of her pockets.

Murien crossed his arms and stood over her, "satiated?"

She looked up at him and made a playful face of affirmation.

"Did the hunters see you coming?"

Lariana laughed and it echoed across the mountains, "what do *you* think? They caught wind of one of the squirrels before they even realized *I* was on them."

"Very good…" Murien turned to Duric, who was taking stock of their supplies. "The Prince?"

"Up there…" Duric pointed towards one of the steep cliff faces.

Murien shook his head in awe, "I didn't even hear him leave."

"He's even subtler than Lariana…" Duric said playfully.

Lariana rose and gazed upwards, "daylight will be upon us in a few hours…how much longer before the First shows himself?"

"Who can say…" Murien said. "The Ancients live by their own rules…"

"Hmmm…" Lariana put a hand to her chin thoughtfully. "I wonder what use they will be to us? Sure, they have ancient wisdom…but times have *changed*. Look around…" she gestured broadly. "This is not the same world it was even a millennia ago."

"You weren't even alive then…" Murien said with a chuckle. He paused and glanced upwards. "But *he* was…"

Lariana moved towards Murien and eyed him carefully, "I sense a change in your attitude towards our sovereign. It seems only yesterday that you could scarcely stand him."

Murien glanced at her with contempt, "he has seen into my heart…seen something that not even *I* dared to see." His voice grew soft. "Perhaps he sees greatness in me…"

Lariana laughed, it was a cruel sound, "*greatness*? Come now Murien, you know yourself better than that."

Murien frowned.

"Our *families* possess greatness…the Empress is a Great One, even our Prince makes us look small by comparison…what possible *greatness* do *we* have? We are the scions of aeon old families that have fought tooth and nail to procure us social standing. On our own…what are we?"

Murien seemed taken aback and appeared lost for words.

Lariana lifted an accusing finger towards him, "I'll tell you what we are: pawns. Pawns in a political game which goes back before we were even conceived. Our families saw an opportunity to win the Empresses' favour and they used us to do it…nothing more."

"You can't truly believe that…" Murien's voice was shaky with uncertainty.

From behind them, Duric watched without intervening.

"I *can*…" Lariana said coldly. "Because my own mother *told* me those words when I was but a child. She made it clear that my sole purpose was to advance the cause of the family, nothing more. It was her purpose and my grandmothers before her."

"So, you would just accept this fate then, would you?" Murien said, anger rising in his voice. "The Prince sees something in us…the *Empress* saw something in us…otherwise we wouldn't be here."

Lariana seemed to consider this for a moment, "perhaps…or perhaps our families merely petitioned the hardest. Regardless, we know our place in our society…do you believe it is stratified by *accident*? We will never truly advance beyond our station, just as the slaves and Sub-Helots will never advance beyond theirs… in fact." She pointed her finger once more at Murien. "We should consider ourselves *fortunate*. Fortunate that we were born into families with wealth and standing. At least we might find a place on the Council of Night one day."

Murien waved her off dismissively, "to *hell* with the Council."

Lariana gasped and Duric smiled slightly with growing amusement.

"Is *that* to be our fate? To serve on some archaic *Council*?" The fire in Murien's eyes was growing. "I don't give a damn about that. I want *more*. I want the freedom to discover. I'm tired of being bound by the fear of the Sun and the fear of our Elders…I want *freedom*. Hell, I've never felt as free as I have on this journey. To see the lands beyond the Enclaves…to walk in the hated sun for the first time in my life…this has made me realize how *small* the world within the Enclaves is…"

Lariana lowered her eyes. When she spoke, much of the fury in her voice was gone and she seemed to have softened considerably, "Murien…our world is what it is…we alone cannot change that."

Murien nodded, "perhaps you're right…but the *First* can."

Lariana's shoulders sagged and she crossed her arms in disappointment, "there you go again…giving your power away to someone else."

Murien shot a dark glare at her, but before he could speak, the voice of Carrinon was heard from behind them.

"Something is coming…" the Prince said.

The others turned to him slowly with fear in their eyes.

"Another Dragon?" Duric asked.

The Prince shook his head, "no…something *else*. A power I've never felt before."

"The *First*…" Murien said reverently.

The Prince nodded, "it's highly poss-"

"NOW!" a voice from behind them shouted.

At that moment, a group of mountain men shambled out of the darkness with weapons brandished.

Carrinon did a quick assessment of the situation and saw that there were nearly fifty men trickling up the mountainside to surround them. It seemed as though their every escape had been covered and the sun was close to the horizon, limiting their ability to climb and avoid their attackers.

Damn...Carrinon thought. *I was so overwhelmed by the growing energy on the mountain; I let these peasants sneak up on us*...

Moments later, they were truly surrounded.

Lariana snarled and extended her claws, ready to cut the nearest throat. Murien stood still as a stone and Duric rose slowly, prepared for anything.

Carrinon quickly came to the stark realization that they were outmatched. There were simply too many adversaries to cut down. Had it been night, the humans wouldn't have stood a chance, but daybreak was imminent and the power of the Vampyres was greatly diminished. The Prince leapt down from the ridge and landed in the midst of Lariana and the others.

In that moment of total understanding, he cursed his Mother. She had sent him to his death, and for what? To awaken her kin? Perhaps it was all just a fever dream, a hope to recover an irretrievably lost former glory.

It mattered not.

If Carrinon was to be slain here, he would take as many of these wretched parasites with him as possible. He sensed the fear in the others, but also the resolution to do the same.

My Mother did one thing right...he thought with a slight smile. *She chose the perfect companions*...

"What are you waiting for!" Murien called out.

As though spurned on by his voice, the mountain men charged forward. Their weapons glinted in the coming daylight and their roars echoed through the mountains.

The first wave was shattered easily. The Vampyres moved in unison and soon they were drenched in the blood of their foes. Lariana and Murien fought with vicious abandon while Carrinon and Duric applied a more strategic and methodical approach, cutting down men left and right while dodging their attacks with ease.

Soon, the Vampyres formed a circle and stood practically back-to-back. They knew they couldn't keep this up and it seemed as though the sun was rising faster by the minute.

One of the mountain men caught Duric off guard, giving him a swift blow to the face with the knob of his axe. The axe shattered in his hand, and while Duric was unharmed against the attack, he lost his balance and stumbled backwards. The circle broke and the victory of humanity seemed assured in that moment. A few seconds later and it would all be over.

Carrinon saw the impossibility of the situation and prepared himself for the end. But it was an end that never came.

There was a huge explosion in the midst of them and the Vampyres glanced up to see human bodies flying in all directions. A shadow moved swiftly among them, cutting down the mountain men like reeds of grass. It all happened so quickly that when the final assailant lay gasping his last breath on the cold earth, the Vampyres were still throwing attacks in defense.

For a moment, all of them were in shock.

"What…what…" Lariana could barely speak.

Murien glanced cautiously around them, but saw only piles of corpses strewn about the black rocks.

"Did you *see* that?" Duric asked. "Did anyone see that?"

"I saw it…" Carrinon said softly. "Or should I say, I saw *him*."

"*Him*?" Lariana was shaking.

Carrinon looked upwards and the others followed his gaze. From a higher peak, looking down on them, was a pair of eyes wreathed in shadow. Indeed, it seemed as though the entire peak was cloaked in darkness despite the onset of the sun.

The others had been so occupied by the sight that they had forgotten all about the Lord of Light and they felt the first stings of daylight assailing their faces. They winced and threw up their magical hoods, looking back up the mountain quickly. To their amazement, the peak was illuminated and the figure was gone.

Lariana's mouth hung open, "was that?"

Carrinon nodded, "we must continue our ascent…" he looked back up the mountain with something close to reverence. "One of the Ancients calls to us…he has shown us where to go."

The Black Mara

"There is a story so old that it has nearly been lost to time. It tells the tale of Slaangrah, the White Snake of the Desert. Guardian of the Black Mara and god of the local Sanna peoples, the legends of Slaangrah predate even the coming of the Ardhians. It is said that the Elder Snake is keeper of ancient wisdom and will indulge those he deems worthy. But woe betide those who fail to meet his lofty standards for they will find their eternal homes in the snake's belly."

-'Legends of the Desert' by Maxima Concera

It was warm outside. Far, far warmer than it should have been.

The Princess was awakened from her light slumber by a sudden onrush of hot air. For a moment she was confused and had forgotten where she was. She gasped and cried out, waking the others. They had all fallen asleep where they sat and had to claw their way back to waking life.

"Where…how…" the Princess muttered. Then the full force of their situation smacked her back to reality. "Oh…oh…we're still…"

"We're still here…" Alexander said softly.

Charlotte glanced around groggily, "we're still in this damn Tower."

Alexander smiled, "well, it's not as though we've made much effort to escape."

Charlotte sighed and her shoulders sagged forward, "enough of this…we've been too exhausted to do anything since we arrived here. Now, we need answers…" she looked hesitantly up towards the dark staircase.

"He's told us where we're going already..." Alexander said. He turned to the great window and noticed the change in the skyline. "Impossible..." he rose and bolted towards it. When he turned back to the others, his face was pale, "you might want to see this."

Charlotte and the Princess rose slowly, almost as though they were trying to delay the inevitable. When they at last made it to the window, they gasped.

The Princess put her hands to her face, "*how*...it's..."

"The desert..." Alexander said, all emotion drained from his voice. "We're already in the desert."

Charlotte turned back to the staircase, "we need answers...*now*." She clenched her fists and began to walk forward, then stopped. It was as though she couldn't will herself to take another step. Memories of her terrifying ordeal came flooding back to her: the sudden adrenaline, the bright, all-consuming lightning. It was too much for her to bear and she collapsed to her knees.

Alexander moved forward quickly, "I'll help you up..." he went behind her and gently put his arms under hers to ease her back to her feet.

She turned to him and smiled wistfully. He was growing up so fast. Perhaps *too* fast for her liking. A small part of her mourned the thought that he would never have a proper childhood. Would never experience a sense of normality.

The Princess moved past them, her eyes fixed on the stairs, "let's go...the longer we delay, the closer his plans come to fruition."

"If we face him together, he might give us answers..." Alexander said, but he could barely hide the fear in his eyes.

Driven by their combined desperation, they made their way towards the dark staircase.

Alexander held onto Charlotte tightly and noticed that she was shaking.

When they arrived in the wizard's main chambers, they saw him seated at a desk with his back towards them. All around them, great machines whirred, whined, and arced with electrical currents. Now that they were rested, they could take in the details of this enormous place. It was as though they were glimpsing into the mind of a madman.

Machines of golden hue and arcane power rose up high into the ceiling and vanished into shadow. The Princess recognized a huge array of alchemical equipment and an enormous forge, larger and more intricate than any she had ever seen, billowed to their left. The golden light it gave off seemed to engulf the room.

Charlotte felt herself stiffen at the sight of the wizard. She felt the urge to either flee back down the stairs or rush forward and assail him while his back was turned. She thought better of the latter as she remembered his earlier warning to her.

"Welcome…" the wizard's voice was surprisingly warm.

"Where are we?" the Princess asked coldly.

"Straight to the point I see…" the wizard kept his head forward. He appeared to be busy writing with a quill on a piece of parchment. "If you must know, we are in the Black Mara Desert. Soon we will reach the Mouth of B'aal."

"Why did you bring us here…" Charlotte said through gritted teeth.

The wizard laughed, "*bring* you here? You brought *yourself* here. I gave you a thousand opportunities to leave, and yet you persisted." He rose slowly from the wooden table and turned towards them, his silver eye glowing preternaturally. "Rather admirable, I will say."

Alexander mustered his courage to speak, "what's in the Black Mara?"

The wizard regarded the boy for a moment, "I see your curiosity remains intact, boy…if you must know, the Temple of Hierophants lies there."

Alexander nodded knowingly, "one of the Relics is in the Temple, then."

The wizard smiled, "yes…hidden behind the Flame of Aman."

Charlotte could contain herself no longer, "take us home…*now*."

"I don't know what I find more amusing, child, your continued stubbornness, or this lingering idea that you *have* a home to go back to."

Charlotte moved forward and Alexander restrained her.

The wizard looked on them and smiled gently, "why not enjoy the journey. Other children your age would give a limb to experience even a *fraction* of the adventure you have."

"*Adventure*?" Charlotte spat. "Is that what this is to you?"

The wizard shrugged, "it is what you make of it, I suppose."

The Princess took a deep breath, "the Temple…I have…read about it."

The wizard frowned but he couldn't hide his amusement, "you have, have you? Tell me about it."

The Princess, suddenly finding herself put on the spot, stumbled over her words, "well…it's…it's…complicated."

The wizard smiled almost indulgently and his demeanour seemed to soften. For a moment, he appeared more like the kindly old guide once more, "yes, it is…as are all things in life, for nothing is black and white." He gestured towards the dark wooden table and the chairs which surrounded it. "Come…sit."

The youths were taken aback. For a moment, they wondered whether the crafty old man was trying to play a trick on them. Slowly, reluctantly, they moved towards the table, picked out a chair, and took a seat. The table was strewn with papers both ancient and new.

The wizard sat in the middle of them and picked up his quill.

Alexander looked at the others in disbelief for a moment, then spoke, "what are you doing?"

The wizard kept his eyes on the parchment, "writing a letter. It is to an old friend whom I have not spoken to in quite some time."

Charlotte crossed her arms, "is it Danyr?"

The wizard smiled slightly, "you've read some of my correspondence, I see…" he looked up and met her gaze with his singular orb. "Yes…we are planning our next move."

"Why write at all?" the Princess asked. "I thought Anturac had magical technology for the purpose of communication."

"We do…" the wizard resumed his writing. "But after the Catastrophe, we understood that technology was not something to be dependent on. We utilize it for our purposes while retaining a healthy respect for more…*simplistic* practices."

Alexander gazed towards the window, lost in thought.

The Princess took a deep intake of breath as the wizard wrote. If there had been any doubt in her mind that he was the author of the Red Book, they were swiftly laid to rest at the sight of that unmistakeable, spidery script. She resumed her line of questioning. She wanted to probe him for any answers she could, “the Flame of Aman…what is it?”

The wizard didn’t look up from his scroll, “legends say that it is the remnant of the fires left behind by the god Antaryan. When he obliterated the ancient Priesthood, the Flame continued to burn eternally.”

“Is it the same as the Arcalypsis Flame?” the Princess asked.

Now the wizard stopped his writing and looked up at her, “no…the Arcalypsis Flame is beyond your comprehension, child…you have read of such things, but you know little about them.”

The Princess was unfazed, “then why don’t you enlighten us.”

The wizard laughed, it had an almost musical ring to it, “I see you and the boy share the same curiosity…” he nodded towards Alexander. “I’m sure your father will be proud you’ve found a worthy suitor.” He resumed his writing.

The Princess gasped and Alexander’s mouth dropped.

“We’re not…we don’t even *know* each other…” the Princess said clumsily.

Alexander remained quiet but his cheeks were flushed with colour.

The wizard smiled slightly, “oh, certainly…I’ve lived long enough to know things as truth when I see them…just remember this prediction when the day comes.”

Charlotte cut through the tension, her impatience getting the better of her, “enough of your mind games…why don’t you just let us go.”

“In the desert?” the wizard said with a sly grin. “How long do you think you would last out there?”

“Longer than we will as your captives.”

The wizard leaned back and crossed his arms, “if dehydration and the local tribesmen didn’t kill you, then the Elder Serpent would.”

Charlotte leaned back in her chair and frowned, “Elder Serpent?”

“He has had many names over the millennia, but in this Age he is known as Slaangrah: The White Mouth of the Sand.”

Charlotte glared at him, “and you’re planning to feed us to this Serpent, no doubt…”

The wizard laughed heartily, “I would do no such thing, I don’t want to give him a stomach ache.”

Alexander smiled despite himself.

The wizard ran his fingers through his beard, “the Serpent and I are old friends…he will grant us safe passage as Druim did.”

The youths were baffled. They had thought they knew what kind of man they were dealing with, but as they learned more about him, the enigma surrounding him grew: he was thousands of years old, a magical adept of the highest order, a member of an ancient and long-dead civilization, a close friend of a legendary Mage Emperor, and now, an acquaintance to a Forest God and a Titan Serpent that stalked the Desert.

“I suppose you wish to know what I intend when I attain one of the Great Relics…” the wizard said softly.

The Princess leaped at the opportunity as though she alone had somehow coaxed the answer from him, “you’re no different than any of the men who are pursuing you then. You want power and you enjoy exerting power over others.”

The wizard raised a hand to her to indicate silence, “please…do not project your own shadow onto me. I have lived through enough Ages on this world to have seen the rise and fall of kingdoms and witnessed the petty power struggles that take place within them. I’ve watched them pass away like dust in the wind.” He fixed them all with a cold glare. “Impermanence is a fact of life. One that cannot be altered. Therefore, why worry about power at all?”

The Princess leaned forward, “then what are your motives?”

The wizard met her glare, “it is no business of yours, my most honoured guest.”

“Bah!” the Princess spat contemptuously. She turned and departed down the dark stairs.

Charlotte followed her, a sour expression on her face.

When they were gone, the wizard turned to Alexander, “…women.” He said with a slight smile. He returned to his writing.

Alexander hesitated for a moment. He contemplated following the girls, but he felt himself drawn to the old man. He had seen a glimpse of the wizard’s humour and he thought this might be the chance to ply him with more questions. Perhaps he could figure out the old man’s true intentions.

The wizard stopped writing, "yes?"

Alexander was momentarily caught off-guard, "I um…I…"

"Ask, boy…"

Alexander's natural curiosity took over, "are you really writing to Danyr?"

The wizard's response was casual, "…yes."

Alexander's eyes widened, "*the* Danyr?"

The wizard offered up a slight smile, "yes…*the* Danyr…Mage Emperor of Anturac."

"He's your…Master?"

The wizard laughed, "no…he's my friend. We go back many millennia."

The boy could scarcely contain himself any longer, "is Danyr going to attack us? Does he *actually* live in Anturac? Are there other towers there like this one and did you build them?"

"Calm yourself boy, you're becoming excitable…" there was no malice in the wizard's tone.

Alexander took several deep breaths and managed to regain his composure. He saw something close to sympathy in the wizard's eyes and realized for the first time that they were not prisoners here, nor had they ever been.

"I will answer your first question…" the wizard said softly. "No…Danyr is not going to attack the Continent. With all the might of Anturac, he could obliterate it many times over, but he never will. What reason would he have for such a rash course of action?"

Alexander shrugged, "I don't know…maybe because of the wars that are going on?"

The wizard dropped his quill and looked at the boy, "most of the wars here are petty and meaningless. They burn hard and fast, then wither out in a flash. In fact, *we* even helped to start a few of them."

Alexander's mouth dropped.

The wizard cocked his head to the side, "don't look so surprised, boy." He leaned back in his chair. "Once, many moons ago, there was a heavy rainfall. I was out walking when I spotted a large worm along the path, struggling to make it to the dirt. It appeared to be drowning in one of the many puddles which had formed. I, out of pity, lifted the poor creature up and placed it in the safety of the grass thinking I had done it a service. The following day, I took the same route and found the worm devoured by ants. I had delivered it to a much more gruesome death than I would have had I allowed it to be left to its fate." He leaned forward. "The point is this: sometimes the path to destruction is already determined."

Alexander placed a hand on his chin thoughtfully, "so…the worm is like the great kingdoms of Man? And you and Danyr are shepherding them towards destruction?"

The wizard snapped his fingers, "precisely! The bloated corpses of the kingdoms have already begun to fester; we are merely directing the vultures. Take Arinönde, for instance: a corrupt, degenerate province which is already on the verge of collapse and which will soon be invaded by one of its many enemies."

"So…you and Danyr *are* attacking the Continent…just not directly."

"That is a fair statement…now…your second question has already been answered, so let us proceed to the third," the wizard gestured around them. "I did not build this tower, per se…but I did oversee its construction. There are no others like it as it was intended for my personal use. Not even the finest architects in Anturac possess the knowledge to build another one as that wisdom has been lost." He crossed his arms. "Anything else?"

Alexander sighed, "yes…what will you do when you attain the Great Relic?"

The question was so genuinely forthright that for a moment, the wizard's eyes widened, then a glimmer of their old mischief shone through, "you know, you remind me of someone. Someone who was very near and dear to me, whom I lost long ago. To those who knew him, he was Ionir…but to me…he was my son."

Alexander gasped, "*you* had a son?"

The wizard frowned, "with all the millennia I have lived, did you imagine that I was always a reclusive wizard living in a dark tower?"

Alexander smiled, "well…I suppose…it's possible."

For the first time, the boy noticed a deep sadness behind the wizard's eyes.

The silver orb shone with a melancholy light, "I had three children…they were born to my second wife…my first wife, my greatest love, was *taken* from me. After that, I never imagined I would love again…until I met a peasant woman in the village of Rhontrist. She was a simple, salt of the earth type and I quickly became enamored of the small farming community she was a part of. We settled down and started a family amongst the great hills and pastures of the hinterlands. Elba, Aonis, and Ionir…two girls and a boy.

"The time passed quickly. My wife, her name was Hela by the way, knew of my Ardhian heritage and that I would outlive her and the entire community from which she came. She hoped, however, that if our children should inherit my traits of immortal life, that they would be in good hands as I would be around to look after them." He lowered his eyes to the hard table and was silent for a moment. When he spoke again it was as though a great weight had come upon him. "And she would have been right…but it was not to be so. I departed on a mission from Anturac to ensure that a renegade tribe would not break through to our dimension. You must understand, boy, that since the Catastrophe, the barriers between dimensions on this plane are tenuous…and sometimes…they *breach.*

"In any case, when I was away, a plague swept through the hinterlands. It devastated every village in the area. When I returned at last, it was to the blackened corpses of my family…" he leaned forward, appearing truly old for the first time. "I…should have been there…but duty called…duty always calls." When he raised himself back up, there was a hardness around him. "Life is transitory, boy…it is a lesson you would do well to learn and one that I was foolish to forget."

They sat in silence for a moment and Alexander didn't dare to break it as he was loathe to sever whatever distant familiarity had caused the wizard to open up to him.

"I suppose…" the wizard said at last. "That I have allowed the three of you to remain out of some intractable and pathetic attempt to cling to the family I have lost…two girls and a boy…" his voice trailed off for a moment, then he caught himself. "Enough for now…leave me be…"

Alexander rose slowly as the wizard returned to his writing. He dared not pester him with further questions.

Outside, night was beginning to fall upon the land.

As Alexander made his way towards the darkened staircase, his mind whirled with thoughts. He felt a bond to this strange man, perhaps even a pull to see him as a father figure and he held him in both awe and fear. Now, however, his thoughts turned towards the Princess and his sister. He couldn't forgive the wizard for his devastating assault on Charlotte and he felt as though the sudden onrush of vengeful thoughts which flooded his mind might overwhelm his reason. For a boy so young, he had endured a great deal of loss and these hard realities had imbued him with a surprisingly cold, calculating rationality.

It was this part of himself that he turned to now, suppressing his growing anger.

The wizard had revealed much during their conversation, but perhaps most important of all: he had revealed that despite his fearsome nature and seemingly god-like power, he was still a man. A man who had a weakness, and as Alexander knew all too well, weaknesses could be exploited.

Ancestral Eyes

"It is written that the First were more akin to gods than mortal beings Their mastery of science and magic was complete. The Ardhians petitioned them for their knowledge and it was the misuse of this knowledge which led to the Days of Fire. During those dark days, the First worked feverishly to contain the rents in space-time which had formed across the world. Many of them sacrificed themselves to prevent total cataclysm. It was this terrible event which cemented the alliance between the remaining First and the survivors of the Ardhian nations. Blood was exchanged and as a result, the race of modern Vampyres emerged. It is said that while only three Ancients remain in our world, the rest have moved to other dimensions beyond the stars. They are rumoured to be finished with this plane of existence and now seek out another realm which they may call their own."

-Inscription on the Tomb of a Vampyre Lord

The path had become more perilous as they climbed. The temperature was dropping, but Vampyres do not feel the cold as mortal men do and their immunity to many of the vicissitudes of life allowed the Prince and his cohorts to climb more in a day than any man would be able to in a week.

Carrinon surveyed the peaks and determined their course from there. He was moving purely on instinct at this point. He had felt the overwhelming psychic might of the Ancient down in the valley and he clung to it now like a guiding beacon.

"You know where you're going?" Lariana asked the Prince.

Carrinon nodded, "we're not far…the Ancient is guiding us."

Duric shrugged, "guiding us on a wild goose chase, to be sure."

Murien chuckled, "could you believe what happened down there? I thought we were done for."

"I've never seen anything like it…" Duric said softly. "There must have been a hundred men…and they were cut down in an instant."

"All the more reason we should tread with respect…" the Prince said caustically. "The only reason we are still alive is by the grace of our illustrious Ancestor."

Murien muttered something to himself, but chose to remain silent. He wasn't sure what he believed anymore and this journey was beginning to fray his nerves. *Had* they been spared from death back there? There was no denying that something had slaughtered the humans en masse and with such an efficiency that they had not even had time to retreat. When the slaughter was over, he had seen that cold, brooding presence near the peaks which had darkened the mountains. Part of him wished to turn back. *Longed* to turn back. But he knew it was out of the question. They were in it until the end, whatever that end may be.

They continued their ascent and the air grew thinner. They were nearing the Dragon's Talon, one of the higher peaks along the mountain chain.

Duric looked up repeatedly to see if any of those saurian beasts after whom the mountains were named were hovering above them, but he saw nothing. The sun was now high in the sky, yet the clouds which enshrouded them seemed to blot out much of its potency.

Lariana stopped for a moment and sat on one of the boulders, "this is pointless…we'll never find what we're looking for."

"Hush…" the Prince said with more than a little irritation. "This is the problem with you fools among the younger generation, you've never fully developed your psychic abilities."

Lariana glared at him, "why would I waste my time with such nonsense? What good have they done *you*?"

The Prince looked on passively. He understood that the nerves of his young cohorts were beginning to wear thin and as such, his royal title started to hold little meaning to them. It was a dangerous situation and one that could lead to mutiny, "listen…let's stop here and rest."

The mood among the group immediately buoyed.

Murien sat on a rock opposite Lariana and breathed deeply, "the air here is…different. It's as though it's more pristine than any I've ever breathed."

"That's because you don't get out enough…" Duric quipped.

That got them laughing and the Prince was somewhat relieved to see the tensions among them dissipate.

"What I don't understand…" Lariana's voice was now brimming with her old vitality. "Is why the Elders didn't build the Enclaves near mountains?" She gestured to the endless vista below them. "It makes for a magnificent view…"

Carrinon let the banter continue for a moment in silence before he spoke, "there is a very specific reason why the Enclaves were built exactly where they were…"

The conversation among the group ceased and the Prince now had their full attention.

"There are certain telluric currents which run across these lands. Currents that your dull senses likely can't detect, but which our Ancestors discovered easily. They built the Enclaves along these lines to harness the natural power sources that dwelled there."

Duric seemed to consider this for a moment, "so…that's why they're able to keep the cities in perpetual night?"

Carrinon nodded, "precisely…the magical currents which charge the Enclaves are the same magical currents that power Anturac."

"Why don't the Eldann and the humans have access to this?" Lariana asked.

Carrinon gave a contemptuous chuckle, "the Eldann, though long-lived, are not even in the same league as us…and as for the humans, their knowledge has been *deliberately* limited by Anturac to prevent them from becoming viable rivals." The Prince stood. "My Father's domain is preserved through the petty rivalries that he fosters among the kingdoms. He is ever conniving to find new ways to keep them fighting amongst themselves."

"What is he like?" Murien asked softly. "Your Father?"

The question caught Carrinon off-guard. He seemed to grasp for an explanation that would satisfy the young enquirer but instead, memories began to flood him.

He remembered the smell of the throne room in Anturac's Crysal Palace and the way the light shone through the gleaming walls. He remembered his joy when his Father took him through the Royal Gardens and he was witness to a vast array of plants that were likely extinct on the Continent.

"These we have preserved from before the Catastrophe..." his Father's sonorous voice trickled down to him.

"Will you replant them on the Continent?" the young Prince asked.

His Father shook his head, *"no, my son...these plants cannot survive in such alkaline soils. Here we use special means to keep them alive."* He gestured towards the gleaming gates which led back into the Palace. *"Come...let us return to the library to continue your studies."*

The young Prince bounded forward eagerly, but then stopped suddenly, *"Father...will you and Mother ever be together again?"*

Even now, looking backward through time, he could see the pained look on his Father's face, *"I don't yet know, my son...that day will come when she chooses it."*

The Prince hadn't had the chance to inquire further as his Father hurried him along towards the Palace.

"Sire?" Murien asked. "Are you alright?"

The Prince's eyes widened.

"You're crying, sire…"

Carrinon lifted a hand to his face and felt the wet streak of a tear. He withdrew his fingers to examine it, his face a mask of shock and disgust. Suddenly, a blinding rage overcame him which he was barely able to suppress, "my Father…my Father…"

Murien put a gentle arm on the Prince's shoulder and to his surprise, Carrinon did not recoil, "it's alright sire…I feel the same way about mine."

Carrinon breathed deeply. He loathed himself utterly in that moment for showing such weakness, especially to these ingrates and Murien's sympathetic tone had only added to his frustration. He had *nothing* in common with these beings. He came from *royalty*. He was their superior in every way.

But you don't really believe that, do you?

The thought was his own, but it had been in his Father's voice. "Enough talk of that…we resume our journey at once…" he turned and began to gather up their supplies.

Lariana watched the Prince carefully, then leaned over to Murien, "I think you might have struck a nerve…"

Murien shrugged slightly, "no kidding…remind me not to ask of such things again."

The climb seemed to go on for an eternity. They were now high enough that their chance of encountering any humans was slim to none. The Vampyres could go long periods without food and while they had gorged themselves on several of the fallen mountain men, the danger of being caught in a position where no sustenance was available to them was now very real.

Lariana had considered all of this prior to their continued ascent and had packed several containers with fresh blood. She handed these out now as they neared the Dragon's Talon, "drink up, boys…it's the last we have."

Murien and Duric sipped away while the Prince held his up for a moment, open but untouched.

"Go on sire…" Lariana said softly. "Drink…"

The Prince, ever averse to the blood curse which afflicted his people, had always been hesitant to indulge it. He could go much longer than his fellows could without blood, but in the end, he shared the same weakness whether he wished to acknowledge it or not. Slowly, reluctantly, he began to sip.

"Does anyone see anything?" Duric asked. "Any signs of life besides us?"

Murien surveyed the desolate landscape before them, "nothing…not even a bird."

The sun was now beginning to crest the horizon once more. Their journey had taken a day and they would need to carefully ration their supplies to make the return journey.

Murien felt exposed at this height. A Dragon could easily swoop down and snatch them from here if it wished. He eyed the forbidding peak of the mountain with a touch of reverence. The way the rock jutted out towards the sky made it look very much like the talon it was named after.

Suddenly, he saw something, a discoloration in the rock. He moved forward and pointed, "look…"

The others followed his hand and their sharp vision revealed the hidden cave which had nearly eluded them.

Carrinon stepped forward and squinted, "ahhh…that *must* be it…"

"We're close, sire…" Duric said. "That cave is a mere hour's climb away."

"Then let us not waste any further time…" the Prince said. "We're expected, after all…"

As they made their way across the perilous chasms towards the cave entrance, the snow began to pick up. The Vampyres considered it little more than an inconvenience.

"Sire…" Duric asked as they leaped between boulders. "If the Ancient is awake, why would he not simply return to the Enclaves?"

The Prince didn't break his stride, "because…we're being *tested*…to prove that we're *worthy* of aid. The Ancients respect my Mother, but they do *not* respect the Houses of Night. They know how corrupt they've become. Therefore, they must see that there are still members of our race who are not contemptuous and weak."

"Makes sense I suppose…" but Duric was beginning to have his doubts. He didn't share the Prince's optimism when it came to the future of their race. He could see the cracks which were beginning to form in the world around them and he doubted that a pair of Ancient Vampyres would be able to set the scales aright on their own. Still, he followed, for what choice did he have. What choice did any of them have?

At last, they came to the cave entrance. It yawned like a great, black chasm before them and the idea that anything could live in such a place was baffling.

Murien eyed the cave with caution. He wondered why the greatest among their race would seek refuge in such a desolate place. Perhaps the Ancients had gone mad as the aeons had passed and their self-imposed isolation was a means of escape from a world that was no longer tolerable to them.

The Prince stood before the great dark of the cave with his hands on his hips. He glanced back to the others and smiled before turning and marching headlong into the shadows.

Murien's shoulders sagged, "you must be joking…"

"Come, boys, we mustn't let his Highness outdo us…" Lariana said snidely as she followed the Prince into the void.

Duric turned to Murien and nodded. Together, they walked into the jaws of darkness, leaving the modern world behind them and facing an archaic past they had thought forgotten.

The Dead City

"It is said that the ancient peoples of the Desert once worshipped the goddess Agagammal. She was a goddess of fertility who was associated with the yearly floods of the great river Anc. The loss of this tradition has been linked to the rise of the Hierophants and other so-called magicians. They replaced the old cults with a new one that praised the wisdom of the Lord of the Deep. It was by His grace alone that the rivers flooded and the oceans swelled and so to Him alone was given all tribute. It is believed that this Deity is the same as the one the Vampyres call the Black Dragon, or Draganathan."

-The Book of Songs

"There's no way that'll work..." Charlotte said. "Not a chance..."

"It might..." Alexander's voice was a low whisper. Even though they were on the lower levels of the Tower, he didn't want to risk the chance of being overheard.

The Princess seemed lost in thought for a moment. She ran her slender fingers along her chin ponderously, "if he *has* taken some sort of liking to us...then perhaps it could work."

Charlotte threw up her hands, "you actually *believe* that nonsense he told you? He's a liar through and through...he's just using us as pawns in his little games."

"Perhaps..." Alexander said. "But perhaps not...it didn't *feel* that way when he was saying it."

Charlotte could barely contain her anger, "it doesn't matter what it *felt* like...feelings can be used as weapons against us..." she lowered her eyes to the floor. "This has been the case many times already."

They were silent for a moment. The right course of action seemed impossible to comprehend.

"I think Alexander is right…" the Princess said, turning to face him. "I think we need to continue to gain our captor's confidence. We have to move carefully…" she gestured around them. "None of us know how to operate this Tower and therefore, we are at our captor's mercy. He has brought us to a distant, strange land and therefore all of the cards are in his hands. However…" she pressed her hands together. "*If* what he revealed to Alexander is true, then that gives us a distinct advantage. We *can* use this sentimentality against him."

Charlotte sighed, "we'd be playing a dangerous game…if he caught on to us…"

"We are already in the thick of it…" the Princesses' tone was firm. "What choice do we have?"

Alexander eyed the large staircase behind them, "we know he seeks one of the Great Relics…" he turned to the Princess. "You read about them, yes? Did you read about the Flame of Aman?"

The Princess reached within the folds of her robe and held the Red Book firmly, "the Flame holds one of four Relics…that much is certain. Which one, however, is anyone's guess. That has never been specified. You must remember that these Relics were crafted from the shards of the Light Spire after the Empyrean War…"

"The *what*?" Charlotte couldn't hide her confusion.

"The Empyrean War…the War in Heaven…the War of the *Gods*." The Princess cleared her throat. "It is written, in texts which are gathered from ancient oral traditions, that there was once a great war in the skies. I have only ever pieced together fragments of what happened but suffice to say, the gods marched against each other. The destruction left a gaping hole in reality and plunged the cosmos into chaos…at least…that's what the old legends say. It is said that the Light Spire came into being during that time…"

"Is the Light Spire a *real* thing?" Alexander asked. "I always thought it was just a symbol?"

"It's real…" Charlotte said softly.

The others turned to her with obvious surprise.

"I read it in one of *his* letters…the one from Danyr *Himself*."

"Danyr mentioned the Light Spire?" the Princess asked.

Charlotte nodded, "that should be reason enough to indicate that it exists…" she pressed one of her hands to her forehead as though stifling a sharp pain. "It's just all…so much…"

The Princess lowered her eyes, "there's…something else…I haven't mentioned."

Alexander and Charlotte frowned.

"Some time ago, before we met…I was…*taken*."

"Taken where?" Alexander asked gently.

"I don't know…but it was a place of darkness…a place which was thrumming with a hidden energy. I met an old crone there…but she didn't appear *human*…" she looked up at the siblings. "You must think me mad."

Charlotte couldn't help but chuckle, "Princess…we're in a floating tower being manned by an ancient wizard…I'm prepared to believe *anything* at this point."

The Princess smiled slightly, "the crone…she said I had been chosen. That I would serve a greater purpose."

Alexander frowned, "chosen by *who*?"

When the Princess spoke again her voice was so low that the siblings had to lean in to hear it, "…the Most High."

Charlotte's blood went cold and when she turned to Alexander, she could see that his face was white, "did you just say…the Most High…did I hear that correctly?"

The Princess nodded, "it's a term I've never heard before or since."

Charlotte gripped the Princesses' shoulders. Her eyes were wide, "when Alexander and I stayed with our great uncle Adair, he mentioned the Most High…" she glanced towards her brother. "He also tried to kill us."

The Princess gasped.

"There was a cult in that village…" Alexander said. "And a black tree that they worshipped. They claimed it was planted by the Most High."

"I *hated* that wretched tree…" Charlotte spat.

Alexander shifted uneasily on his feet, "I…saw something…a vision of that tree…only it was distorted into some great, black-tendrilled thing which reached up into the heavens."

He looked into the Princesses' eyes, but saw no judgement there.

"I believe you…" she said softly.

"In one of the letters I read on the wizard's table, it said something about the **Others**." Charlotte said. "I think it was from a necromancer, or something like that…regardless…he said something along the lines of "if the **Others** find out what we're doing then the entire solar system will be in jeopardy."

The Princess seemed to consider this deeply for a moment, "I don't think we can fathom the forces that are involved in this…we can only speculate at this point. Suffice to say there is a far, far larger game being played here…one that defies our comprehension."

Charlotte seemed to consider all of this for a brief moment. It was too much for her mind to handle and she needed something tangible to bring her back to reality. "Regardless…we need to stay focused on the task at hand." She turned to Alexander. "If you can gain the wizard's trust, then that might be our best option at this point…"

The boy nodded nervously, "I'll do my best…"

Charlotte smiled, "just be yourself..." she tousled his hair playfully. "It's never failed you before."

When Alexander ascended the stairs, he was greeted by an empty room. Confused, the boy moved among the whirring machines, seeking his quarry. He didn't feel comfortable calling out, so he searched silently between the large devices and even behind the bookcases at the window.

Nothing.

He was prepared to turn back and head down the stairs when a sudden whoosh of air brushed across his back.

"Yes?" the wizard's soft voice echoed from behind him.

The boy turned quickly, his face a mask of shock. He found himself unable to form words.

"Don't look so surprised boy…I was merely ensuring that we are on schedule…" the wizard said.

Alexander nodded as though he understood what that meant. It was clear that whatever his previous intentions had been, they were swiftly dashed. By this simple act, the wizard had proven that he was capable of nearly anything. It was as much an assertion of his power over them as it was a means for him to achieve his own ends.

The wizard stood with his hands behind his back, waiting for the boy to muster the courage to speak.

Alexander at last forced the words out, “I…came to see what you were doing.”

“Did you now?” the wizard’s tone was almost sympathetic. “You *are* curious aren’t you…” he gave the boy a hard look. “Or nosy…perhaps?”

Alexander shook his head furiously, but he felt utterly exposed. It was as though his every thought was transparent to this man, “no, not at all…I can leave if you like.”

“Stay…” the wizard turned towards the enormous window which loomed before them. “We are nearly there…”

“We’ve passed the Black Mara?”

“We are in the *heart* of it, boy…” the wizard rocked on the balls of his feet. “The City of Lucia…the City of the Dead.”

Alexander considered this for a moment, then plunged forward, “so what is the Arcalypsis Flame?”

The wizard’s musical laughter echoed through the enormous room, “for one so young, you have both gumption and gall…a dangerous combination…” the wizard’s silver eye glowed as he turned and met the boy’s gaze. When Alexander didn’t flinch from it, the wizard smiled. “I could tell you what the Arcalypsis Flame is…but I doubt you would be able to comprehend it.”

Alexander smiled slightly. He knew it was a subtle barb but it was said in such a way that it was almost teasing him to continue prying, “…try me.”

“Very well…” the wizard moved towards the dark, oaken desk at the center of the room and beckoned the boy forward. “Sit.”

Alexander took a chair and faced the old man.

“Now…” the wizard said. “It took me many years to understand the nature of the Flame and it will take you many more to do the same…therefore I will only give you hints along the path…” he folded his hands. “What do *you* think it is?”

“A weapon of some sort…”

The wizard frowned, “what makes you say that?”

Alexander shrugs, “what else could it be…”

The wizard smiled slightly, “you imagine me to be a megalomaniac of some sort?”

“What does that mean?”

The wizard leaned back in his chair, "you think I'm on some quest to dominate the Continent."

Alexander shrugged, "I suppose…"

The wizard sighed. It was as though he was mildly offended by the comment, "I do not seek the Flame…for no man nor god can wield it…now…we were guessing what it was and thus far, we seem to be tunneling into the abyss."

The boy smiled, "alright…it's an actual Flame then."

"Wrong again…" the wizard snapped his fingers.

Alexander frowned, "it's a concept?"

"You're getting a little closer…"

"It's an idea…"

The wizard smacked the table slightly, "you're right…and very wrong at the same time."

The boy huffed, "I feel like I'm going in circles."

"Exactly…you are making a valiant effort, but how do you expect me to convey the ineffable to you. I cannot tell you what the Flame is…I can only tell you what it is not. This is called apophatic reasoning."

"Apo-what?"

The wizard's silver orb shone brighter as he spoke, "it's a process of reduction…you are trying to add things to the Flame. Do you not see that you were so very close before you attempted to describe it. Even as you circled around to it again by applying concepts and all of that other jargon you were still miles from it." The wizard leaned closer. "Don't you see, boy, the Arcalypsis Flame is not something that can be found…it must instead be *experienced*."

Alexander's eyes were wide, "…how?"

"That…you shall have to discover for yourself."

The boy threw up his arms in protest, "oh, come on!"

The wizard laughed, "now…as we near our destination, I shall require that you and your little co-conspirators make your way to the lower levels. We won't be landing as there is nowhere stable enough to do so."

Alexander caught the subtle jab. '*Co-conspirators,*' the wizard had said.

Suddenly, one of the black-winged creatures flew through the great window and landed next to them.

Alexander recoiled in horror at the sight of the yellow-eyed beast which dwarfed both of them by several feet.

The creature said something to the wizard in a guttural language and the old man nodded. He turned to Alexander "we have arrived…as I said, you'd tell the others to make their way to the lower levels."

The boy shrank from the creature's baleful gaze and barely managed to will himself to step back. He had the distinct feeling that the beast would've reached out and grabbed him had the wizard not been present. It made his stomach turn and he could barely prevent himself from bolting and falling down the stairs.

The wizard turned to the creature and smiled, "children nowadays…" he glanced out the window. "I will not need you and the others…you may remain here and watch the Tower. The children will come with me…"

The creature bowed and was gone seconds later, soaring through the window like a shadow.

The wizard turned to the boy and grinned, "where were we?"

Alexander tried to pull the threads of his memory back together, "we were…discussing the Flame."

"Ahh…of course…" the wizard ran his fingers along the dark table. "You are young, so you should be able to understand it far better than you would were you an adult…suffice to say that the Flame is nearer than you think."

Alexander scratched his head, "how so?"

"Come…we must make our way to the lower levels…" the wizard rose and beckoned the boy forward. "There will be time for questions…let us gather up the other two."

As they descended the stairs, Alexander suddenly realized how warm the air was. He had paid it little heed before and now the understanding began to dawn on him that they had truly made their way to a land that was utterly alien to anything he had ever known. A feeling of dread ran through him at the mere thought.

The wizard led the way into the observatory where the Princess and Charlotte waited. "Shall we?"

"Shall we what?" Charlotte asked.

"You children have seen several wondrous sights on your journey, but I can promise you, you haven't seen anything like the City of the Dead…" the wizard's mouth creased in a slight smile.

The Princess glanced at Charlotte, her eyes wary.

Charlotte kept her gaze fixed on their captor, “I suppose you’re going to give us the grand tour, then?”

The wizard grinned, “a better guide, you could not ask for, my dear.” He pulled a small, glowing orb from his robes and glanced at it. “Now… let’s see…”

The Princesses’ eyes widened, “the orb from my Father’s Vault!”

The wizard grinned, “yes…it had been most helpful in allowing me to retrace my steps…the landscape has changed, you see.”

The Princess crossed her arms and frowned.

The wizard chuckled softly, “do not be troubled, Princess…the orb never belonged to your father to begin with…he was merely safeguarding it until its true master returned.”

First

"Metanoia is called the Black City because it was constructed from the volcanic obsidian which proliferated the desolate landscape. The Eldann cities stand in stark contrast with their fine, white quartz walls and domes. That the two races should be such ferocious foes is no surprise when one understands their history. War after war has been waged between them and while their common citizens imagine that there is no greater threat to their sovereignty than their hated foes, their rulers have a different view. It would shock the commoners to know that the real war ended long ago and what remains is but a shadow play designed to ensure that the populace remains occupied."

-The Secret War, forbidden document written anonymously

The cave was surprisingly warm. It was as though they had entered an alternate reality which teemed with strange life and hidden secrets.

Duric had created a makeshift torch before they had entered and its gentle glow illuminated every crevice. The Vampyres had excellent night vision and could have navigated the cave with ease even in the pitch black, the torch seemed a mere formality.

The Prince ran his hands along the walls of the cave, "do you hear that?"

The others listened intently and soon enough the familiar sound of water could be heard.

"There must be a natural spring here…" the Prince turned back towards the tunnel and continued.

"What use would one of our Ancestors have for water?" Murien wondered aloud.

"You forget that they were never afflicted with the blood curse as we are…" the Prince said softly. "They may very well have drunk water instead."

Murien nodded. "Ahh…"

"Sounds rather bland, if you ask me…" Lariana could scarcely hide the disgust in her voice.

The Prince turned and smiled, "it's because you've never known anything else."

They pressed on into the cave, the torchlight illuminating their path. Soon, they reached what appeared to be a wide-open space with a high ceiling.

Duric lifted the torch, "by Draganathan…look."

The walls, every inch of them, were covered in images.

"What do you make of that?" Lariana asked, her eyes wide with awe.

The Prince examined the images closely, "they're hieroglyphs and pictographs…created using red ochre and perhaps charcoal."

"Magnificent…" Murien said. He had never seen such artistry even in the hallowed halls of the palace in Metanoia.

The Prince examined the images carefully, "it appears to be a history of our race…perhaps from the earliest days…look." He pointed towards the ceiling. "My Mother taught me these hieroglyphs when I was very young. They were our original form of writing before letters took over."

"What does it say?" Duric asked, barely able to contain his curiosity.

The Prince squinted for a moment, "it says: 'in the first days, there was the void, and the void reigned over the world, we drove back the void and moulded it to create, in creating…we imbued spirit into form."

Murien nodded slightly, "my…that *is* something, isn't it?"

The Prince nodded and indicated to the pictographs, "this looks like a representation of the Dark Days…the Days of Fire."

The Vampyres followed his hand and what appeared to be armies marching forth in vast columns. They were drawn in ochre and iron oxide while the strange creatures they were arrayed against were drawn in charcoal. The mere sight of the beasts filled the Vampyres with dread.

"I know very little of that time…" Duric said softly. "Only myths and legends."

"Consider yourself fortunate..." Carrinon's voice wavered with emotion. "My Mother and Father were both present during those times...as was the Ancient who drew this, it seems."

The others looked around, feeling suddenly very exposed.

"Where...where *is* the Ancient?" Duric asked, his voice barely a whisper.

The Vampyres glanced around them but saw only shadows.

"Perhaps he is gone and will return soon..." the Prince said. His attention returned to the images on the cave wall. "It seems that we have several formulas written here...formulas for...a weapon...of some sort."

Lariana moved forward and stood beside the Prince. She pointed to a large circle which was drawn in red with an outline of black. It looked like a great eye staring back at them. "What *is* that?"

The Prince shuddered at the sight of it, "according to the hieroglyphs, it's called a Blood Singularity. I can't imagine what that is, but it appears to be the power source for some sort of device."

They moved back slightly and examined the wall from a different perspective. The great, red circle was at the center of a large, megalithic structure. The gears and pulleys which surrounded it gave no doubt that it was a machine of some sort.

Murien breathed deeply, "perhaps we should go..."

The Prince turned to him, "you mean to turn back?"

Murien shook his head, "no...I don't mean return to the Enclaves, I mean perhaps we should leave this cave...it feels..."

"It feels as though we're intruding on hallowed ground."

Murien nodded nervously.

The Prince was mildly irritated by his comrade's loss of nerve, but part of him agreed with the assessment. They had walked into someone else's home uninvited and it might be deemed an insult if the Ancient returned and found them here without proper introduction. He nodded to the others, "very well...let's make camp outside of-"

There was a rustling noise in the shadows. The Vampyres turned as one to see the source of it. To their relief, it was only a small cave salamander. They sighed collectively as the little creature scurried away into the darkness.

The Prince nearly laughed that something so small had startled them. As he watched the creature go, he noticed two orbs shining out at him from the blackness. His blood went cold as his mind registered that it was a pair of eyes staring at them.

The same eyes they had seen after the slaughter of the mountain men.

The others were still laughing amongst themselves when the tall figure stepped forward. Lariana noticed the dark creature and let out a scream which she managed to stifle only through an application of will. Duric and Murien backed away and the Prince seemed frozen in place.

The figure was tall. Tall enough to be head and shoulders above them. Its eyes were piercing, even in the twilight of the cave. The creature had a bald head and skin the colour of charcoal. Its ears were large and pointed and its face resembled one of the bats that perpetually circled the Enclaves.

The Prince noticed that the figure appeared to be garbed in a great, illustrious cloak and it was only as it approached that he realized it was a pair of black-feathered wings.

Wings akin to the ones his Mother had.

The creature stood before them and the air seemed to be sucked out of the cave. Duric, Lariana, and Murien fell to their knees in awe while the Prince was barely able to remain standing. It took every ounce of his will to prevent his knees from buckling.

The creature spoke. It was a harsh, guttural voice from the abyss, "Melan drag'in din drag'or."

For a moment, the Prince found himself unable to speak. It took him a moment to realize that this was indeed the Ancient they had been searching for and he was speaking the primal tongue of the Vampyre race. A tongue his Mother often spoke to him from the time he was a boy. He mustered his courage and replied haltingly, "danim…er…danim'nos veratu nostramos."

The eyes of the Ancient glistened for a moment and he nodded slightly, "dragor'in domamm nosfer nomas."

Lariana, her voice shaking, managed to speak, "what…what is he saying?"

The Prince took a deep intake of breath, "he is asking us who we are…and…and why we've come." He remembered the words his Mother had spoken to him before they had left. They were words which he was to relay at just this moment. “Drana…er…drana’nim drao ganda…Freya Draconnis.”

At the mention of the name of the Empress, the Ancient smiled broadly. Suddenly, all of them heard his voice although his lips did not move, *“the Empress sent you here…”*

Carrinon squinted at the strength of the Ancient’s telepathic speech, but he managed to focus his mind enough to channel his own psychic powers. He nodded slowly, *“yes, Great One...we come to seek your aid. I am the son of the Empress...my name is Carrinon.”*

“Carrinon...” the Ancient seemed to be pondering the significance of the name. *“You have come far...young Prince. Your Mother must be desperate indeed if she has sent her only son to me.”*

“She is, Master...” Carrinon lowered himself and bowed. *“There has been a disturbance...one which troubled her enough to reach out to you.”*

The Ancient nodded, *“I am Apophanis...your Mother was my finest student and a close friend. I will assist her in any way that I can.”*

Duric and Murien were too stunned even to speak. They knew that there was communication occurring between the Prince and the Ancient but they hadn’t the faintest idea of what was being said.

Lariana was able to pick up shards of the conversation. A few more words were exchanged which she could only just understand: *“the Machine...Others...imminent.”*

Suddenly, the telepathic banter ceased and the Prince turned to them, “may I introduce Apophanis, my Mother’s teacher…he has agreed to accompany us.”

Duric blinked a few times, “well…that’s…that’s excellent!”

Lariana was the first to rise to her feet, “can he…speak our language?”

Carrinon nodded, “yes…but he disdains the current decayed language of our people. He prefers the soft resonance of the mother tongue.”

Lariana shook her head, “what I mean is… is he able to communicate telepathically…”

"Yes..." the Prince turned back to Apophanis. "Master...the trip back will be a mere inconvenience to you should you travel by foot. Flight will see you to the Enclaves much quicker."

Apophanis shook his head, "dranam duran'im goss."

"What did he say?" Lariana asked.

The Prince turned to her, "he wishes to see us back. He says that if we had the courage to make the trip here, then we are worthy of his protection."

She frowned, "he said all of that in so few words?"

The Prince laughed, "I told you...our mother tongue is much purer and more profound than the decayed wreckage our language has become."

"Fair enough..." she glanced towards the Ancient cautiously. "Would you tell him...that I would very much like to learn it from him...our old language."

The Prince folded his arms and smiled, "he can read your very thoughts, child..." he turned towards Apophanis. "You just told him yourself."

The Dust Settles

"The ancient Ardhians were masters of disguise. There are myths that tell how they could change form at will, moulding their appearance to suit their mysterious purposes. As such, they have ever remained an elusive people whose whims and desires can never fully be known."

-'A Treatise on Magic' by Athair Shan

How they had managed to make their way from that enormous, floating fortress to the ground below was a mystery which they would never be able to fully comprehend. They had followed the wizard to the bottom floor of the Tower and had been drawn into a blinding light. The next thing they knew, they were standing in the hot desert winds and the heat of the blazing sun.

Alexander felt disoriented and stumbled forward. Charlotte managed to catch him before he landed flat on his face.

The Princess felt nauseous, but was able to get her bearings enough to stave off retching. She was in awe of what she was looking at: a vast city of black stone.

Charlotte groaned as she lifted Alexander to his feet and they gasped at the sight of the City of the Dead.

"Behold…" the wizard said with a gesture. "Lucia."

Two large rock formations stood like sentinels on either side of the city itself. It was as though a mountain had been carved down to make room for the spires and temples which now stood in its place. The twin formations did indeed give the impression of a great mouth which seemed poised to swallow the city whole.

"Come…" the wizard turned and proceeded forward.

Charlotte glanced back towards the Tower and saw it floating above them, the black-winged ones flying around it in endless permutations. She turned and shielded her eyes and face against the harsh desert air.

The Princess caught up to the wizard as they strode across the sands, "is this where the Flame is?"

The wizard cocked one of his eyebrows slightly, "the Flame of Aman…yes…this is where it resides."

"And you will seek to claim its power?"

"I will seek what resides *within* it…"

As they approached the dark city, the sense of dread among them continued to grow. Every building was ancient beyond imagining and falling into ruin.

The youths huddled closer as the wizard led the way.

Without turning, he regaled them with the history of this place, "you have perhaps read that Antaryan, son of the Sky Father, is the reason that this place was destroyed. You have perhaps imagined that this story is an old myth, but I will tell you now that it was as real as anything written in the histories of the Bright Church.

"The black stone of this city used to be purest white and this place was known as the City of Light. The greatest scholars from far and wide studied here and the granaries of this land fed not only the empires of the East but the Continent as well. It was a prosperous place…until the corruption began to infiltrate it. You see, the Old Religion of the people worshipped the Sky Father and His Son, Antaryan, Lord of Cosmic Flame. Antaryan rewarded the people by giving them abundant light and imbuing His fire into the ground to bring it to life, allowing a fertile land to blossom into being. He also allowed the magical currents to flow freely through here, perhaps more so even than anywhere else save for Ardhia itself."

Alexander interrupted, "Antaryan was *real*?"

The wizard held up his hand, "listen carefully boy…now…the Old Religion could not possibly last forever, for all things change. It was when the Hierophants began to rise in power. They manipulated the magical currents and began to horde the knowledge for themselves. The average person was forbidden from practicing magic and within a few generations, the knowledge of it had been all but lost. The Priesthood grew mighty beyond imagining and they ensured that their knowledge was passed down amongst themselves and those they initiated into the mysteries. Soon, the people began to worship them as living gods and they basked in the adulation. The land began to die as Antaryan withdrew His blessings, but the people had faith in their Priests that a Golden Age was just around the corner.

"They were convinced by their overlords that the only way to appease the gods was to sacrifice the weakest among them on the altar. This they did and when it did not bring about the Golden Age, they were told it was *their* sin which was holding them back. In an orgy of bloodlust and wanton abandon, the people began to tear each other apart. They roamed the streets like mad dogs, hunting and killing without pity. Lording over it all were the Priests themselves, directing the angry mobs to greater and greater acts of decadence.

"Antaryan was so disgusted by the sight of the land He had once blessed that He appeared in dreams to the few decent citizens who remained in hiding, warning them to take what supplies they could carry and flee before first light. Those who could, did so without question, abandoning their beloved home to the wolves."

The wizard stopped for a moment and stared at the black towers before them, his voice was so soft against the desert winds that the youths had to strain to hear him, "at first light…a stranger appeared at the city gates. He arrived dressed as a simple mendicant and made his way towards the Central Sanctum. The crowd, having sated much of their bloodlust on their fellow citizens and curious as to who this stranger was, allowed him passage, but followed him closely. They knew the Priests would likely condemn this intruder to death and they were anxious to be there to witness his torment, for they were now little better than demons.

"As the stranger approached the Sanctum, the Priests emerged from their temple and lambasted him as a fool for approaching the sacred city. The stranger replied that the city had *once* been sacred, but was now a festering pit of depravity. The Priests, offended, passed judgement on him there and then and declared that he would be tortured and executed for his blasphemy.

"It was then that the stranger threw away his robes and shone with the light of a hundred suns, for he was Antaryan Himself, come to bring His reckoning at last. The Priests cowered before the Son of Light, but it was too late. Antaryan unleashed His sacred fire and for a day and a night the city burned. The stones themselves were charred black and the citizenry consumed in a holocaust of righteous fury. When it was over, Antaryan went to the Sanctum and cursed the once sacred flame which He had blessed. The flame burned black and the remnants of the vile Priesthood was condemned to watch over it. Thus were the Black Hierophants born."

The youths were so absorbed by the wizard's story that they had forgotten how thirsty they were. Their lips were parched in the dry desert heat and they regretted not having a drink before they had left the Tower.

The wizard seemed to sense this and passed them a sheepskin bag with water in it. The children passed it around and drank deeply from it, feeling a sense of renewal afterwards.

Charlotte returned the bag to the wizard and he took it swiftly. She coughed as the sandy wind slapped her face, "so, the Black Hierophants are still guarding the temple?"

"There were twelve original Priests…" the wizard said. "Only one is designated a Black Hierophant every twelve hundred years…then he gives up his soul and another takes his place. The last of them will perish at the end of the solar cycle."

The winds began to pick up and it whistled eerily through the blackened spires before them.

The wizard stopped and stared at the ruined city, "Danyr and I came here once…it was *he* who plunged one of the Great Relics into the Black Flame. To keep it safe from any who would attempt to seize it…from those who are unworthy." He turned to the youths. "Today…you will witness something few mortal eyes have seen. You will need every ounce of courage to face it and once you have crossed the threshold, there is no going back."

Alexander looked at the girls and saw that they were terrified. His own fear rose like a great shadow inside of him and threatened to consume him. But what choice did they have?

Behind them lay the endless desert which stood like a great barrier against them, propelling them inexorably forward.

"When you get the Great Relic…" the Princess could barely force the words from her lips. "What will become of us?"

The wizard turned towards her slowly, his black robes billowing in the wind, "that will depend, Princess…what would you wish to become of you?"

She lowered her eyes and tears began to spill from them, "I…I'd like to return home."

The wizard sighed, "I give you my word that your wish shall be granted…but Princess…" he moved towards her and gently lifted her chin until her eyes met his. "When you return, you may find it a different place than the one you left…" he lowered his hand and began to walk towards the city.

Charlotte watched him go, "what is *that* supposed to mean?"

The Princess wiped her eyes with her robe, "I don't know…but it can't be good."

"If he gets the Relic, there will be *nothing* we can do to stop him…" Charlotte clenched her fists.

"We'll have to make our move before then…" Alexander said. "But it could result in all of us being killed."

"That's a gamble I'm prepared to take…" Charlotte frowned. "What do I have to lose. I'd rather be dead than a slave."

The Princess turned to her, "you can't be serious? He gave me his word he would take us home..."

Charlotte nearly laughed at the Princesses' naivete, "his *word?* Bah! What does his word mean? Nothing! How many deceits has he ensnared us in since we met him?" She could feel her anger engulfing her. "And even if he weren't a lying snake…he promised to bring *you* home…what will become of my brother and I?" She glanced at Alexander but the boy lowered his eyes. "We don't *have* a home anymore…we have *nothing*…"

"You could come and stay in the castle…" the Princess whispered.

Now Charlotte *did* laugh and it was a despair-filled, awful sound, "you must be joking…do you think *King* Animrens will allow two orphan children to stay with you? As what? As *servants*?" She turned her gaze back towards the wizard who was now approaching the great entrance of the city. "No…no…I'll take my chances here…" she marched forward without saying another word, her face a mask of stone.

Alexander looked almost bashfully at the Princess, "thank you…for the offer."

Princess Rionéolas reached forward and clasped his hand tightly, "I wish I was as strong as you are…" she glanced almost fearfully at the city. "Perhaps your sister is right…perhaps we need to make our stand here…"

The boy nodded slightly and pulled her forward. Together, they raced after Charlotte and the wizard. What they would find once they reached the city was unknown to them, but they knew it would alter their destinies forever

EPILOGUE

The Fall of Arinönde

"The fox never accesses the hen house when the farmer is awake and on guard. He waits until the cover of darkness to stake his claim, and stake it he does, with furious precision."

-Old country aphorism

The assault came swiftly and without warning. The main bulk of Arinönde's armies were still many leagues away in Valleyhold. The teleportation of so vast a force had exhausted the energies of the Sanctum and as such, the capital was left completely undefended when the Móg Flagen attacked.

Mabinogan had timed his assault well. He had elected to move with a much smaller force than he had originally intended and this allowed them to pass swiftly through the provinces practically undetected. When they at last arrived at the capital, there weren't even enough defenders on hand to bar the gates.

The Móg Flagen swept into the city with ease and moved towards the castle. Their goal was to capture the King.

Mabinogan himself led his men under cover of darkness and within an hour's time, they had breached the castle and stormed the King's throne room. Animrens was caught unaware in his study. The King's face turned to horror as he realized that the castle was compromised.

Mabinogan entered the book-lined room, his large frame filling the doorway, "we meet again…Highness."

The King was still seated at his desk, "what is the meaning of this? I didn't summon a Barbarian delegation."

"Who said we were a delegation?" Mabinogan grinned broadly. He moved towards the great window and looked out on the city, breathing in the cool night air. "I left this city a child in disgrace…and I return to it a conqueror."

The King rose from his seat, “you have no claim to this kingdom…”

“I have *all* the claim to this kingdom…” the Lord of the Móg Flagen turned and met the King’s gaze. “This land is part of the *Unterwilt*…it was taken by your ancestors in ages past…we mean to reclaim it once more.”

The King’s eyes shifted towards the group of Barbarians that were guarding the doorway. He felt his stomach tighten as the gravity of the situation dawned on him, “our armies will be-”

Mabinogan raised his hand, “nowhere near the capital for several days…you shouldn’t have sent your best forces away so suddenly…it was rather careless.” He moved towards the King’s desk and picked up one of the books. He opened it and thumbed through the pages. “The bulk of our armies will be here tomorrow…we will fortify the city against any incursions from the outside.” He turned his baleful gaze to the King, “messengers will be sent out and it will be made known that if the forces of Arinönde do not surrender unconditionally and relinquish their arms, then we will begin to execute its citizenry…”

Animrens gasped, “you *can’t* do that…”

Mabinogan laughed, “tell the new Sovereign of Arinönde what he can and cannot do…”

The King’s eyes darted back and forth nervously.

At that moment, a group of Barbarians entered the study with Korazon at their head. They bowed to Mabinogan and Korazon spoke, “my Lord, we have searched the castle but there is no sign of the Princess.”

Mabinogan nodded slightly, “so, she truly did vanish. It wasn’t just some ruse, was it Animrens?”

“She’s not here…” the King said softly.

Mabinogan grinned, “you couldn’t protect your own city from me, *Highness*… what makes you think you can protect your daughter?”

The King mustered the courage to face his captor, “she left on an errand…she is nowhere near the capital nor its surrounding provinces…the best trackers in your retinue would not be able to find her…” there was a hint of triumph in the King’s voice.

Mabinogan crossed his arms and was silent for a moment, when he spoke it was with a degree of resignation, “he speaks the truth…" he turned to Korazon. "Search the castle regardless…we have what we came for."

Korazon nodded and departed.

"This will never stand…" the King said. "You cannot occupy the capital without incurring the wrath of Anturac…"

Mabinogan brushed him away contemptuously, "aren't you the *King*? I thought you more adept when it came to the political situation in your own province…"

Animrens ignored the barb, "Anturac will not hear of it…they will send their armies…"

Mabinogan grinned broadly, "you damn fool…it was *Anturac* which gave us their blessing!"

The King's mouth dropped, "they…they *what*?"

Mabinogan put his powerful hand on the King's shoulder almost tenderly, "ahhh…I see you've lost favour with the Mage Emperor. Perhaps this kingdom needs an injection of new blood into it…perhaps the time of the Móg Flagen has come round again."

The King moved back, his face was white, "how…how can this be? We did everything that was expected…"

"Did you?" Mabinogan crossed his arms. "Look around at the decadence that has overtaken this kingdom…your people have lost their way." He gestured to his guardsmen who stood at the door. "*This* is the future…and the hour of reckoning has come."

The King's shoulders sagged slightly, as though the full weight of the situation had now settled upon him, "what will you do? Ransack the city and take your share of the spoils?"

Mabinogan laughed heartily, "ahhh, *Highness*… you give me no credit. Why would I destroy my own kingdom? I intend to *reshape* it."

The King looked at him listlessly.

Mabinogan smiled cruelly, "perhaps I should have rephrased my earlier statement…I left this city a child in disgrace…" his eyes flashed in the twilight. "And returned to it, a *King*."

Within her private quarters, the Empress of the Vampyre Enclaves sat pensively. She knew that her son had been successful and also knew that events were now in motion which could not be stopped. The Great Cycle was well underway and the coming of a New Age was inevitable.

She glanced out the enormous, arched window which looked out onto the Enclaves and wondered if any among them could sense the magnitude of what was coming. Her greater knowledge and wisdom had always been a heavy burden for her to carry. But now that she was to be reunited with her brother and her beloved teacher after untold ages, she felt the weight around her heart loosen.

She looked out into the perpetual night, *and what of you, my Husband...where do you stand in all of this?*

There was no doubt that he was busy with his machinations. He and his fellow Serpent had always been cunning and secretive. It was one of the traits which drew her to him in the days of old. The fact that their union had resulted in a long separation did not bother her in the least, for what was time to an immortal?

She smiled slightly. She knew the hour of their reunion was approaching. In many ways, despite the devastation that was surely coming, she was *excited.* She despised the political machinations of the Court and chafed at the limitations imposed upon her in her role as Empress.

But every role must be played to its conclusion.

The Quantum Sea was infringing upon the very fabric of reality and soon they would have a great many difficult decisions to make. This would not be a time for half-measures.

The Empress turned from the window and began to pace through the throne room. The Days of Fire had been terrible, to be sure...but how much worse would the coming days be?

She turned and looked at the inscription above the throne. It was written in the classical Vampyre language which preceded the modern tongue. It was far inferior, she thought, to their *original* speech which had been purely telepathic, but she supposed it would have to suffice. The inscription said: *"by the might of Draganathan, we are delivered."*

"Delivered indeed..." she said aloud.

She wondered if the Elders realized just how deeply they had been deceived. The First had fallen for the same ruse and paid dearly for it.

She looked up at the nine headed statue of the Black Dragon which towered over the throne. It sent a chill down her spine. She had loathed sitting beneath it but it was expected of her and so she did it without complaint. The Great Beast loomed over all, guiding and manipulating lesser beings to its whims from the shadows.

She frowned and breathed deeply. She wondered what it would be like to see inside the mind of a god. What kinds of endless patterns and permutations from time immemorial must be hidden there and how unfathomable they must be to even *her* daunting intellect.

She brushed these thoughts from her mind. She needed to focus on her own plans lest they slip away from her. Her teacher was already on his way. She reached out with her incredible psychic might and felt for her brother's presence. She would need him by her side when the final hammer stroke came.

She turned back towards the window and imagined that she could see the Crystal Palace of Anturac in the distance. She had told Danyr what a ridiculous idea that was, but then, he always did have a taste for the theatrical and the grandiose. By their combined wills, this globe-spanning empire was maintained and strengthened.

*How much longer can we continue...*she wondered. *Before the end comes? To what star-system will we flee this time, Husband? To what dimension?*

She found that she did not know, but neither did she care. So long as her family was by her side, she would venture forth into any reality, even beyond time itself. Some of her people were already preparing the way for them. She imagined the poor souls who would be left behind and found that she felt pity for them, yet this did not dissuade her from her path.

She knew that her Husband would want to fight, as he always had, for this place they had made their home.

But how much would you be willing to sacrifice?

She already knew the answer, and while it disturbed her, she was prepared for whatever may come.

Appendix

On the Kingdoms

The various kingdoms of the empire are more akin to city states and principalities than vast regions. All kingdoms on the Continent have a degree of autonomy and are able to engage in trade with one another freely. They can levy their own taxes and govern their peoples internally, free from interference. One constant among them, however, is the tribute which must be sent monthly to Anturac. The tributes and tithes change based on the unfathomable will of the Mage Emperor and failure to meet them can result in heavy penalties.

No kingdom, as of yet, has been foolish enough to risk the wrath of Anturac for they could not stand against the technological might of that supreme nation. Therefore, all tithes and tributes are given without complaint and on schedule. This keeps a steady stream of wealth flowing into Anturac while providing a subtle reminder to the lesser kingdoms that they are vassal states and nothing more.

Anturac's sway extends across the Continent all the way to the Eastern Desert where there are statues and shrines to the Mage Emperor to honour His passage through that desolate land in ages past. The once great empire of the desert now lies in ruins and its people have been reduced to either a nomadic existence or eking out a living in small villages. Slaangrah, legendary guardian of the Black Mara, has been a potent barrier against incursions from outside forces.

The most prosperous kingdom in the empire is Arinönde, which has both the greatest standing army and the largest concentration of wealth. Arinönde has exerted its strength over the centuries and has even made a vassal state of its neighbour, Calchie. Calchie pays a steady tribute to Arinönde for protection from the Beastmen of the Lower Wastes. The Wastes themselves are generally uninhabitable and extend beyond into what the Barbarians call the *Unterwilt.*

Greater Valleyhold, Aringyle, and witch-haunted Bandover have all fallen under the influence of Arinönde through the machinations of the Bright Church which exerts significant power in the court of Animrens. The immense prestige and strength of the kings of Arinönde has imbued them with a natural sense of superiority which has made them both feared and despised by their neighbours. Several times they have imagined themselves mighty enough to challenge Anturac itself, but have been swiftly chastened by that great nation's supremacy.

The kingdoms beyond the south are ruled first by the Eldann and then by the Vampyres, both of whom are at war with one another perpetually.

The once great Dragon empire is no more, though Dragons are still said to nest in the Dragon's Teeth. Their role in saving the world in ages past is remembered only by the immortals themselves and through myths and legends. Most common citizens refuse to believe that such creatures even exist, although the people of the mountains pay them tribute in order to live upon those treacherous slopes.

The Kingdom of the Giants was said to have been wiped out in the very first days, although Giants are still said to roam the edges of the Great Sea.

The enigmatic Skeags have not been seen since the Days of Fire, though they are rumoured to reside deep within the earth. None have ever encountered them and lived to tell of it as they are a secretive race of unfathomable will and unimaginable antiquity.

Anturac itself remains the great beacon of culture and strength. In ages past, the peoples of the Continent used to venture there to be schooled in the ancient arts and to receive the lost knowledge. Five centuries ago, however, the Mage Emperor suddenly put a stop to all travel to the island and as a result the Continent stagnated into a Dark Age which saw the rise of the Bright Church and the vilification of the magical sciences. Whether such an occurrence was a result of the Mage Emperor's policies or was something He intended all along is known only to Him.

On the Ardhian Peoples

The Ardhian people have been natural users of magic since the days of antiquity. The books and legends claim that the destruction of their homeland was the result of a cataclysm brought about by their great technological achievements. The Days of Fire left a mark on them that has never fully been washed away. The oldest among them, few as they are now, were present during that dark time and aided in the battles which saved the world.

All pure-blooded Ardhians are immortal and can change their appearance as they wish, seeming to be young or old. When they have seen all there is to see of life and grown weary of it, they can simply give up their body and move into the realm of spirit at will. They can pass their immortality onto their children if they are of pure blood. When they first arrived in the desolate lands which would become the Continent, much of their population had died in the devastation of the Cataclysm. As such, they mingled and mixed with the local peoples and while their offspring were not immortal, they had many years of long life and vigour, some even living as long as five hundred years.

With time, this longevity has diminished significantly, however, those with Ardhian ancestors can expect to live to one hundred and be in ruddy good health. Nearly all pure-blooded Ardhian people live on the Isle of Anturac and generally swear off contact with the Continent unless it suits their purposes.

Flaming red hair, pointed ears, and natural magical aptitude are all signs of Ardhian ancestry among the common people. Some may have one or several of these traits depending on the strength of their genetic inheritance.

The knowledge which the Ardhians brought with them has generally been kept secret in Anturac, although they are known to have shared the techniques of farming and agriculture on the mainland. Ancient Ardhian artifacts, some of great power, can still be found across the Continent and are hoarded by those who long for greater magical understanding, particularly the Bright Church and its adjacent secret societies.

In Anturac, the Mage Emperor reigns supreme. A hero to His people and a legend on the mainland, Danyr's word is law. Being one of two great Serpent Priests, His mystical council was highly sought after by people across the lands before Anturac went into self-imposed isolation. The Council of Five, a powerful group of Archimages, rule in Danyr's stead when He attends to His unfathomable works.

The island itself is powered by a blazing tesseract of magical energy which never diminishes and also allows for interdimensional travel. It is believed to be a minor replica of the device which began the Great Cataclysm.

On Religious Belief

There is a wide variety of religious beliefs across the Continent and beyond. In Arinönde and most of its surrounding provinces, the Bright Church possesses enormous influence. Through their famous Bright Seminary, they have disseminated many of their most deeply entrenched principles. They have an almost autocratic control over magic and the way magic is perceived and they ruthlessly punish renegade magicians. In its early days, the Church had no qualms about exterminating entire villages if it meant consolidating their power.

The Church is funded by both the Von Richter Banking Clan as well the infamous Barrows Family. There is a secret order within the Church itself called the Brotherhood of the Golden Way and they reside over many important Church functions. The Light Father is believed to be the one true God and He is always associated with Light Spire iconography. Danyr is viewed as one of His prophets and many believe that when the Mage Emperor at last returns to the Continent, the Final Judgement will begin.

Unbeknownst to the common people, a small, fringe group known as the Noumenons were the original founders of the religion which became the Bright Church. They believed in the Formless God who transcends time and space. They were nearly destroyed by their brethren in the early days and now exist on the margins of society.

The Eldann or the Shining Ones, worship Aryavartha and His eternal fire which they believe dragged the world out of the primeval void. Their religion is in stark contrast to the Vampyres who worship Draganathan, the Outsider. They believe that the Black Dragon has been intimately enmeshed in the world for millennia and that His defeat in the Empyrean War was part of a cosmic plan to renew the Cycles.

What little is known of Dragon beliefs tells of how they worshipped the Cosmic Egg which gave rise to all life. Their religious system was deeply integrated with their astronomy and mathematics. A science so advanced that it was called the Supreme Science by the Ardhians who took up its study.

The Alderamin worship the Star Mother, Aenith, and Her demi-goddess avatar, T'anis. It is said in ancient legend that T'anis was once married to a great Ardhian mage until her sudden disappearance.

There are many other religious beliefs too numerous to name here, ranging from the Giants and their worship of the Eternal Principle all the way to the Sea Peoples known as the Drya'Din who believe in the ocean as a representation of the Original Primordial Waters.

The Ardhians, ever mysterious and secretive in their ways, were said to worship the Fiery Current of Being or the Immutable Flame. The truth of these beliefs was said to be available only to initiates of the Serpent Priesthood.

The Skeags, those unfathomable creatures of the Inner Earth, are said to worship their Immortal Kings. Little else is known about their culture and many scholars have brought their very existence into question, believing that they are merely the product of myth.

www.ingramcontent.com/pod-product-compliance
Lightning Source LLC
LaVergne TN
LVHW091037080826
845145LV00002B/531

9781738051540